THE SIXTH Galaxy READER

THE SIXTH
Galaxy
READER

Edited by H. L. Gold

DOUBLEDAY & COMPANY, INC.

GARDEN CITY, NEW YORK

*All of the characters in this book
are fictitious, and any resemblance
to actual persons, living or dead,
is purely coincidental.*

"The Nuse Man" by Margaret St. Clair, "Success Story" by Earl Goodale, "Lex" by William T. Haggert, "License to Steal" by Louis Newman, "Thing of Beauty" by Damon Knight, "Personnel Problem" by H. L. Gold, "the IFTH of OOFTH" by Walter S. Tevis, Jr., reprinted by courtesy of the authors.

"A Husband for My Wife" by William W. Stuart, "Insidekick" by J. F. Bone, "The Number of the Beast" by Fritz Leiber, "Flower Arrangement" by Rosel George Brown, reprinted by courtesy of Harry Altshuler and the authors.

"Love Called This Thing" by Avram Davidson and Laura Goforth, "True Self" by Elisabeth Mann Borgese, reprinted by courtesy of John Schaffner and the authors.

"The Genius Heap" by James Blish, reprinted by courtesy of Kenneth S. White and the author.

To Rip and Carla Camp—real snookies

Contents

INTRODUCTION:

How to Write Science Fiction

Few things are demonstrably more wrong than the linear theory of history. This theory argues that everything in the future will be the same as in the present, only more so, that to extrapolate we have only to extend the present upward on a graph. It worked that way in the past, says this concept; therefore it will work in predicting the future.

It did nothing of the sort. In actual fact, history is a constant process of reversals. Revolutions are followed by periods of intense conservatism, after the revolution has devoured its own children. Lax morality leapfrogs into strict puritanism. War brings peace, and peace—at least this far—leads to war.

The transitions are never gradual. They may not happen overnight, though sometimes they do. But they invariably gain momentum in direct proportion to the looseness of the times, or the severity of the repression, or whatever. Reversals of all sorts will distinguish the twenty-first century from the twentieth, for, as in the physical sciences, each social action causes an equal and opposite reaction. Let's take some random examples:

Just when civil rights everywhere are in greatest peril, there is less intergroup friction than ever. Paradoxically, Hollywood, which habitually shies away from such controversial issues, helped bring this about; these themes were rebellions against the bland pablum that preceded them, and in which they fed.

The economic interests of the anti-Communist bloc are savagely competitive, and yet the extent of co-operation against the common danger is seemingly limitless.

The Communist bloc is theoretically free of such bitter competition, and yet it is riven by internal disputes, jealousies, rivalries, and schisms on national scales.

TV is killing the reading habits of millions, yet more books and magazines are sold in TV areas than ever before.

Only one person out of five is self-employed now, as against four out of five in 1900, and never has there been so much employment.

Security regulations are hampering the physical sciences, and yet decade outdoes decade in the wealth of discoveries, so that the first half of this century saw more change than all the previous millenniums.

The trick in writing good science fiction is to find the paradoxes in advance—and then use the linear approach to history. This is the way business and government extrapolations are made: all things being equal (which they never are), there will, for instance, be more cars than people in 2000 A.D., more food and fuel than they can consume, more housing than they can occupy, and the like. These extrapolations are more than useful. They are absolute necessities. The trick is to rule out the reversals beforehand and proceed as if traffic laws wouldn't limit the sale and operation of vehicles, fuel deposits were not being depleted, and the certainty that single-generation houses will produce unthinkable slums, and then ride hell for leather as far as the trend can be made to go.

Here is the final paradox:

No matter how far you make them go, you probably will still be underestimating. If you want proof of that, consider how timid were the most extravagant nineteenth-century predictions of what mid-twentieth-century life would be like—linear predictions all.

—H. L. GOLD

THE SIXTH Galaxy READER

The Nuse Man

BY MARGARET ST. CLAIR

I don't know why, really, the nuse man comes to call on me. He must realize by now I'll never order a nuse installation or an ipsissifex from him; I consider them as dangerous as anything our own lethal age has produced. Nuse, which is a power source that the nuse man describes as originating on the far side of 3000 A.D., is the worse of the two, but the ipsissifex, a matter duplicator, is bad enough. And though I listen to the nuse man's stories, I can hardly be considered a sympathetic audience. I suppose he drops in because I can always be depended on for a cup of tea and some toast and marmalade.

"Hello," he said as I answered the bell. "You've aged in the last six months."

Before I could wrap my tongue around the obvious *et tu* (he was looking terrible—his clothes looked as if they had been slept in by machinery, and there were bruises and cuts and lumps all over his face)—he had pushed past me into the living room and was sitting down in my husband's easy chair. The dachshunds, who have never liked the nuse man, were growling at him earnestly. He put his feet up on the fireplace and lay back in the chair on his spine.

"Ahhhhhh!" he sighed, and then, to me, "Put more butter on the toast than you did last time."

When I came back with the tea, he was standing by one of the bookcases looking at Woolley's little book, *Ur: The First Phases.*

"Silly book," he grumbled. "That stuff about the plano-convex bricks is all wrong."

"What do you know about it?" I asked him.

"I sold a nuse installation to King Nebu-kalam-dug of Ur of the Chaldees on this last trip."

"Oh, yes? Well, the home office ought to be pleased with you. Perhaps they'll give you a vacation back in your own time."

The nuse man made no direct answer, but his battered, lumpy face grew dark. He bit into a slice of toast so savagely that I feared for his iridium alloy teeth.

"Don't tell me that something went wrong with the nuse *again!*" I cried.

This time he couldn't have answered if he had wanted to. He had choked over some toast crumbs, and I had to beat him on the back and pour tea down him before he could speak.

"Why are you so prejudiced against nuse?" he demanded at last. "The nuse had nothing to do with it. It was the king and the priests that birded it up."

"I'll bet."

The nuse man's face turned even redder. It was a shade or two darker than the lapels around the waist of his trousers. "I'll tell you all about it!" he said passionately. "You be the judge!"

"Oh, Lord." There was no polite way of getting out of it. "All right," I said.

"Everything was going fine," the nuse man began, "until the old King, Nebu-kalam-dug, died. I'd sold him a nuse installation—"

"General or special?"

"Special, of course. Do I look like fool enough to put a general nuse installation into the hands of a lot of 3000 B.C. yaps? I sold him a special nuse installation in exchange for a stated number of Sumerian gold artifacts, so many on installation and so many each lunar month until the price was paid."

"What were the artifacts?"

"Gold wreaths and necklaces and jewelry. Of course, gold's nothing. Only good for lavatory daïses. But the workmanship was interesting and valuable. I knew the home office would be pleased. Then the old yoop died."

"What killed him?"

"His son, Nebu-al-karsig, poisoned him."

"Oh."

"Everybody in the court knew it, but of course nobody would talk about it. I was sorry the old king died, but I wasn't worried, because I thought I could work out the same sort of deal with the new king. Even when I saw how scared the court ladies looked when they were getting ready for the funeral, I didn't apperceive. And then the soldiers came and arrested me!"

"What had you done?" I asked suspiciously.

"Nothing. They were short little tzintes with big muscles, and they wore sort of skirts out of sheepskin with the wool twisted into bunches to look elegant. They wouldn't say a word while they were arresting me. Then I found out I was supposed to be strangled and put in the royal tomb with the dead king."

"Why?"

"Because I'd been one of the old man's special friends. At least, that was what young Nebu-al-karsig said. The prime minister and two or three of the councilors were being strangled along with me."

"Gosh."

"I argued and argued, and talked and talked. I told the young king we hadn't been such good friends as all *that*. And finally he said, very well, I could go with the court ladies in the death pit."

"Were you scared?"

"Of course I was scared," the nuse man said irritably. "I didn't have my chronnox—they'd arrested me in too much of a hurry for that—so I couldn't get into another time. And I had no way of getting in touch with the home office. Certainly I was scared. And then there was the indignity—somebody from when I come from, to be killed by a lot of primitive button heads. It made me sore."

He slurped at his tea. "When we got to the pit," he continued, "they were just closing the old king's tomb up. You understand, the tomb was at the bottom of the pit, and there was a ramp leading down into it. They hung matting over the sides of the pit, to cover the earth, and then they backed old Nebu-kalam-dug's war chariot down the ramp; he'd want his chariot in the next world. Then the rest of us went down the ramp into the pit."

"Who was 'us'?" I asked curiously.

"Oh, harpists and singers and court ladies and slaves and soldiers and attendants. If anybody didn't want to go, the soldiers had spears they used for prodding. I counted, and there were fifty-eight of us."

"Pretty barbarous," I said sympathetically.

"Nobody from your period has any right to call *anything* barbarous," the nuse man said severely. "I've seen some bad ages, but yours—! Anyway, there we were.

"The funeral services began. The harpists twanged on their harps and the singers sang in high falsetto voices. It sounded awful. The priests chanted prayers from the edge of the pit above. The soldiers passed around an opiate in little bronze cups for us to drink. The priests prayed some more. It was beginning to get dark. Then they started shoveling earth in on us."

"Were you sorry for the others?" I asked.

"I was more sorry for myself. It was their era, and if they wanted to die in it, that was their business. After all, they thought that when they woke up they'd go on serving old Nebu-kalam-dug in the next world. *I* didn't—and even if I had, he was nobody I'd want to serve."

"How did you get out?" I asked quickly. I did not like the thought of the scene in the death pit, even if it had taken place so many thousands of years ago.

"I got under the car of the chariot to shelter myself from being crushed. After a long while, the earth stopped coming in and I decided the mourners had gone away. I didn't have my chronnox, and, as I told you, I couldn't get in touch with the home office. But I was wearing an ipsissifex. I started materializing myself up through the earth of the pit."

"You *didn't!*" I said incredulously.

"I did, though. Each 'me' was a little farther up through the earth layer of the pit."

"You mean there are five or six 'you's buried back there in Ur of the Chaldees?"

"Seven. Of course they weren't *really* alive—you know how an ipsissifex is."

It was the first time I had ever heard the nuse man admit that one of the devices he was peddling might have a flaw.

"I clawed my way up through the last few inches of dirt without any more materializations," he said, "and started walking up the ramp. There was a soldier on guard at the top. When he saw me, his spear began to shake. It shook so much he could hardly hold it. The moon was coming up, and my shadow fell in front of me on the ramp.

"He licked his lips and swallowed before he could say anything. 'Get back in the pit and die,' he said finally. 'What are you doing out here? You're supposed to serve our lord Nebu-kalam-dug in the other world. Go on back and be dead.'

"I didn't say anything. I just kept walking closer to him. When I was about two feet away, he dropped his spear and ran.

"I didn't have any trouble getting in at the palace, either. Young Nebu-al-karsig was playing checkers on a fiddle-shaped board with one of his girls when I walked into the great hall. When he saw me, he jumped up and the board fell to one side and the pieces rolled over the floor. I said, 'My lord Nebu-al-karsig, I am harder to kill than your noble father was.'

"He had turned a dirty greenish tan. He said, 'I saw—I saw—'

"I sat down on the floor in front of him and bumped my head on it a couple of times to show I was going to be polite. Then I said, in a deep, serious voice, 'A magician cannot die until his time has come, my lord. Shall we discuss extending the nuse installation I made for your respected sire?' And he said, 'Yes, let's.'"

"It's a wonder he didn't try to poison you," I commented.

"Scared to," the nuse man said briefly. "Anyhow, we agreed I was to increase the nuse installation by one third, and in return Nebu-al-karsig was to pay me twice as many gold artifacts each lunar month as his father had, and for half again as long. It took a lot of figuring and explaining by the royal scribes before the king could understand the terms of the agreement, but he finally was satisfied with the arithmetic. Oh, and I got my old rooms in the palace back."

"What did the special installation do?" I poured the last of the tea into the nuse man's cup and went out to the kitchen to put water on to heat for more.

"It made bricks," he said when I came back. "Beautiful, even, true, symmetrical mud bricks. Nebu-kalam-dug had been crazy about those bricks, and even Nebu-al-karsig thought they were pretty neat. You should have seen the adobe junk the brickmakers had been turning out by hand—sloppy, roundish affairs, all different sizes, with straw sticking out of them. Yes, my installation made bricks."

"What did they use the bricks for?" I asked.

"For ziggurats—stepped temple pyramids. They made the first story black, the second white, the third red, and the last blue. Sometimes, just for a change, they'd do an all-blue or an all-red pyramid.

"For a while, everything was fine. Ziggurats were going up all over the place, and the skyline of Ur altered rapidly. The priests were pleased because all those ziggurats meant more priests were needed. Nebu-al-karsig was pleased because he was going down in history as the greatest ziggurat builder of his dynasty. And I was pleased because I was getting a lot of elegant artifacts. Then things started to go sour."

"The nuse," I murmured. "I knew it."

The nuse man glared at me.

"It . . . was . . . not . . . the . . . nuse!" he said, biting off the words. "What happened was the brickmakers started to get sore. They were out of jobs, you see, because of the nuse. And the bricklayers were almost as badly off. They were working twelve hours a day, seven days a week, without any overtime, trying to use up all the bricks. Pretty soon there would be riots in the streets.

"Nebu-al-karsig asked me what I thought he ought to do. I told him, let the brickmakers into the bricklayers' guild. That way he'd have twice as many men to build ziggurats. So he issued a decree. And then there *were* riots in the streets.

"'What,' said the bricklayers, 'let those dirty sheep's livers into our union? When they haven't served a seven years' apprenticeship?' 'What,' said the brickmakers, 'be forced to give up our noble art, sacred to Nintud since time immemorial, in exchange for slicking mud paste over heartless mechanical bricks?' Then both sides shrieked 'Never!' and barricades, made out of brick baskets and cobblestones, began to go up everywhere.

"I suppose the fuss would have died down in time. People—as your age has learned—can get used to anything. But Nebu-al-karsig was sleeping badly. Palace gossip had it that he'd wake up screaming from dreams about his father. He asked the priests what the cause of the trouble was, and they told him that some of the minor gods, those who hadn't got ziggurats yet, were mad at him. The people in Ur had about four thousand gods. So he decided to have the nuse installation turn out more bricks.

"Every morning, as soon as it was daylight, a bunch of shave-headed priests would file into the nuse factory. They'd stand in front of the installation, concentrating, for an hour, and then a new batch of priests would come. They kept that up all day. Nuse, of course, is basically a neural force. By the end of the day, bricks would be simply pouring out of the brick hoppers. Even to me, who had nothing to do with laying them, seeing all those mountains and mountains of bricks was very discouraging.

"I tried to argue with Nebu-al-karsig about it. I told him as politely as I could that he was endangering his throne. But he'd never liked me, and after the episode of the brickmakers' guild, he hadn't trusted me. He wouldn't listen. I decided it was time I got out of Ur.

"I had one more installment of artifacts due me. I would collect that and then leave. By now the chest of artifacts in my bedroom was almost full.

"The day of the installment came and went, and no artifacts. I mentioned it to Nebu-al-karsig and he showed his teeth at me. But on the next day, ten or twelve priests came to my rooms with a little box. The head priest opened it and gave it to me. In it were the missing artifacts.

"They weren't quite what my contract called for, but I was glad to get them. I thanked the head priest for them as nicely as I knew how, and he smiled and suggested that we have a drink. I said fine, and he poured it out. One of the minor priests was carrying goblets and the wineskin. I put out my hand for the cup and the head priest—did I tell you I'd put a small general nuse installation in my rooms?"

I thought back. "No, you didn't."

"Well, I had," said the nuse man. "I wasn't going to be bothered with slow, stupid slaves waiting on me. I put out my hand for the cup and the priest went sailing up in the air. He hit on the ceiling with a considerable thump. Then he went around the room, floating just at eye-level, and whacked solidly against each of the four corners. He hit the fourth corner harder and faster than he had the first. I could see that his mouth was open and he looked scared.

"There was a kind of pause while he hovered in the air. Then he went up and hit the ceiling, came down toward the floor, up to the ceiling, down again, up, hovered, and then came down on the floor for the last time with a great crashing *whump!* He landed so hard I thought I felt the floor shake. I knew he must be hurt.

"I stood there frozen for a moment. I couldn't imagine what had happened. Then it came to me. The drink in my cup had been poisoned. I suppose Nebu-al-karsig hadn't had nerve enough to do it himself. And the nuse installation in my room hadn't let the head priest get away with it.

"'A nuse never makes a mistake. 'The airy servitor. Don't think, use nuse.' The more I sell it, the more I'm convinced that it's wonderful stuff. This time it had saved my life. I couldn't help wishing for a minute, though, that it had just tipped over the poisoned cup quietly, because banging a priest around like that was sure to be sacrilege.

"The other priests had been as surprised as I was. Now they began to mutter and heft the clubs they were carrying. The nuse might be able to handle all of them at once, but I didn't wait to find out. I made a dash into the next room and bolted the door.

"I was wearing my chronnox. All I had to do was grab my chest of artifacts and go to some other time. I made a dive under the bed for the chest. And it wasn't there."

"Stolen?" I asked helpfully.

The nuse man shook his head. "No, I don't think so. Not with a nuse installation on guard. I think the nuse had levitated the chest to some safe place for extra security. I concentrated on getting the nuse to bring the chest back, and I did hear noises, levitation noises, as though it were trying to obey me. But it had all it could do to handle the priests in the next room.

"By now there was a considerable commotion in the palace. Doors were opening, people were shouting, I heard soldiers outside in the hall. Thumps and bumps from my sitting room showed that the nuse was still doing what it could with the priests, but several people were throwing themselves as hard as they could against the connecting door. I didn't know how much longer the bolts would hold.

"I tried concentrating on getting the nuse to abandon the priests and bring me my chest. I'm sure it would have worked in another minute. But then there was a lot of yelling and they began using a ram on the door. One of the panels busted. The hinges were sagging. I had to go."

The nuse man looked so depressed that I poured him out more tea. Just as I had suspected in the beginning, the nuse—always incalculable, always tricky, the essence of unreliability—the nuse had been at the bottom of his troubles. It always was. I had too much sense to say so, though.

"What was the point you were making about the plano-convex bricks?" I finally asked.

The nuse man looked even more gloomy. I wished I hadn't mentioned it. He picked a leaf out of his tea with his spoon and frowned savagely at it.

"I went back to Ur," he said finally. "I wanted to see what had happened about the bricks, and of course I wanted my chest. I picked a time about ten years later."

"Well?"

"The first thing I noticed was the skyline. Every one of the ziggurats Nebu-al-karsig had put up was gone. I walked up to where one of them had been, and there was nothing but a heap of bricks, and the bricks looked as if people had pounded them with hammers.

"I walked on to the center of town where the royal palace had been. It was gone, too, and what looked like a new royal palace was going up to the north of it. It was plain what had happened. There had been a revolution, Nebu-al-karsig had been over-

thrown, Ur had a new king. I ought to have gone then. But I was
still curious about my chest.

"The nuse factory had been just outside the palace walls. It
had been razed too—my beautiful installation!—but I could see
people working around where it had been. I went over to talk
to them.

"When I got up to them, I saw they were making bricks. Making them by hand, in the dumb, inefficient, old-fashioned way.
But these weren't rectangular bricks, the way the ones before my
nuse bricks had been. These were rectangular on the sides and
bottom, but they had round tops, like loaves of bread."

"In other words," I said, "plano-convex bricks."

"Yes. It was the most impractical idea in the world. Their
changing to such a silly shape made me realize how much the
brickmakers had hated the nuse bricks. By the way—I know how
curious you are—you'll be interested to learn that walls made with
bricks of that kind don't look especially different from ordinary
walls."

"Oh," I said. "I'd been wondering about that."

"I thought you'd be glad to know," said the nuse man. "Well, I
went up close to one of the brickmakers and watched him working. The pace he was going, he'd be lucky if he got ten bricks
done in a day. He smoothed his brick and rounded it and patted
it. He put more mud on it and stood back to watch the effect. He
pushed a wisp of straw into the surface with the air of an artist
applying a spot of paint. He just loved that brick.

"I cleared my throat, but he didn't seem to hear me. I said, 'Say,
I heard where they found a chest with gold and jewels in the
ruins of the old palace yesterday.'

"'Another one?' he answered, without looking up. 'You know,
they found one on the south side of the palace about five years
ago. Full of treasure. Some people have all the luck. Me, I never
find anything.'

"The south side of the palace was where my rooms had been.
I made a sort of noise.

"Up to then the worker had been too busy patting his round-
topped brick to pay any attention to me. Now he looked up. His

eyes got wide. His jaw dropped. He stared at me. 'Aren't you—are you—' he said doubtfully.

"Then he made up his mind. 'Brothers! Brothers!' he shouted. 'It's the foreign magician, come back to curse us again! Hurry! Kill him! Kill him! Kill the stinking sheep liver! Quick!'

"You wouldn't have thought that people who were working as slowly as they were could move so quick. As soon as they heard the words 'foreign magician,' they went into action, and before he got to the second 'Kill him!' the air was black with flying bricks."

"So that's how your face—"

"Yes. Of course, not all the bricks were dry. If they had been—but even a wet brick can be painful."

"And you never got your chest back."

"No. All I got was the artifacts the priest brought me just before the nuse levitated him. Would you like to see them?"

He sounded as if he wanted to show them to me. I said, "Yes, I'd like to."

He got out a little box and opened it. Inside was a piece of lapis lazuli that he said was a whetstone, two crude gold rings with roughly cabochon cut blackish stones, and a handsome gold necklace with lapis lazuli beads and gold pendants shaped like some sort of leaf.

"Very pretty," I said, examining them.

"You should have seen the stuff I had! But this is better than nothing. The home office will be glad to see it. I don't usually get even this much."

This was true, and he looked so depressed when he said it that I felt a burst of sympathy for him. I didn't know what to say.

He picked up the last piece of toast on the plate and looked at it.

"Burned," he said sourly, "and one of the other slices was, too. Listen, why don't you let me put in a nuse installation for you? Then your toast would never be burned. It's this housework that's getting you down. You might get so you didn't look any older than your real age if you used nuse."

"You should live so long," I said.

Success Story

BY EARL GOODALE

Once my name was Ameet Ruxt, my skin was light blue, and I was a moderately low-ranking member of the Haldorian Empire. Or should I say I was a member of the lower income group? No, definitely "low-ranking," because, in a warrior society, even one with as high a technological level as a statistician sits low on the totem pole. He is handed the wrong end of the stick—call it what you will; he's the one who doesn't acquire even one wife for years and he hasn't a courtesy title. He's the man they draft into their Invasion Forces—the Haldorians are always invading someone—and turn him into a Fighter Basic in a third of a year.

"Look," I'd complained to the burly two-striper in the Receiving Center, "I'm a trained statistician with a degree and . . ."

"Say Sir, when you address me."

I started over again. "I know, Sir, that they use statisticians in the service. So if Haldor needs me in the service it's only sensible that I should work in statistics."

The Hweetoral looked bored, but I've found out since that all two-stripers looked bored; it's because so many of them have attained, at that rank, their life's ambition. "Sure, sure. But we just got a directive down on all you paper-pushers. Every one of you from now on out is headed for Basic Fighter Course. You know, I envy you, Ruxt. Haldor, what I wouldn't give to be out there with real men again! Jetting down on some new planet—raying down the mongrels till they yelled for mercy—and grabbing a new chunk of sky for the Empire. Haldor! That's the life!" He glanced modestly down at his medalled chest.

"Yes, Sir," I said, "it sure is. But look at my examination records you have right there. Physically I'm only a 3 and you have to have a 5 to go to Basic Fighter. And besides," I threw in the clincher, though I was a bit ashamed of it, "my fighting aptitude only measures a 2!"

The Hweetoral sneered unsubtly and grabbed a scriber with heavy fingers. A couple of slashes, a couple of new entries, and lo, I was now a 5 in both departments. I was qualified in every respect.

"See," he said, "that's your first lesson in the Service, Ruxt. Figures don't mean a thing, because they can always be changed. That's something a figure pusher like you has to learn. So—" he shoved out that ponderous hand and crushed mine before I could protect myself—"good luck, Ruxt. I know you'll get through that course—alive, I mean." He chuckled heartily. "And I know men!"

He was right. I got through alive. But then, 76.5 per cent of draftees do get through the Basic Fighter Course, alive. But for me it took a drastic rearrangement of philosophy.

Me, all I'd ever wanted was a good life. An adequate income, art and music, congenial friends, an understanding wife—just one wife was all I'd ever hoped for. As you can see, I was an untypical Haldorian on every point.

After my first day in Basic Fighter Course I just wanted to stay alive.

"There's two kinds of men we turn out here," our Haldor told us as we lined up awkwardly for the first time (that scene so loved by vision-makers). We new draftees called our Trontar our Haldor because he actually had the power over our bodies that the chaplains assured us the Heavenly Haldor had over our liberated spirits. Our Trontar looked us over with his fatherly stare, flexing his powerful arm muscles so that his three tattooed stripes rippled and danced. "Yeah," he went on, "two kinds of men: Fighting men and dead men!" The Trontar grinned that fighting Haldorian grin you see all your lives on the Prop Sheets. "And I'll tell you something, men. When you leave here—all Fighters Basic—I'm going to envy you. Yeah, I'll really envy you gutsy killers when you go out in that big Out-There and grab yourselves a new chunk of sky." He paused and studied our faces. "Now we're gonna run, and I do mean run, two full decades. The last four men in get to do it over again, and pull kitchen duty tonight too."

I tried, as others have tried, to slip quietly out of Basic Fighter. I tried being sick, but following sick report one found oneself doing a full day's training—after the understanding medics had shoved some pep pills into you. I demanded a physical examination. They weren't going to push me around.

After a couple of days in solitary, I asked in a nice way for physical evaluation.

Well, I asked. I wasn't very smart in those days.

They weren't interested in my story of how my records had been falsified or in my fighting aptitude.

"Look, draftee," the psycho-man said after I finally got to him, "the fact that you've got to see me shows you have enough of a fighting aptitude. Your Trontar didn't encourage you to request evaluation, did he? And he isn't going to like you very much when you report back to your platoon, is he?"

I shuddered. "Not exactly."

"Call me Sir."

"No, Sir. But I was desperate, Sir. I don't think I can stand . . ."

"Draftee, you know that some unfortunate men break down in training and that we have to take them out. Maybe you've already lost some that way. Suppose you were brought in here, gibbering, yowling, and drooling—I guess we'd have to cure you and send you back home as non-fighter material, eh?"

Someone up here liked me! Here was a tip on how to escape back to the old quiet life. I nodded agreeably.

"But you know, don't you," he said softly, "that first we run a thorough test on our drooling draftee? Say it's you . . ."

I nodded again.

"We most always detect fakers. And you know there's a death

penalty for any Haldorian attempting to escape his duty." He smiled sadly, and reminiscently.

I nodded. Maybe someone up here didn't like me.

"So we'd shoot you dead with one of those primitive projectile weapons, as an object lesson for both you and the draftees we had remaining."

I nodded and tried to show by my countenance how much I approved of people being shot dead with primitive weapons.

"But suppose," he went on, "that you'd really cracked up or that you'd faked successfully?"

"Yes, Sir?" Hope returned, hesitantly and on tip-toes, ready to flee.

"Then we'd cure you," he said. "But the cure unfortunately involves the destruction of your higher mental faculties. And so there'd be nothing for it but to ship you off to one of the mining planets. That's standard procedure, if you didn't know. But I think you'll be all right now, don't you?"

Hope fled. I assured him that I'd be just fine and reported back, on the double, to my training platoon.

"Just in time, Ruxt," my Trontar greeted me. "Back for full duty, I take it? That's the Haldorian spirit!" He turned to the platoon which was lined up like three rows of sweaty statues. "Men, remember what I told you about taking cover when you're under fire—and staying under cover? Just suppose we suddenly came under fire—flat trajectory stuff—out here on this flat exercise ground with no cover except in that latrine pit over there. Would any of you hesitate to dive into that latrine pit? And once in there, safe and sound, would any of you not stay there until I gave the word to come out?"

A perceptible shudder passed like a wave over the platoon. We knew the Trontar did not ask pointless questions.

"Of course you wouldn't," he assured us, "and you'd even stay in there all day under this hot sun if you had to. Ruxt! You're rested and refreshed from visiting the hospital. You demonstrate how it's done."

It was a long day, even though my Trontar kindly sent some sandwiches over to me at high noon. I didn't eat much. But I did do a lot of thinking.

There was one last hope. I wrote a letter to a remote clan relative who was supposed to have a small amount of influence.

It was a moving letter. I told how my test results had been falsified, what beasts our trainers were, how the medics refused to retest me—very much the standard letter that new Haldorian trainees write. As I went out to mail this plea, one evening, I met two of my fellow trainees starting out on a night march in full field equipment.

"How come?" I asked, instantly fearful that I'd missed some notice on the bulletin board.

"We wrote letters," one of them said simply.

"The Trontar censors all our mail," said the other. "Didn't you you know? Oh, well, neither did we."

As they marched off, I made a small bonfire out of my letter after first, almost, just throwing it away—before I remembered that the Hweetorals checked our waste cans. What a man has to do to hold two measly stripes!

Acceptance of the inevitable is the beginning of wisdom, says the ancient Haldorian sage. I put in an application for transfer to the Statistical Services to be effective upon *completion* of Basic Fighter Course.

"Statistical Services?" the Company Clerk asked. "What's that? Anyhow, you're going to be a Fighter Basic, if you get through this training," he said darkly. The Company Clerk was a sad victim of our Haldorian passion for realistic training; he had lacked one day of completing Basic Fighter when he'd let his leg dangle a bit too long after he'd scaled a wall, and the training gentlemen had unemotionally shot it off. As it turned out, our efficient surgeon/replacers had been unable, for some technical reason, to grow back enough leg for full duty. So there was nothing for it but to use the man as could be best done. They'd made him a clerk—mainly because that was the specialty they were shortest of at the time.

"Who says you can put in for Statistical Services?" the Company Clerk demanded.

"Reg 39-47A." I was learning my way around. The night before I was on orderly duty in the office. I had tracked down the chapter and verse which, theoretically, allowed a man to change his destiny.

"Know the Regs, do you? Starting to be a trouble-maker, huh? Yeah, Ruxt, I'll put in your application."

I turned away with some feeling of relief. This might possibly work.

The Company Clerk called me back. "You know the Regs so good, Ruxt," he said. "How come you didn't ask me for permission to leave? I'm cadre, you know." He leaned back in his chair and grinned at me. "Just to help you remember the correct Haldorian deportment, I'm putting you on kitchen duty for the next three nights. That way," he grinned again, "you can divide up your five hours of sleep over three nights instead of crowding them all into one."

Poor deluded Company Clerk! I actually averaged three hours of sleep every one of those three nights—after I found out that the Mess Trontar would accept my smoking ration.

I felt that I was beginning to understand the system, a little and at long last, particularly after I saw my co-workers in the kitchen doing what should have been my work.

II

Then we started combat training, and then we started losing our normal 23.5 per cent.

It wasn't too bad as long as they stuck to the primitive stuff. I mean, you can see arrows and spears coming at you, and even if you have had only the five hours of sleep you can either duck the projectiles or catch them on your shield. And with the medics on the alert, the wounds are painful but seldom fatal. You just end up with a week's hospitalization and slip back to the next training group. But when they go up to the explosively propelled solids, when the Trontar smirks and says: "Men, this is called a boomer, or a banger, or maybe sometimes a firestick, depending on what planet you're fighting on," and when he holds up a contraption of wood and metal with a hole at one end and a handle on the other—then, Draftee, look out!

It takes time to learn. It isn't till you associate a bang in the distance with a perforated man beside you that you do learn. And when you finally come under fire from our regular production weapons like rays—well!

You might wonder why they run us through the entire history of weapons starting with the sling and ending with the slithers—the name servicemen give to those Zeta Rays that diverge from line of sight to drop in on a dug-in enemy. The usual explanation is that Haldorians are still invading places where the natives still use such things as bows and arrows. But I think, myself, that it's something the Mil Prop guys figured out. The idea is, as I see it, to run you right through the whole course of our fighting, invading Haldorian history, and in that way to make a better fighter out of you. And you do get rid of the death-prones before there's much time or work invested in them—or before their inevitable early death means the failure of a mission. Haldoria—most practical of Empires!

But they didn't make a fighter of me. All they did was to reinforce my natural survival instinct considerably, acquaint me with the tortuous ways of the service, and give me a great urge for a peaceful existence. But to all appearances, as I stood in the orderly room after graduation, I was the ideal poster-picture of a Haldorian, completely uniformed with polished power boots and rayer, a crawler to the higher-ups and a stomper on the lower-downs, a Fighter Basic with no compassion but with a certified aptitude for advancement to at least the rank of Trontar.

"Fighter Basic Ruxt," the Dispositions Hweetoral announced. "Here, Sir!"

"Your application for transfer to Statistical Services has been disapproved." The two-striper's expression showed what he, as a fighting man, thought of the Statistical Services. "But we've got a real assignment for you, Ruxt! The 27th Invasion Force is all set to drop on a new system. You're lucky, Ruxt, that you put in that application. We had to hold you till it bounced. Your buddies got shipped to those rear-echelon guard outfits, but you're going to a real fighting one. It should be a good invasion—this new system's got atomic fission, I hear. And I'd like to tell you something, Ruxt . . ."

"I know what, Sir," I said. "You envy me."

The 27th was a real fighting unit all right: they had their own neckerchief, their own war cry, and a general who was on his way up. Now they had me.

And they were going to get another system for the Haldorian Empire.

You see, those intelligent worms, or maybe they are slugs—I'm a bit vague on universe geography—over on the next galaxy but one, give us Haldorians all sorts of difficulties. They insist on freedom, self-determination, and all that sort of thing. That's all very well, but they insist on them for themselves. Our high-level planners decided that another solar system would make a better offensive set-up for Haldoria. The planners, I understand, have all sorts of esoteric theories about the ideal shape and size of an offensive unit. They ring in time and something related to time which makes galaxy distances differ according to which direction you are travelling. As I say, esoteric.

The only thing that mattered to me was that some technicians had fed some data into a computer and it had hiccuped and said: "You'll need such-and-such a planet to control such-and-such a solar system, and that will give you a better offensive set-up." Then the computer hiccuped again and said: "You'll need to draft and train Ameet Ruxt to help on this little job of taking over this planet called Terra, or Earth."

That's what it amounted to, anyhow. Consequently I joined the 27th Invasion Force.

"So you've got an application in for transfer to the Statistical Services, huh?" Trontar Hytd, my new platoon three-striper, asked when I reported in for duty with the 27th.

"Yes, Sir." I'd learned, along the line, that one should never give up when applying for a transfer—just keep one in the mill.

"Huh, Borr, this new guy likes to work with figures," Trontar Hytd growled at Hweetoral Borr, my new squad leader. "Thinks he doesn't want to be a Fighter." Trontar Hytd looked at me questioningly.

I didn't say anything. I'd learned a lot in Basic Fighter Course.

"Figures?" asked Hweetoral Borr. I could see a train of thought had been started in the Hweetoral's mind.

"Yeah, figures," snapped Trontar Hytd. "He likes to count things, Borr. Get it?"

"Guess we need all our ray charges counted, for one thing," suggested Hweetoral Borr. "I get all mixed up with them figures."

"After training hours, of course," Trontar Hytd said.

"Of course, Trontar. And someone's gotta jawbone some kind of report on ammo expenditures every training day. Maybe after the rest of us have sacked in, for instance?"

"Of course. Okay, Hweetoral, I guess you got the idea."

Invasion was almost a relief after that brief bit of refresher training the 27th was going through.

Our General-on-the-way-up had outlined his plan of attack: "Drop'm, hit'm, lift'm and drop'm again." So I dropped, hit the defenders, was lifted to a new center of resistance, and dropped again. I understand it was a standard type of invasion. There's only one way to do simple things.

Once in a while, these days, I remember those sadistic and battle-hardened comrades of mine. Hard, gutsy Trontar Hytd stayed on his feet to direct his platoon underground after our Kansas force collapsed, and one of those little fission weapons separated his body parts too widely for even our unsentimentally competent surgeon/replacer to reassemble him. Well, they had a go at the job, but they had to ray down what they created—some primitive regression had set in and the creature was hungry.

And rough and tough Hweetoral Borr incautiously scratched his hairy ear just when one of those rude projectile weapons was firing at him. The slug slipped through that opening the Hweetoral had made in his body armor. With the brain gone—or such brain as Hweetoral Borr possessed—our kindly old surgeon/replacer was foxed again.

Then there were the new germs . . .

But these things are as nothing to the creative military mind. A swarm of regulations, manuals and directives issue forth from headquarters, and force fields cease to collapse, and fighters keep their body armor on and adjusted. When something like the influenza germ wipes out half a platoon, the wheels turn, a new vaccine is devised, and no more Haldorians die from that particular germ. All the individual has to do is to live from one injection to the next (any civilized enemy always cooks up new diseases), move from one enemy strong point to the next, and dream of the day when he can return to his old life. For me it was a dream of returning to that quiet tiny room with its walls lined with the best of Haldorian art—just cheap reproductions, of course

—and never again to handle a rayer or to wear armor. Real life, meanwhile, went on.

"Fighter First-Class Ruxt! Take these men and blast that strong point!" That would be the order somewhere in Missouri, or maybe in Mississippi—I never was much good on micro-geography. "Hweetoral Ruxt! Take your squad and clean out that city. New Orleans they call it. Get their formal surrender and make damn sure there are no guerrillas left when the colonel comes through to inspect."

By the time I was Trontar Ruxt the invasion was practically over. As I say, it was the standard thing with one or two countries holding out after all hope was gone—England never did formally surrender, not that it mattered—and our successful General was made a Sub-Marshal of the Haldorian Empire.

A real promotion and a great honor. Much good it did him when he ventured his battle fleet too far into the Slug lines a year later.

With the fighting over—the real fighting, I mean—the ever-efficient Haldorians started moving their troops off Earth to get ready for a new and bigger invasion that the computers had decreed. Only a few troops were to be left behind for occupation and guard stuff.

I had a talk with a fat Assignments Trontar in his plush office.

"You know, Trontar," I said, "I was hoping to see more of this world here, and the rumor is that all of us excess combat types are being shipped to a training world to be shaped into new invasion forces."

"Tough," he said. He should know. He'd requisitioned a mansion complete with servants and everything. He even had a native trained to drive one of their luxuriously inefficient ground vehicles. What a deal! That Trontar had no worries, *his* anti-grav ray was working.

"I heard that a man doesn't even need any money if he's stationed down at our headquarters," I said, and I hauled out a handful of Haldorian notes from my pocket. "Guess I wouldn't need this stuff if I was transferred down to our headquarters."

"Who needs money?" he asked. "Guys all the time trying to

bribe me, Trontar. You'd be surprised. Sure glad you aren't, though, because I do hate to turn anyone in."

I put the money back in my pocket. "Speaking of turning in people," I said casually, "you ever have any trouble with the undercover boys about all this loot you've picked up?" This, I thought, would shake him—and at the same time I marvelled at how I'd changed from a simple, naive statistician to a tough and conniving combat NCO.

He yawned all over his fat face and swung his swivel chair so that he could better admire the picture beside his desk. I recognized the picture as a moderately good reproduction of a Huxtner, a minor painter of our XXVth. "No," the Assignments Trontar said, "it turns out that one of my sept brothers runs the local watch birds. He often drops in here to visit with me. But anything I can do for you, Trontar?"

"No," I said, and I fired at the only possible loophole left, "I'll just leave quietly so you can admire your Huxtner."

He swung back to me with a start. "You recognize a Huxtner? You're the first man I've ever met in the service who ever heard of Huxtner, let alone recognizing one of his masterpieces! Hey, did you know I brought this all the way from home in my hammock roll? And just look at the coloring of that figure there!"

The loophole had been blasted wide open. "You're lucky," I said, and I went on to lie about how I'd lost my own Huxtner prints in the invasion. "No one," I continued, "ever got quite that flesh tint of Huxtner's, did they?"

Huxtner, by the way, is notorious for using a yellow undercoat for his blue flesh colors, unlike every realistic painter before or after who have all used green undercoats—what else? Imagine a chrome-yellow underlaying a blue skin color. All Huxtner's figures look like two-week corpses—but Huxtner enthusiasts are unique.

The Assignments Trontar and I had a nice long chat about Huxtner, at the conclusion of which he insisted on scratching my name from the list of combat-bound men and putting me on a much smaller list of men scheduled for our guard outfit, stationed at the old Terran capital of Washington.

I had an un-Haldorian feeling of having arranged my own life after that incident. That feeling persisted even after I took over one of the guard platoons and discovered that life in a guard outfit is rather similar to Basic Fighter Course.

"Trontar Ruxt! Two men of your platoon have tarnished armor. Get them working on it, and maybe you'd better stay and see that they do it properly."

"Yes, Sir."

One lives and learns. I turned the job of supervising the armor cleaning to the Hweetorals of the squads and then I went home to my native woman. Yes, this guard's outfit life was like Basic Fighter Course.

But only for the lower ranks.

III

Life wasn't too unendurable in those days. The duties were incredibly dull, of course, but the danger of sudden death had receded, since only a few fanatics still tried to pick off us occupation troops. And this new world of Haldoria's was rich in the things a sensitive and artistic man appreciates: painting, sculpture, music. Then there was this new and pleasing thing of living with a woman . . .

But it wouldn't last long.

Soon there'd be another planet to invade and maybe a space battle with the great enemy. More years of cramped living and lurking danger, for in the Empire one was drafted for the duration, and this duration was now some four hundred years old. The most Trontar Ruxt could expect, the very most, was to somehow keep alive for another fifty years and then to retire on a small pension to one of the lesser worlds of the Empire.

"Trontar Ruxt! Your records show that you're a statistician." My commanding officer stared at me suspiciously, for a fighting man, even one on guard duty, distrusts office personnel. And as everyone knows, "Once a fighting man, always a fighting man." I think my C.O.'s last action had been thirty years ago.

"I was a statistician before I got in the service, Sir."

"Well, they're screaming over at headquarters for qualified office personnel, and we have to send them any trained men we have—of any rank."

"It's for Haldor, Sir," I said. By now I knew the correct answer was most often the noncommittal one.

I reported to the Headquarters, 27th Invasion Force. The rumor was that Phase II, Reduction of Inhabitants to Slavery with Shipment to Haldorian Colonies, was about to start. And also, our Planners were supposed to be well into Phase III, Terraforming, already. Terraforming was necessary, of course, to bring the average temperature of Earth down to something like the sub-arctic so that we Haldorians could live here in comfort. We lost quite a few fighters during invasion when their cooling systems broke down. Rumor, as always, was dead right; and the Headquarters was a mad rat-race.

The Senior Trontar of the office was delighted to get another body.

"Took your time getting here, Ruxt! You guard louts don't know the meaning of time, do you?"

I remained at attention.

"So you're a statistician, are you? Well, we don't need any statisticians now. We just got in a whole squad of them. Can you use a writer, maybe?"

"Yes, Sir." I did not remind the Senior Trontar that using a writer was a clerk's job, not a Trontar's, not a combat three-striper's, because the chances were that he knew it, for one thing. And he could easily make me a clerk, for another thing.

"Okay. Now that we understand each other," the Senior Trontar grinned, "or that you understand me, which is all that matters, here's your job." He handed me a stack of scribbled notes, some rolls of speech tape and a couple of cans of visual stuff. "Make up a report in standard format like this example. Consolidate all this stuff into it. This report has to be ready in two days, and it has to be perfect. No misspellings, no erasures, no nothing. Got that?"

"Yes, Sir."

"Yes, Sir," he mimicked. "Haldor only knows why they couldn't send me a few clerks instead of a squad of statisticians and one guard Trontar. Do you know what this stuff is that you're going to work up? It's the final report on our invasion here!"

I looked impressed. Strange how you learn, after a while, even the facial expression you are supposed to wear.

"Do you know why this report has to be perfect in format and appearance?" I wouldn't say the Senior Trontar's manner was bullying, quite. Perhaps one could call it hectoring. "Because the Accountant is out in this sector somewhere and we have to be ready for him if he drops in."

This time I didn't have to try to look impressed. The Accountant is the man who passes judgment on the conduct of all military matters—though of course he's not one man, but maybe a dozen of them. Armed with the invaluable weapon of hindsight, he drops in after an invasion is completed. He determines whether the affair has gone according to regulations, or whether there has been carelessness, slackness or wasting of Haldorian resources of men or material. Additionally he monitors civil administration of colonies and federated worlds. There are stories of Generals becoming Fighter Basics and Chief Administrators becoming subclerks after an Accountant's visit.

I got the report done, but it took the full two days—mainly because fighting men make such incomplete and erroneous reports while action is going on. I got to understand the exasperated concern of office personnel who have to consolidate varied fragments into a coherent whole. And adding to the natural difficulties of the task was the continual presence of the Senior Trontar, and his barbed comments and lurid promises as to what would follow my failure at the work.

But the report was done and sent in to the Adjutant.

It came back covered with scribbled changes, additions, and deletions—and it came back carried by a much disturbed Senior Trontar.

"Who in Haldor do they think I am?" he moaned. "I just handed on to you the figures that they gave me. Me! And threatening me with duty on a space freighter . . . and one into the Slug area at that!"

I thought, as I looked at my ruined script, that guard duty wasn't so bad, and that even combat wasn't rough *all* the time.

"See, Trontar," the four-striper said, calling me by my proper rank for the first time, "you did a good job, the Adjutant himself said so. But these figures . . ." he shuddered. "If the Accountant should see these we'd all be for it. Space-freighter duty would be getting off light." The Senior Trontar seemed almost human to me right then.

"I just put down what you gave me," I said.

"Yeah, sure, Ruxt. But I didn't realize, nobody realized, how bad the figures were till they were all together and written up. Look, this report shows that we shouldn't Terraform this planet —that we can't make a nudnick on the slavery proposition—and that maybe we shouldn't have even invaded this inferno at all."

"So what do you want me to do?"

"I'll tell you what you're going to do . . ." The Senior Trontar had regained his normal nasty disposition. "You're going to re-do this report. You're going to re-do it starting now, you're going to work on it all night, and you're going to have it on my desk and in perfect shape when I come in in the morning, or, by Haldor, the next thing you write will be your transfer to the space freighter run nearest the Slug Galaxy." The Senior Trontar ran momentarily out of breath. "And," he came back strongly, "you won't be going as no Trontar, neither!"

"It'll be on your desk in the morning, Sir," I said.

Deck hands on the space freighter run were, I'd heard, particularly expendable.

By the middle of the third watch I had completed a perfect copy of the report complete with attachments, appendices, and supplements. And also by this time I knew from the differences between the original report and this jawboned version that someone had goofed badly in undertaking this invasion, and then had goofed worse in not calling the thing off. Now there was to be considerable covering-up of tracks. The thought suddenly came to me that a guard's Trontar named Ruxt knew rather a lot of what had gone on. Following that mildly worrying thought came a notion that perhaps a guard's Trontar named Ruxt might be considered by some as just another set of tracks to be covered up. That far-off retirement on a small but steady income became even more unlikely, and the possibilities began to appear of a quick end in the Slug-shattered hulk of a space freighter.

Had the Senior Trontar changed in his attitude toward me, toward the end of the day, perhaps acted as though I were a condemned man? Possibly. And had some of the officers been whispering about me late in the afternoon? Could have been.

Shaken, I wandered down to the mess hall and joined a group of third-watch guards, who were goofing off while their Trontar was checking more distant guard posts.

"It's easy," one of them was telling the others. "All you got to do is to slip some surgeon/replacer a few big notes and he gives you this operation which makes you look like a native. And then you just settle down on Astarte for the rest of your life with the women just begging you to let them support you."

"You mean you'd rather live on some lousy federated world than be a Haldorian in the Invasion Forces?" There was a strong sardonic note in the questioner's voice.

"Man, you ever been on Astarte?" the first man asked incredulously.

"Yeah, but how are you going to be sure that the surgeon/replacer doesn't turn you in?" objected one of the others. "He could take your money, do the operation, and have you picked up. That way he'd have the money and get a medal too."

"I'd get around that," the talky guy said, "I'd just . . ."

At this point he was jabbed in the arm by one of his buddies who had noticed my eavesdropping. The man shut up. All four of them drifted off to their posts.

I went reluctantly back to the office. From then till dawn I dreamed up and rehearsed all manner of wild schemes to take me out of this dangerous situation. Or was it all perhaps just imagination? A Haldorian Trontar should never be guilty of an excess of that quality. But I made sure when the Senior Trontar sneaked in a bit before the regular opening time, that I was just, apparently, completing the last page of the report. The impression I hoped to convey was that I had spent the entire night in working and worrying.

"It's okay," the Senior Trontar growled after he had studied the completed report. "Guess you can take a couple of days off, Ruxt. I believe in taking care of my men. Say," he asked casually, "I suppose you didn't understand those figures you were working up, did you?"

"No," I said, "I didn't pay any attention to them; they were just something to copy, that's all." I felt confident that I could out-fence the Senior Trontar any time at this little game, but what had he and the Adjutant been whispering about before they had come in?

"But you used to be a statistician, didn't you?" He looked at the far corner of the room and smiled slightly. "But you take a couple days off, Ruxt. Maybe we'll find something good for you when you come back." He smiled again. "Don't forget to check out with the Locator before you go, though. We don't want to lose you."

I stumbled home, not even noticing the hate-filled glances my armor and blue skin drew from the natives along the streets. The glances were standard, but this feeling of being doomed was new.

They were going to get me. I felt sure of that, even though my Sike Test Scores had always been as low as any normal's. But how could a Haldorian disappear on this planet? Aside from skin color, there was the need to keep body temperatures at a livable level. The body armor unit was good only for about a week. Find a surgeon/replacer and bribe him to change me to an Earthman? I saw now how ridiculous such an idea was. But was there nothing but to wait passively while the Senior Trontar and the Adjutant, and whoever else did the dirty work, all got together and railroaded me off?

Haldorians, though, never surrender—or so the Mil Prop lad would have us believe. Right from the time you are four years old and you start seeing the legendary founders of Haldoria— Bordt and Smordt—fighting off the fierce six-legged carnivores, you are told never to give up. "Where there's Haldor, there's Hope!" "There's always another stone for the wolves, if you but look." I must confess I'd snickered (way deep inside, naturally) at these exhortations ever since I'd reached the age of thinking, but now all these childhood admonitions came rushing back to give me strength, quite as they were intended to do. I found that I could but go down like any Haldorian, fighting to the last.

IV

So I put on my dress uniform the next day, and made sure that
nothing could be deader than the dulled bits, or brighter than
the polished ones. A bit of this effort was wasted since I arrived
at Headquarters looking something less than sharp. The cooling
unit in my armor was acting up a bit; and, also, three Terran city
guerillas had tried to ambush me on the way. You take quite a
jolt from a land mine, even with armor set on maximum. Some
of those people never knew when they were licked. No wonder
their Spanglt Resistance Quotient was close to the highest on
record.

I got through the three lines of guards and protective force
fields all right, checking my rayer here, my armor there—the
usual dull procedure. By the time I reached the Admissions Officer I was down to uniform and medals.

"You want to see the Accountant?" the Admissions Officer
asked incredulously. "You mean one of his staff! Well, where's
your request slip, Trontar?"

"I've come on my own, Sir," I said, "not from my office, so I
haven't a request slip."

"Come on your own? What's your unit? Give me your ID card!"

Let's see, I thought, I've abstracted classified material from
the files and carried it outside the office, I've broken the chain
of command and communication, and, worst of all, I'd tried to see
a senior officer without a request slip. Yeah, maybe I'd be lucky
to end up as a *live* deckhand on a space freighter.

A bored young Zankor with the rarely seen balance insignia of
the Accountant's Office rose from behind the Admissions Officer.

"I'll take responsibility for this man," he said casually to the
A.O. "Follow me, Trontar. I was wondering when you'd turn up."

"Me?"

"Well, someone like you. Though usually it's scared sub-clerks
that we drag up. And that reminds me." He turned to another
young and equally bored Zankor standing nearby. "Take over,
Smit, will you? They're bringing in that sub-clerk who's been writing those anonymous letters. I've reserved the Inquisition Room
for a couple of hours for him."

I followed the Zankor as he strode away, wondering as I did if they had more than one Inquisition Room.

He led me into a small room just off the corridor and motioned me to a chair. "Before you see the Accountant, Trontar," he said, "I'll have to screen what you have. It may be that we won't have to bother the Accountant at all."

The smooth way the Zankor talked and his friendly manner almost convinced me that we should both put the interests of the Accountant first. But then it occurred to me that a man with the gold knot of a Zankor on his collar wasn't often friendly with a mere Trontar. That thought snapped me out of it and I knew I should only give the minimums.

"I've got documents," I said—"document" is such a lovely strong word, "which prove that the official report on the invasion and occupation of this planet is false." That, I thought, was as minimum as one could get.

"Ah, and have you?" The Zankor still looked bored. "Well, let's see them, Trontar," he said briskly.

The Zankor had that sincere look the upper class always uses when they are about to do you dirt. They blush that heavy shade of blue, almost purple, and they look you straight in the eye, and they quiver a bit as to voice . . . and the next thing you know, you're shafted.

"I'm sorry, Sir," I said, "but what I have is so important that I can give it to the Accountant only."

He stared at me for rather a long moment, pondering, no doubt, the pleasures of witnessing a full-dress military flogging. Then he shrugged and picked up the speaker beside him. He didn't call the Trontar of the Guard to come and take my documents by force. I could tell that even though he spoke in High Haldorian, that harsh language the upper class are so proud of preserving as a relic from the days of the early conquerors. No, he was speaking to a superior—there's never any doubt as to who is on top when people are speaking High Haldorian—and then I caught the emphatic negative connected with the present-day Haldorian phrases meaning Phase II and Phase III, Terraforming. So even though I don't know High Haldorian, and would never be so incautious as to admit it if I did, I knew roughly what had been said.

And I was frantically revising my plans.

"Follow me," the Zankor said, after completing the call. "We'll see the Accountant now, and—" he looked at me sincerely— "you'd better have something very good indeed. You really had, Trontar."

The Accountant turned out to be a tall and thin Full Marshal, the first I'd seen. He was dressed in a uniform subtly different from the regulation, and he wore only one tiny ribbon, which I didn't recognize. He had the slightly deeper-blue skin you often see on the upper classes, though this impression may have been due to the green furnishings of the room. It was, in fact, called the Green Room, when the Terrans had used it as one of their regional capitals.

I saluted the Accountant with my best salute, the kind you lift like it was sugar and drop as if it were the other. The Accountant responded with one of those negligent waves that tell you the saluter was a survivor of the best and bloodiest private military school in existence.

"Proceed, Trontar," the Accountant said, leaning back and relaxing as if he didn't have a care in the universe.

I launched into my speech, the one I'd been mentally rehearsing. I told him I knew I was breaking the chain of communication, but that I was doing it for the service and for Haldoria, etc. Any old serviceman knows the routine. I was, as I ran through this speech, just as sincere and just as earnestly interested in the good of Haldoria as any Haldorian combat Trontar could be. But, deep inside me, the old Ameet Ruxt was both marveling at the change in himself and cynically appreciating the performance.

The Accountant interrupted the performance about halfway through. "Yes, yes, Trontar," he said brusquely, "I think we can assume your action is for the good of Haldoria, may the Empire increase and the Emperor live forever. Yes. But you say you have material dealing with the overall report on our invasion and occupation of this planet. You further say this material shows discrepancies in the official report—which you imply you have seen."

"Yes, Sir," I said, and I handed over the several sheets of paper which comprised the old report and the changes of the new. Meanwhile, behind me, the Zankor was invisible but I had not a doubt but that he was there, keeping the regulation distance from me.

These people knew their business.

The Accountant took the collection of papers and compared them with some others he had on his desk. I continued to stand at Full Brace. Once you've been chewed out for slipping into an Ease position without being so ordered, you never forget.

The Accountant laid down the papers, scanned my face, got up and walked to the far end of the room. In front of a mirror he stopped and fingered that one small ribbon, quite, I thought, as if he were matching it with another one.

He came back quickly and sat down again. "Zankor," he said, "set up a meeting with the top brass for this afternoon. I'll talk with the Trontar privately."

The Zankor saluted and was on his way out the door when the Accountant spoke again. "And Zankor . . ."

"Yes, Sir?"

"I should be very unhappy if the top brass here—the *present* top brass—found out about this material the Trontar brought."

The Zankor swallowed hard and assured the Accountant that he understood . . . "Sir."

Then we were alone and the Accountant was suddenly a kindly old man who invited me to sit down and relax. I did. I really let go and stretched out, I forgot everything I'd ever been taught as a child or had learned on my climb to the status of Trontar. I relaxed and he had me.

I had been caught on the standard Haldorian Soft/Hard Tactic.

"Disabuse your mind, Trontar," the Accountant snapped, and he was no longer a kindly old man but a thin-lipped Haldorian snapper, "of any idea that you have saved the Empire—or any such nonsense!" Having cracked his verbal whip about my shoulders he just crouched there, glaring at me, his mouth entirely vanished and his eyes—well, I'd just as soon not think about some things.

Yes, and then he gave me the Shout/Silence treatment, the whole thing so masterfully timed that at the end he could have

signed me on as a permanent latrine keeper on a spy satellite in
the Slug Galaxy. A genius, that man was. The sort of man who
could—and probably did—control forty wives without a weapon.

"Your information, as it happens," he said after I had regained
my senses, "checks with other data I've received. It might be, of
course, that the whole thing is a fabrication of my enemies. In
that case, Trontar—" he looked at me earnestly—"you can be
assured you'll not be around to rejoice at or to profit from my
downfall."

"Of course, Sir," I said, quite as earnestly as he.

"But we both know that you are only a genuine patriot," he
said with a hearty chuckle, a chuckle exactly like that of a Father
Goodness—that kindly old godfather who brings such nice pres-
ents to every Haldorian child until they are six, and who on that
last exciting visit brings, and enthusiastically uses, a bundle of
large and heavy whips to demonstrate that no one can be trusted.
Efficient teachers, the Haldorians.

"Just a genuine patriot," the Accountant repeated, "who has
rendered a considerable service to the Empire. Trontar," he said,
all friendly and intimate, "the Empire likes to reward well its
faithful sons. What would you most like to have or to do?"

"To serve Haldoria, Sir!" I was back on my mental feet at last.

He dropped his act then. He was, I think, just practicing anyway. We had a short talk then, the kind in which one person is
quickly and efficiently pumped of everything he knows. After
about ten minutes of question and answers, the Accountant
leaned back and studied my face carefully.

"Have you considered Officers' Selection Course, Trontar? I
might be able to help you a little in getting in."

Officers' Selection Course was, I knew, Basic Fighter Course
multiplied in length and casualties. Less than 20 per cent gradu-
ate . . . or escape.

"No, Sir," I said. "I wondered if I mightn't be of more value to
Haldoria in some way other than being in the combat services."
So now I'd said it, and there was nothing to do but to go on.
"Perhaps," I ventured, "I might be of some help in the adminis-
trative services."

The Accountant said nothing, his face was immobile, his hands still. He'd learned his lessons well, once.

"In fact," I said, deciding to go for broke, "with my knowledge of the language and the customs here, I might be of most service to Haldoria right here on this planet."

"Had you guessed, by any chance, Trontar," the Accountant's voice was neutrally soft, "that we won't be Terraforming this world? And that we may not even exploit the slavery proposition?"

"I thought both those possibilities likely," I admitted.

"But you know that in such a case we would have no administrative services on this world? Thus you are, in fact, asking for a position that wouldn't exist." The Accountant, without a change of position or expression, somehow gave the impression of looming over me.

"I thought," I said, trying to pick exactly the right words, and at the same time all too conscious of a twitching muscle in my left eyelid, "that there might be an analogous position, even so."

The Accountant loomed higher.

"If only," he said, "you hadn't come to us, Trontar. I mean that you, in effect, sold your associates out to me. And I hold that once a seller, always a seller. If I could be certain that you are and will be perfectly loyal to the Haldorian Way . . ."

I managed to quiet the twitching eyelid and to look perfectly loyal to the Haldorian Way.

"Yes, Trontar," the Accountant said decisively, "I'll buy it."

The results of my conference with the Accountant were not long in appearing.

The Haldorian troops were called in, along with the military governors and the whole administrative body, and they all shipped out, somewhere into the Big Out-There they all love so much. A surprised Earth was informed that she was now a full-fledged and self-governing member of the Haldorian Empire. The Terrans were not informed of the economic factors behind this decision, though it might have been cheering for them to know that their Spanglt Resistance Quotient indicated they would make unsatisfactory slaves. Nor did the high cost of Terraforming the planet get mentioned. We Haldorians prefer the gratitude of others toward us to be unalloyed with baser, or calculating, emotions.

Not all the Haldorian personnel went out to fight or to administer. I understand the space-freighter run to the battle fleet in the Slug Galaxy gained many new deck-hands, among them one whose uniform showed the marks where Trontar's stripes had perched.

As for myself?

Well, a relatively minor operation changed me into a black-skinned Terran, though the surgeon/replacers could do nothing, ironically enough in view of my new color, to increase my resistance to heat. I remember those stirring days of combat sometimes, usually when I am making my semi-annual flight between Churchill, Manitoba, and Tierra Del Fuego. In fact, during those flights when I am practically alone is the only time I have to reflect or remember, because on both of my estates there is nothing but noise, children, and wives.

But it's a good life when the snow is driving down out of a low gray overcast, just like it does back on Haldor. It's a good life being Resident Trader on Terra, especially when one is, on the side, a trusted agent of the Accountant. It would be a perfect life—if the Accountant hadn't been right about people being unable to stop selling out.

Right now I'm up to my neck in this Terran conspiracy to revolt against the very light bonds Haldoria left on this planet. But how could I resist the tempting offer the Terrans made me? The long sought-for good life, it now occurs to me, isn't so much in escaping from something, but in knowing when to stop. But that I know. I'm drawing the line right now. I'll just tell that agent of the Slug Galaxy that I have no intention of selling out both this solar system *and* Haldoria!

A Husband for My Wife

BY WILLIAM W. STUART

Soon, very soon now, the time will come for me to meet my wife's husband. I can hardly wait. Every dog has his day and Professor Thurlow Benjamin has just about had it. Every day has its dog, too, and I am going to return to him with full five years' interest the bad time he gave to me. The dog.

Dog? Look, he stole my girl not once but twice. The second time he, you might say, took his time to beat my time—and left me behind to the bad time that belonged to him. Benji is—or he was and he will be—a scientifically sneaky, two-timing dog, and a dog's life is what he gave me. But now, after nearly five years, time is on my side. He will get what, minute by minute, is coming to him not soon enough, but soon.

Benji—Professor Thurlow Benjamin—was my oldest, closest friend. I was his. We hated each other dearly in the way that only two boyhood pals can and by chance or mischance that quality of bitter-friendly, boyish rivalry never left our relationship. Why? A woman, naturally.

The first time we met, he was a tall, gangling, red-headed, big-nosed kid of nine. I, Bull (for Boulard) Benton, was shorter, stockier, heavier. Maybe not handsome exactly, but clean cut, very clean cut. Benji knocked a chip off my shoulder and I knocked his block off, but not without collecting a few lumps doing it. From then on, we fought together against anyone else. When no one else was handy, we fought each other. And naturally we each wanted what the other had.

After high school, we roomed together at Burnington University right there in our home town, Belt City. Benji was a brain, a scholar. I was an athlete. So he broke nearly every bone in his body trying to be a six-foot-three, one-hundred-and-thirty-nine-pound scatback, while I nearly sprained a brain that was deep, definitely deep, but maybe not quite as quick on its feet as some, trying for scholarship.

The last year and a half at the university, the competition between us narrowed down to a battle for Vera Milston, old Dean Milston's statuesque daughter. That was all a mistake. I can see it now. So can Benji. But not then.

Dean Milston was the dourest, sourest, meanest old tyrant ever to suspend a football captain for a couple of unimportant "D"s. One afternoon in junior year at basketball practice—Benji was out, dragging around a cast—Jocko Bunter bet me ten I didn't have the nerve to date the dean's daughter. Well, hell, I'd seen her around, visiting the dean as regularly as I had to. She was a lot of girl. Tall, honey-blonde—a little on the regal, commanding side, and maybe her lips were a mite set over a chin that the old man should have kept to himself—but there are times when a young man doesn't analyze the details as carefully as he might. She was built like nothing I had tackled all fall.

So I took a chance, got a date, won ten, and that might and should have been that. She had a way of saying "No!" that made me think of her father. But, the thing was, Benji didn't know about the bet. I dated her once. So he had to date her twice. Again, I didn't analyze. I jumped to the conclusion Benji had the hots for her and went to work to cut him out.

That kept us busy the next year and a half and I led all the way. Vera and I got engaged at the spring prom to be married right after my graduation—which improved the odds on my graduating considerably. The dean was a grim old devil who considered Hamlet a comedy and could refuse anything to anyone—

except Vera, and how could I have known it was fear rather than affection that made him give in to her?

Anyway, perhaps the strain of passing me a diploma was too great. The next day the old devil passed on himself, and no matter where he may be sitting, I know he is happy as long as he can watch the others fry. But I shouldn't grumble. He saved me, unintentional though it was.

Vera, possibly having second thoughts as she looked over the Dean's List, said she couldn't marry me till after a reasonable period of mourning. The Army took me and rejected Benji. He stayed on for post-graduate study in physics. I told you he was a brain.

A brain, but not equally acute in all fields. When I got back to Belt City three years later, Benji was already an assistant professor of physics—and Vera's husband. They were settled in the old dean's big, ancient house just off the campus and Benji was aiming—or being aimed—at a distinguished academic career. I came back to town with the idea of winding up the family insurance and real estate business and pulling out, mostly to keep away from them.

It wasn't, you understand, that I was carrying such a heavy torch for Vera. She hadn't blighted my life; not then, that is. But it seemed to me that living in town with her and Professor Thurlow Benjamin—a gloating, triumphant Benji, laughing at me because he'd succeeded in marrying my girl—would be a real annoyance. But, of course, when I hit town I had to call them and they had to invite me to dinner.

For one time, anyway, I figured I had to accept. I gritted my teeth and went. I never had a sweeter, more enjoyable evening in all my life.

I got there about seven in the evening and walked up the steps to the big old porch on the dean's house feeling a bit nervous and upset. I'd walked up those same steps often enough before, feeling nervous and upset, but this was different. I lifted the oversized brass knocker and rapped. Vera's voice, coming from the back of the house someplace, cut through the evening air. "Thurlow! Answer the door!"

"Yes, sweets. I'm on my way, Vera hun bun." That was Benji.

Hun bun, yet! And his voice was misery. It cringed and whined. I grinned to myself and began to feel more cheerful.

Benji let me in. His glasses were thicker and his hair thinner and he looked a lot older. But it was Benji, the same old lanky, gangling redhead; yet not the same, too. He had a hang-dog look that was new and suddenly I felt so good, I punched him playfully in the ribs. He winced—and didn't even counter. If the fight hadn't gone out of him, it had sure been watered down. We went on in to the parlor across the hall from the dean's old study. Vera joined us. She didn't look bad—at a glance. But if you checked right close, and I did, there was something in her look— a sharpness I hadn't noticed before; her nose seemed bigger, beak-like; the broad, solid shoulders; deep-down grooves at the corners of her mouth.

She threw her arms around me and kissed me. My temperature stayed steady and cool.

"Boulard! Boulard, darling! You look marvelous!"

I felt great, too. "Vera, girl. You're as gorgeous as ever, radiant, blooming, still the campus goddess. And Mrs. Thurlow Benjamin now, hm-m? Old Benji is sure a lucky dog."

Benji forced a hollow laugh. Vera smiled a positive agreement.

Then Benji sort of coughed out a faint note of hope and pleaded, "Vera, sweet, this is a—uh—an occasion, don't you agree, dear? Don't you—ah—do you think maybe I ought to—fix us all a drink?"

"Thurlow! You drink far too much! You had a highball before dinner at Professor Dorman's only night before last."

Almost—but not quite—I felt sorry for him.

"Ah, well, Vera doll," I said, "this *is* an occasion, after all. And I *do* want to drink a toast to you and Benji."

"Hmph."

"Especially you, the love of my life, lost now, but lovelier than ever."

"Boulard! . . . Well, Thurlow, don't stand there like an idiot. Go mix us some drinks. And mind the line on the bottle."

And then she turned back with some more gush for me. I enjoyed it, knowing now what I had been saved from. In fact, as I said, I enjoyed the whole evening; my playing up to Vera made her just that much rougher on Benji. Revenge on Benji plus relief at what I had escaped made life seem pleasant, and right there and then I changed my mind about leaving town. I decided to stay and settled down.

Well, I did settle, but not too far down. Instead of selling out Uncle George's insurance and real estate firm, I went to work in it. It was prosperous enough and light work. There were plenty of girls around town if you got around, and I did.

Looking back, those were the happy years. Naturally I kept seeing quite a bit of Vera and Benji. Rubbing it in? Sure, why not? Hell, half the pleasure in any success comes from giving a hard time to those who gave you a hard time. It may not be nice, but it is normal.

I lolled in the shade and laughed; Benji sweated and suffered. His boss's whip cracked merrily. He plodded ahead in the University Physics Department and fiddled around his lab whenever he could escape into it.

Then there came a black Friday evening in early autumn. I was due at Benji's for dinner, just him and me. Vera had gone up to Chicago that morning to see her ever-dying Aunt Bella and do some shopping. She would not be back till the next day so she called on me to keep an eye on Benji.

So I was due for a quietly pleasant early evening listening to Benji talk about his sorrows. Then, I figured, Benji would go to his lab in the old dean's study and I would go out on the town. I had a date, one of the very best, Starlight Glowe, formerly Daisy Hanzel, formerly an office clerk. She was a pert little strawberry blonde, cute, with a lot of good humor and a lot of everything else too; about as unlike Vera as a girl could be. That week she was between nightclub engagements, back in her old hometown. And back in the old groove with me, too. I looked forward to the evening—first Benji's troubles and then my own pleasures.

I pulled up in front of Benji's old place just at dusk. A late working lineman from Beltsville Power was fiddling around on the pole outside Benji's lab room. "Hey, Mac," he hollered, "you going in there? Look, tell the prof they'll cut it in at seven ayem, huh? Can't make it a minute sooner."

I nodded as I went up the steps and across the porch; knocked once. Walked on in—and stopped dead in the hallway to stare up the stairs. It was Benji, but not the Vera's Benji I was used to. He was dressed in the evening clothes Vera got him to wear only at major faculty functions. He carried a cane, wore a flower. Tonight he was Benji, man about town, knight of the evening. Sharp. Cool. Cocky.

He strutted on down the stairs and past me. He winked, grinned that dirty, sneaky grin of his I remembered all too well from the old days. At the door, he looked back over his shoulder, still grinning, and said, "Stick around a minute, Bull boy. I have something to show you." The door slammed shut.

I couldn't believe it; he wouldn't dare. Then I heard my car, my new sport car, starting outside and I swore, grabbing the doorknob.

"Wait, Bull. You couldn't catch me."

I spun around. Damned if it wasn't old Benji, coming down the stairs again just as though it wasn't impossible. This time he looked himself, but worse. He had on an old lab smock and a new hangover. He looked awful—but with a hint of satisfaction too, like remembering the time he'd had getting into such lousy shape.

"Well, Bull boy," he mumbled, wavering on down the steps, holding the top of his head on with one hand, "come on out in the lab. Maybe we could find a little nip. And I have something to show you."

"So you said."

"Eh? Oh, yes, so I did. Last night, when I was going out."

"It was just now—only you went out all dressed up, and here you are all beat up. What's this all about?"

"Come *on*," he said with a flash of temper. "When I get a hair or two of the dog, I'll explain it to you."

I followed him into his lab, the dean's old study. It was the only thing Benji could call his own. Vera let him have it on the off-chance that he might find something important enough to give their social and financial position a boost.

In the lab, Benji fished an amber-filled flask from the wastebasket under the old rolltop desk and poured himself a double, me a single, in a couple of big test tubes. I only half saw him out of a corner of the eye.

What I was really looking at was a damned peculiar rig that

filled up about a third of the space along the side wall next to the kitchen. It was—I couldn't figure it. It looked something like one of those jungle gym outfits in the kids' playgrounds. But there were wires running from it to half a dozen wall plugs, and a seat up in the middle with a bunch of dials and things.

It was all odd, and oddest was the way it all sort of shimmered and blurred as I watched it.

"What in hell is that?" I walked across the lab toward it, reaching out.

"Better not touch it, Bull. You might knock something out."

Since he put it like that, I raised my hand to grab hold of one of the cross bars by the seat in the center of the thing—and there I was resting comfortably on a small cloud in far outer space, watching a great spiral nebula whirling in infinite majesty through the vast, empty blackness, and I thought about the mystery of the universe. I felt that if I could just reach out, I would have in my grasp the final answer. But then it drifted away and the nebula slowly narrowed and evolved into a great system of suns, planets, moons—and finally into the big, old chandelier in the dean's study.

When it all seemed to stabilize at that point, I sat up a little shakily. The room, Benji's lab now, was still there. I stood up and felt lousy. My head ached. I looked around. Benji was sitting at the desk slumped over, his head on his folded arms. The flask of whiskey, half gone, was on the desk beside him. I emptied it out a little more, into me, and checked my watch. Six o'clock and the sky showed gray outside. I had been out all night.

I put my foot on the base of Benji's swivel chair and shoved hard. The chair rolled back, out from under him. He slumped down with a pleasing thud on the floor. He woke up with a pained expression that helped my headache a little.

"Damn you, Benji," I said, "you did that out of spite, to break my date with Daisy, I bet."

He yawned. "I told you you'd better not touch it."

"Because you knew then I'd have to go ahead and do it. It's a wonder, with me knocked out, you didn't go try to steal my girl."

"I did. I am."

"You what?"

"I did go out with Daisy. I am with her now."

"Are you cracked? You are right here with me."

"True, but I am simultaneously with Daisy." He grinned reflectively. "And I don't mind saying Daisy is much better company than you . . . Now wait, Bull. I know this is difficult for you to grasp, but it is a fact that I am in two places at the same time—only on different circuits. This is big, Bull, really big! After you help me with one or two details, I am going to share it with you. Listen to me."

Sometimes I can be sickeningly gullible. "All right. Start explaining."

"Think, Bull! Last night you saw me go out the front door. At substantially the same time, you also saw me, dressed quite differently, come down the hall stairs. It should be obvious. I have built a time machine."

I looked down at my watch and then back at him, with raised eyebrows.

"No, Bull. Not a machine for telling time; a machine for traveling through time or, actually, more or less around it. You see my machine there."

The jungle gym rig was still at the side of the room, blurred and shimmering. "Yeah, I see it. And don't bother telling me not to touch it again. I won't."

"Your own fault. Ordinarily you could touch even one of the bars; it is perfectly safe. But just now the machine is there twice. That creates further static force fields."

"Benji—"

"Look at it. Looks as though you were seeing double, hm-m? And you are. You see, Bull, this coming morning at ten to seven, I took—and will take—the machine and I traveled back to ten to five yesterday afternoon. At that time the machine was already there. Actually, I should have moved it just before I used it this morning, to limit the overlaps. But I was rushed. You'll see. Daisy and I will be here shortly." He grinned. It was an expression I had never particularly cared for. "Have another drink, Bull."

That was an expression I liked better. I did have one. His story was unbelievable. But I was beginning to believe it—partly because of the machine there and the fact that I had seen two of him practically at once the evening before, partly because I knew

Benji would be capable of almost anything if it would let him steal a girl from me and get away from Vera besides.

He took a short nip himself and went on. "I won't strain your limited facilities by trying to give you the technical side of it. More or less, it is a matter of setting up the proper number of counteracting magnetic force fields, properly focused, in a proper relationship each with the other to bend the normal space factors in such a way as to circumvent time. Is that clear?"

"Not to me," I said. "Is it to you?"

"Not altogether. But what is clear is this. My machine works. I can jump through time. To any time."

"Got any special messages from Cleopatra?"

"The amount or period of time is a question of power. With only the regular house current I have connected now, about a day at a step is the limit. That is as far as I have gone. Of course I could go one day and then another and then another, forward or back, indefinitely. With more current, there would be no such limitations."

"How about taking a run up to the end of the week and let me know how the World Series is going to come out?"

"Ah, now you begin to see! I told you this is a big thing—tremendous! And all I ask is just a little help from you, and you will share in the proceeds."

"What, me help? How?"

"I had the power company run in a special power line yesterday. It will cut in this morning at seven. With this added power, the machine can travel five years. Five years at a jump, which as far as I—we, that is—want to go."

"Well, just suppose what you say is true, Benji. If it is, then you used your sneaky machine to two-time me with Daisy last night, eh? I like that. Vera will like that, too. But you expect to bribe me with a share in your rig to help you out. How? With what?"

"Bull, it's like this. I did go out last night, my first time in a long time. You know Vera. So, considering the past few years, you can understand that I was—uh—maybe a bit reckless last night, ran into a few little problems. Nothing serious, of course. And besides, with your help, the police won't be able—"

"The police?"

"Yes. But, Bull, you've been right here with me all night. You can swear to that. So I couldn't possibly have driven your car up the steps and through the glass doors into the ancient history section of the museum."

"My car!"

"Now, Bull, we'll make money—you can get *lots* of cars. And I didn't mean to smash up yours. I simply wanted to give Daisy a rough idea of a time trip back into the past. But you can tell the police I was right here when someone broke out through the window by the Neanderthal exhibit while the police were coming in the front door after us. So someone else must have driven off in the police car."

"You stole the police car?" I yelped.

"Oh, we won't keep it," he said airily. "But perhaps they are upset about our borrowing it and about the duet of 'As Time Goes By' that Daisy and I sang over the police radio."

"Lord! And when did you finish all this fun and games?" I demanded.

"When? Let's see. It's 6:40 A.M. So we—Daisy and I—are on our way back here now. In the patrol car."

"Now? You and Daisy? In the patrol car?"

"The one we borrowed. The police—they seem to have a lot of cars—are not far behind. I believe they think they recognized me. You can tell them how wrong they are."

He stopped to listen. I heard it too, a sound of sirens in the distance, coming closer.

"So, Benji. In a minute or so, you—a second edition of you, when one has always been plenty—you are coming here, with all the cops in town on your tail, *and* with my girl. And you expect me to step forward and, lying in my teeth, tell these enraged cops that you are innocent. This is quite a request, Benji."

There was the roar of a car racing down the quiet, Saturday-dawn street. Benji looked at me anxiously. "Here we come. Bull, please! You wouldn't turn me over to the police. Would you?"

No, I didn't want the cops to get him. I wanted to get him myself—and let Vera finish him.

There was a sound of running footsteps up the porch stairs. The hallway door opened. Arm in arm, laughing like a pair of idiots, in came Benji—Benji II—and my girl, Daisy. They staggered across the room. Benji II threw his arms around Daisy and kissed her with conviction and assurance. Then, quickly, he stepped away from her and walked over to the time-machine rig.

"Hurry it up," said the first Benji, "quick. The power will cut off any second now, until they switch in the new line."

Drunk or not, Benji II knew what he was doing. He dragged the straight chair by the wall to the side of the machine and climbed it. He swayed, almost fell. Then, without touching any of the bars, he managed to step from the chair into the seat of the machine rig. He fiddled with a dial or knob—and vanished. The double exposure look of the machine disappeared too.

"Benji," said Daisy, staring blankly at the machine.

"Daisy," said the leftover Benji, walking toward her. The sound of sirens outside sounded loud and louder—and then moaned to a stop in front of the house.

"Benji," Daisy said again, giving me and the sirens about as much attention as an individual ant gets at a family picnic, "Benji, it was *true* then! All that you were telling me about going through time was true! And we can—"

"Of course, sweet. I told you I'd be with you, that everything will be all right, with good old Bull to help us. What time have you, Bull?"

"Hah?" I was dazed.

"The time? What time is it?"

"It's just about seven. But—"

Heavy footsteps pounded up the front stairs and across the porch. The front door knocker thundered.

"Bull," said Benji, "Bull, old friend. I think there may be someone at the door. Would you see who it is?"

I don't know why I didn't make him go answer. I still don't know. But I walked out into the hall from the lab and opened the front door—and nearly got trampled by a squad of four cops, headed by big, tough Sergeant Winesap. There were, I saw through the open door, two squad cars parked out front and another coming down the block, just behind a taxi.

"Oh," said Winesap, "it's you, Benton. Say, you weren't in this crime wave, too, were you? We only saw two, that madman friend of yours, Professor Benjamin, and the girl, in your car . . . Look, you know what they did? They knocked off three hydrants whooping about time and the fountain of youth, and wrecked the museum, and the police car—and what they did to Officer Durlin . . . Maybe you weren't in on it, Benton, but we know they came in here. Friend or no friend, don't try to obstruct justice. Where are they?"

"Yes, officer?" inquired Benji, bland as could be, from the lab door. "What seems to be the trouble? Did you wish to see me?"

His manner must have been disarming. At least they didn't shoot him on the spot. They just advanced, loosening guns in holsters, like a thoughtful lynching party. Benji strolled back into the lab and over to Daisy, who was standing by the machine at the side of the room.

The officers were confused. Benji, sober or nearly so, in his old lab smock, looked a good deal different to them from the wild man they'd been chasing all over town. But there was Daisy in her evening gown.

"That's them, all right," said a young rookie with a fine-blooming shiner. "She's the one that threw the eggplants. I'd know her anywhere."

"And that's Benjamin," said Winesap, grimly. "Okay, both of you, don't try to run. Come along and no more nonsense."

Benji held up one hand—and slipped the other arm around Daisy's waist. "Gentlemen, please! I have no idea what this is about. But surely it can have nothing to do with me. Mr. Benton and I have been right here in my laboratory all night, working. He can verify that."

They looked at me. I opened my mouth. I didn't say a word.

Vera did. She stood there in the doorway. It must have been her in the cab, coming back bright and early from Chicago. She took in the whole scene. Benji. Daisy. Police. Me.

"Benji!!!" she said. You couldn't imagine what she put into that one word.

Everyone turned then to look at her. Slowly and with infinite menace, she started across the room.

"Now, dear," said Benji nervously, "now, sweet, take it easy. This is only a little experiment. Not what you are thinking at all."

We swung back toward Benji. He had boosted Daisy onto the

seat of his time rig and swung up beside her. Vera yelled and started to run toward them.

Benji twisted a knob and grinned. "Good-by now," he said. And they were gone.

Benji was gone again. Daisy was gone. The whole rig was gone.

Vera, looking a little forlorn and foolish, ended up her dash stumbling into the empty space where the thing had been. I expect we all looked a little foolish, standing there, gaping. But I had to carry foolishness to the ultimate of idiocy.

Vera at that single moment seemed sort of sad and helpless. And, Lord knows, I was mixed up. I walked over and put an arm around Vera, saying, "There, there, Vera, hon. It's all right. I'm here."

I should never have called her attention to it. There I was—and, the hell of it was I had kept playing up to her all this time just to needle Benji. When, that morning, I put my arm around her, I never had a chance.

I was married. To Vera. I still am. It has been a long, long time. Almost five years by the calendar, centuries by subjective time.

I am Vera's husband, sitting by the light of a kerosene lamp in Dean Milston's old study, which had been Benji's lab, writing. Benji and Daisy got away and I got caught. But now I can smile about it. Now, after nearly five years.

You understand?

With the power he got into his machine from the new power line, he said he could go just five years at a jump. Of course, away from Vera. Probably he figured on going further, that he would go the power limit of five years, stop, and then jump again, and again, far enough for complete safety.

But I have had a lot more time to figure than he did. I am figuring on a little party; a little reception in honor of our first intrepid time traveler. A surprise party.

It will be five years to the hour since Daisy and Benji left. Benji will be the surprise, since only I know that he will pop up in our midst. It will surprise Benji. It will surprise Vera—and our guests, among whom I have included Sergeant (Captain now) Winesap and the others of his squad.

Eccentric, a party like that? I suppose. But, to Vera and the others, it is a breakfast anniversary party—the anniversary of the very moment of our engagement. Vera is flattered enough to be tolerant and even pleased at this romantic notion. And, since I know I have only one out and that it is coming, I am a dutiful —cringing and servile, that is—husband. So Vera indulges me in a harmless eccentricity or two.

My other little eccentricity is electric power—I don't favor it. I use Benji's lab, the old dean's study, as my den. I claim to be writing a historical novel. I need realism, atmosphere. I have had all electric power lines removed from that entire section of the house. There is no power. None.

That's why I'm writing by lamplight.

Our anniversary party will be here. The lamps and candles and the dawn of a bright new day will be light enough when, to the total astonishment of Vera and our guests, Benji and Daisy and the time rig suddenly appear among us. I will greet them with enthusiasm—but this will be as nothing to the greeting they will get from other sources. Benji will work his dials and controls, frantically. Nothing will happen. No power.

Vera will step forward. The hell with whether the statute of limitations may or may not have run out on Benji's assorted legal crimes and misdemeanors. The wrath of Vera accepts no limitations.

Benji will have run out of time and it will be my time then.

Insidekick

BY J. F. BONE

Shifaz glanced furtively around the room. Satisfied that it was empty except for Fred Kemmer and himself, he sidled up to the Earthman's desk and hissed conspiratorially in his ear, "Sir, this Johnson is a spy! Is it permitted to slay him?"

"It is permitted," Kemmer said in a tone suitable to the gravity of the occasion.

He watched humorlessly as the Antarian slithered out of the office with a flutter of colorful ceremonial robes. Both Kemmer and Shifaz had known for weeks that Johnson was a spy, but the native had to go through this insane rigmarole before the rules on Antar would allow him to act. At any rate, the formalities were over at last and the affair should be satisfactorily ended before nightfall. Natives moved quickly enough, once the preliminaries were concluded.

Kemmer leaned back in his chair and sighed. Being the Interworld Corporation's local manager had more compensations than headaches, despite the rigid ritualism of native society. Since most of the local population was under his thumb, counter-espionage was miraculously effective. This fellow Johnson, for instance, had been in Vaornia less than three weeks, and despite the fact that he was an efficient and effective snoop, he had been fingered less than forty-eight hours after his arrival in the city.

Kemmer closed his eyes and let a smile cross his keen features. Under his administration, there would be a sharp rise in the mortality curve for spies detected in the Vaornia-Lagash-Timargh triangle. With the native judiciary firmly under IC control, the Corporation literally had a free hand, providing it kept its nose superficially clean. And as for spies, they knew the chances they took and what the penalty could be for interfering with the normal operations of corporate business.

Kemmer yawned, stretched, turned his attention to more important matters.

Albert Johnson fumbled hopefully in the empty food container before tossing it aside. A plump, prosaic man of middle height, with a round ingenuous face, Albert was as undistinguished as his name, a fact that made him an excellent investigator. But he was neither undistinguished nor unnoticed in his present position, although he had tried to carry it off by photographing the actions of the local Sanitary Processional like any tourist.

He had been waiting near the Vaornia Arm on the road that led to Lagash since early afternoon, and now it was nearly evening. He cursed mildly at the fact that the natives had no conception of time, a trait not exclusively Antarian, but one which was developed to a high degree on this benighted planet. And the fact that he was hungry didn't add to his good temper. Natives might be able to fast for a week without ill effects, but his chunky body demanded quantities of nourishment at regular intervals, and his stomach was protesting audibly at being empty.

He looked around him, at the rutted road, and at the darkening Vaornia Arm of the Devan Forest that bordered the roadway. The Sanitary Processional had completed the daily ritual of waste disposal and the cart drivers and censer bearers were goading their patient daks into a faster gait. It wasn't healthy to be too near the forest after the sun went down. The night beasts weren't particular about what, or whom, they ate.

The Vaornese used the Vaornia Arm as a dump for the refuse of the city, a purpose admirably apt, for the ever-hungry forest life seldom left anything uneaten by morning. And since Antarian towns had elaborate rituals concerning the disposal of waste, together with a nonexistent sewage system, the native attitude of fatalistic indifference to an occasional tourist or Antarian being gobbled up by some nightmare denizen of the forest was understandable.

The fact that the Arm was also an excellent place to dispose of an inconvenient body didn't occur to Albert until the three natives with knives detached themselves from the rear of the Sanitary Processional and advanced upon him. They came from three directions, effectively boxing him in, and Albert realized with a sick certainty that he had been doublecrossed, that Shifaz, instead of being an informant for him, was working for the IC. Albert turned to face the nearest native, tensing his muscles for battle.

Then he saw the Zark.

It stepped out of the gathering darkness of the forest, and with its appearance everything stopped. For perhaps a microsecond, the three Vaornese stood frozen. Then, with a simultaneous wheep of terror, they turned and ran for the city.

They might have stayed and finished their work if they had known it was a Zark, but at the moment the Zark was energizing a toothy horror that Earthmen called a Bandersnatch—an insane combination of talons, teeth and snakelike neck mounted on a crocodilian body that exuded an odor of putrefaction from the carrion upon which it normally fed. The Bandersnatch had been dead for several hours, but neither the natives nor Albert knew that.

It was a tribute to the Zark's ability to maintain pseudo-life in a Bandersnatch carcass that the knifemen fled and a similar panic seized the late travelers on the road. Albert stared with horrified fascination at the monstrosity for several seconds before he, too, fled. Any number of natives with knives were preferable to a Bandersnatch. He had hesitated only because he didn't possess the conditioned reflexes arising from generations of exposure to Antarian wildlife.

He was some twenty yards behind the rearmost native, and, though not designed for speed, was actually gaining upon the fellow, when his foot struck a loose cobblestone in the road. Arms flailing, legs pumping desperately to balance his toppling mass, Albert fought manfully against the forces of gravity and inertia.

He lost.

His head struck another upturned cobble. His body twitched once and then relaxed limply and unconscious upon the dusty road.

The Zark winced a little at the sight, certain that this curious creature had damaged itself seriously.

Filled with compassion, it started forward on the Bandersnatch's four walking legs, the grasping talons crossed on the breast in an attitude of prayer. The Zark wasn't certain what it could do, but perhaps it could help.

Albert was mercifully unconscious as it bent over him to inspect his prone body with a purple-lidded pineal eye that was blue with concern. The Zark noted the bruise upon his forehead and marked his regular breathing, and came to the correct conclusion that, whatever had happened, the biped was relatively undamaged. But the Zark didn't go away. It had never seen a human in its thousand-odd years of existence, which was not surprising since Earthmen had been on Antar less than a decade and Zarks seldom left the forest.

Albert began to stir before the Zark remembered its present condition. Not being a carnivore, it saw nothing appetizing about Albert, but it was energizing a Bandersnatch, and, like all Zarks, it was a purist. A living Bandersnatch would undoubtedly drool happily at the sight of such a tempting tidbit, so the Zark opened the three-foot jaws and drooled.

Albert chose this precise time to return to consciousness. He turned his head groggily and looked up into a double row of saw-edged teeth surmounted by a leering triangle of eyes. A drop of viscid drool splattered moistly on his forehead, and as the awful face above him bent closer to his own, he fainted.

The Zark snapped its jaws disapprovingly. This was not the proper attitude to take in the presence of a ferocious monster. One simply didn't go to sleep. One should attempt to run. The biped's act was utterly illogical. It needed investigation.

Curiously, the Zark sent out a pseudopod of its substance through the open mouth of its disguise. The faintly glittering thread oozed downward and struck Albert's head beside his right eye. Without pausing, the thread sank through skin and connective tissue, circled the eyeball and located the optic nerve. It raced inward along the nerve trunk, split at the optic chiasma, and entered the corpora quadrigemina where it branched into innumerable microscopic filaments that followed the main neural paths of the man's brain, probing the major areas of thought and reflex.

The Zark quivered with pleasure. The creature was beautifully complex, and, more important, untenanted. He would make an interesting host.

The Zark didn't hesitate. It needed a host; giving its present mass of organic matter pseudo-life took too much energy. The Bandersnatch collapsed with a faint slurping sound. A blob of iridescent jelly flowed from the mouth and spread itself evenly over Albert's body in a thin layer. The jelly shimmered, glowed, disappeared inward through Albert's clothing and skin, diffusing through the subcutaneous tissues, sending hairlike threads along nerve trunks and blood vessels until the threads met other threads and joined, and the Zark became a network of protoplasmic tendrils that ramified through Albert's body.

Immediately the Zark turned its attention to the task of adapting itself to its new host. Long ago it had learned that this had to be done quickly or the host did not survive. And since the tissues of this new host were considerably different from those of the Bandersnatch, a great number of structural and chemical changes had to be made quickly. With some dismay, the Zark realized that its own stores of energy would be insufficient for the task. It would have to borrow energy from the host—which was a poor way to start a symbiotic relationship. Ordinarily, one gave before taking.

Fortunately, Albert possessed considerable excess fat, an excellent source of energy whose removal would do no harm. There was plenty here for both Albert and itself. The man's body twitched and jerked as the Zark's protean cells passed through the adaptive process, and as the last leukocyte recoiled from tissue that had suddenly become normal, his consciousness returned. Less than ten minutes had passed, but they were enough. The Zark was safely in harmony with its new host.

Albert opened his eyes and looked wildly around. The landscape was empty of animate life except for the odorous carcass of the Bandersnatch lying beside him. Albert shivered, rose unsteadily to his feet and began walking toward Vaornia. That he didn't run was only because he couldn't.

He found it hard to believe that he was still alive. Yet a hurried inspection convinced him that there wasn't a tooth mark on him. It was a miracle that left him feeling vaguely uneasy. He wished he knew what had killed that grinning horror so opportunely. But then, on second thought, maybe it was better that he didn't know. There might be things in the Devan Forest worse than a Bandersnatch.

Inside the city walls, Vaornia struck a three-pronged blow at Albert's senses. Sight, hearing and smell were assaulted simultaneously. Natives slithered past, garbed in long robes of garish color. Sibilant voices cut through the evening air like thin-edged knives clashing against the grating screech of the ungreased wooden wheels of dak carts. Odors of smoke, cooking, spices, perfume and corruption mingled with the all-pervasive musky stench of unwashed Vaornese bodies.

It was old to Albert, but new and exciting to the Zark. Its taps on Albert's sense organs brought a flood of new sensation the Zark had never experienced. It marveled at the crowded buildings studded with jutting balconies and ornamental carvings. It stared at the dak caravans maneuvering with ponderous delicacy through the swarming crowds. It reveled in the colorful banners and awnings of the tiny shops lining the streets, and the fluttering robes of the natives. Color was something new to the Zark. Its previous hosts had been color blind, and the symbiont wallowed in an orgy of bright sensation.

If Albert could have tuned in on his fellow traveler's emotions, he probably would have laughed. For the Zark was behaving precisely like the rubbernecking tourist he himself was pretending to be. But Albert wasn't interested in the sights, sounds or smells, nor did the natives intrigue him. There was only one of them he cared to meet—that slimy doublecrosser called Shifaz who had nearly conned him into a one-way ticket.

Albert plowed heedlessly through the crowd, using his superior mass to remove natives from his path. By completely disregarding the code of conduct outlined by the IC travel bureau, he managed to make respectable progress toward the enormous covered area in the center of town that housed the Kazlak, or native marketplace. Shifaz had a stand there where he was employed as a tourist guide.

The Zark, meanwhile, was not idle despite the outside interests. The majority of its structure was busily engaged in checking and cataloguing the body of its host, an automatic process that didn't interfere with the purely intellectual one of enjoying the new sensations. Albert's body wasn't in too bad shape. A certain amount of repair work would have to be done, but despite the heavy padding of fat, the organs were in good working condition.

The Zark ruminated briefly over what actions it should take as it dissolved a milligram of cholesterol out of Albert's aorta and strengthened the weak spot in the blood vessel with a few cells of its own substance until Albert's tissues could fill the gap. Its knowledge of human physiology was incomplete, but it instinctively recognized abnormality. As a result, it could help the host's physical condition, which was a distinct satisfaction, for a Zark must be helpful.

Shifaz was at his regular stand, practicing his normal profession of guide. As Albert approached, he was in the midst of describing the attractions of the number two tour to a small knot of fascinated tourists.

"And then, in the center of the Kazlak, we will come to the Hall of the Brides—Antar's greatest marriage market. It has been arranged for you to actually see a mating auction in progress, but we must hurry or—" Shifaz looked up to see Albert shouldering the tourists aside. His yellow eyes widened and his hand darted to his girdle and came up with a knife.

The nearest tourists fell back in alarm as he hissed malevolently at Albert, "Stand back, Earthman, or I'll let the life out of your scaleless carcass!"

"Doublecrosser," Albert said, moving in. One meaty hand closed over the knife hand and wrenched while the other caught Shifaz alongside the head with a smack that sounded loud in the sudden quiet. Shifaz did a neat backflip and lay prostrate, the tip of his tail twitching reflexively.

One of the tourists screamed.

"No show today, folks," Albert said. "Shifaz has another engagement." He picked the Antarian up by a fold of his robe and shook him like a dirty dustcloth. A number of items cascaded out of hidden pockets, among which was an oiled-silk pouch. Albert dropped the native and picked up the pouch, opened it, sniffed, and nodded.

It fitted. Things were clearer now.

He was still nodding when two Earthmen in IC uniform stepped out of the crowd. "Sorry, sir," the bigger of the pair said, "but you have just committed a violation of the IC-Antar Compact. I'm afraid we'll have to take you in."

"This lizard tried to have me killed," Albert protested.

"I wouldn't know about that," the IC man said. "You've assaulted a native, and that's a crime. You'd better come peaceably with us—local justice is rather primitive and unpleasant."

"I'm an Earth citizen—" Albert began.

"This world is on a commercial treaty." The guard produced a blackjack and tapped the shot-filled leather in his palm. "It's our business to protect people like you from the natives, and if you insist, we'll use force."

"I don't insist, but I think you're being pretty high-handed."

"Your objection has been noted," the IC man said, "and will be included in the official report. Now come along or we'll be in the middle of a jurisdictional hassle when the native cops arrive. The corporation doesn't like hassles. They're bad for business."

The two IC men herded him into a waiting ground car and drove away. It was all done very smoothly, quietly and efficiently. The guards were good.

And so was the local detention room. It was clean, modern and —Albert noted wryly—virtually escape-proof. Albert was something of an expert on jails, and the thick steel bars, the force lock, and the spy cell in the ceiling won his grudging respect.

He sighed and sat down on the cot which was the room's sole article of furniture. He had been a fool to let his anger get the better of him. IC would probably use this brush with Shifaz as an excuse to send him back to Earth as an undesirable tourist—

which would be the end of his mission here, and a black mark on a singularly unspotted record.

Of course, they might not be so gentle with him if they knew that he knew they were growing tobacco. But he didn't think that they would know—and if they had checked his background, they would find that he was an investigator for the Revenue Service. Technically, criminal operations were not his affair. His field was tax evasion.

He didn't worry too much about the fact that Shifaz had tried to kill him. On primitive worlds like this, that was a standard procedure—it was less expensive to kill an agent than bribe him or pay honest taxes. He was angry with himself for allowing the native to trick him.

He shrugged. By all rules of the game, IC would now admit about a two per cent profit on their Antar operation rather than the four per cent loss they had claimed, and pay up like gentlemen—and he would get skinned by the Chief back at Earth Central for allowing IC to unmask him. His report on tobacco growing would be investigated, but with the sketchy information he possessed, his charges would be impossible to prove—and IC would have plenty of time to bury the evidence.

If Earth Central hadn't figured that the corporation owed it some billion megacredits in back taxes, he wouldn't be here. He had been dragged from his job in the General Accounting Office, for every field man and ex-field man was needed to conduct the sweeping investigation. Every facet of the sprawling IC operation was being checked. Even minor and out-of-the-way spots like Antar were on the list—spots that normally demanded a cursory once-over by a second-class business technician.

Superficially, Antar had the dull unimportance of an early penetration. There were the usual trading posts, pilot plants, wholesale and retail trade, and tourist and recreation centers—all designed to accustom the native inhabitants to the presence of Earthmen and their works—and set them up for the commercial kill, after they had acquired a taste for the products of civilization. But although the total manpower and physical plant for a world of this size was right, its distribution was wrong.

A technician probably wouldn't see it, but to an agent who had dealt with corporate operations for nearly a quarter of a century, the setup felt wrong. It was not designed for maximum return. The Vaornia-Lagash-Timargh triangle held even more men and material than Prime Base. That didn't make sense. It was inefficient, and IC was not noted for inefficiency.

Not being oriented criminally, Albert found out IC's real reason for concentration in this area only by absent-mindedly lighting a cigarette one day in Vaornia. He had realized almost instantly that this was a gross breach of outworld ethics and had thrown the cigarette away. It landed between a pair of Vaornese walking by.

The two goggled at the cigarette, sniffed the smoke rising from it, and with simultaneous whistles of surprise bent over to pick it up. Their heads collided with some force. The cigarette tore in their greedy grasp as they hissed hatefully at each other for a moment, before turning hostile glares in his direction. From their expressions, they thought this was a low Earthie trick to rob them of their dignity. Then they stalked off, their neck scales ruffled in anger, shreds of the cigarette still clutched in their hands.

Even Albert couldn't miss the implications. His tossing the butt away had produced the same reaction as a deck of morphine on a group of human addicts. Since IC wouldn't corrupt a susceptible race with tobacco when there were much cheaper legal ways, the logical answer was that it wasn't expensive on this planet—which argued that Antar was being set up for plantation operations—in which case tobacco addiction was a necessary prerequisite and the concentration of IC population made sense.

Now tobacco, as any Earthman knew, was the only monopoly in the Confederation, and Earth had maintained that monopoly by treaty and by force, despite numerous efforts to break it. There were some good reasons for the policy, ranging all the way from vice control to taxable income, but the latter was by far the most important. The revenue supported a considerable section of Earth Central as well as the huge battle fleet that maintained peace and order along the spacelanes and between the worlds.

But a light-weight, high-profit item like tobacco was a constant temptation to any sharp operator who cared more for money than for law, and IC filled that definition perfectly. In the Tax Section's book, the Interworld Corporation was a corner-cutting, profit-grabbing chiseler. Its basic character had been the same for three centuries, despite all the complete turnovers in staff. Albert grinned wryly. The old-timers were right when they made corporations legal persons.

Cigarettes which cost five credits to produce and sold for as high as two hundred would always interest a crook, and, as a consequence, Earth Central was always investigating reports of illegal plantations. They were found and destroyed eventually, and the owners punished. But the catch lay in the word "eventually." And if the operator was a corporation, no regulatory agency in its right mind would dare apply the full punitive power of the law. In that direction lay political suicide, for nearly half the population of Earth got dividends or salaries from them.

That, of course, was the trouble with corporations. They invariably grew too big and too powerful. But to break them up as the Ancients did was to destroy their efficiency. What was really needed was a corporate conscience.

Albert chuckled. That was a nice unproductive thought.

Fred Kemmer received the news that Albert had been taken to detention with a philosophic calm that lasted for nearly half an hour. By morning, the man would be turned over to the Patrol in Prime Base. The Patrol would support the charge that Albert was an undesirable tourist and send him home to Earth.

But the philosophic calm departed with a frantic leap when Shifaz reported Johnson's inspection of the oiled-silk pouch. Raw tobacco was something that shouldn't be within a thousand parsecs of Antar; its inference would be obvious even to an investigator interested only in tax revenues. Kemmer swore at the native. The entire operation would have to be aborted now and his dreams of promotion would vanish.

"It wasn't my supply," Shifaz protested. "I was carrying it down to Karas at the mating market. He demands a pack every time he puts a show on for your silly Earthie tourists."

"You should have concealed it better."

"How was I to know that chubby slob was coming back alive? And who'd have figured that he could handle me?"

"I've told you time and again that Earthmen are tough customers when they get mad, but you had to learn it the hard way.

Now we're all in the soup. The Patrol doesn't like illicit tobacco planters. Tobacco is responsible for their pay."

"But he's still in your hands and he couldn't have had time to transmit his information," Shifaz said. "You can still kill him."

Kemmer's face cleared. Sure, that was it. Delay informing the Patrol and knock the snoop off. The operation and Kemmer's future were still safe. But it irked him that he had panicked instead of thinking. It just went to show how being involved in major crime ruined the judgment. He'd have Johnson fixed up with a nice hearty meal—and he'd see that it was delivered personally. At this late date, he couldn't afford the risk of trusting a subordinate.

Kemmer's glower became a smile. The snoop's dossier indicated that he liked to eat. He should die happy.

With a faint click, a loaded tray passed through a slot in the rear wall of Albert Johnson's cell.

The sight and smell of Earthly cooking reminded him that he hadn't anything to eat for hours. His mouth watered as he lifted the tray and carried it to the cot. At least IC wasn't going to let him starve to death, and if this was any indication of the way they treated prisoners, an IC jail was the best place to be on this whole planet.

Since it takes a little time for substances to diffuse across the intestinal epithelium and enter the circulation, the Zark had some warning of what was about to happen from the behavior of the epithelial cells lining Albert's gut. As a result, a considerable amount of the alkaloid was stopped before it entered Albert's body—but some did pass through, for the Zark was not omnipotent.

For nearly five minutes after finishing the meal, Albert felt normally full and comfortable. Then hell broke loose. Most of the food came back with explosive violence and cramps bent him double. The Zark turned to the neutralization and elimination of the poison. Absorptive surfaces were sealed off, body fluids poured into the intestinal tract, and anti-substances formed out of Albert's energy reserve to neutralize whatever alkaloid remained.

None of the Zark's protective measures were normal to Albert's body, and with the abrupt depletion of blood glucose to supply the energy the Zark required, Albert passed into hypoglycemic shock. The Zark regretted that, but it had no time to utilize his other less readily available energy sources. In fact, there was no time for anything except the most elemental protective measures. Consequently the convulsions, tachycardia, and coma had to be ignored.

Albert's spasms were mercifully short, but when the Zark was finished, he lay unconscious on the floor, his body twitching with incoordinate spasms, while a frightened guard called in an alarm to the medics.

The Zark quivered with its own particular brand of nausea. It had not been hurt by the alkaloid, but the pain of its host left it sick with self-loathing. That it had established itself in a life-form that casually ingested deadly poisons was no excuse. It should have been more alert, more sensitive to the host's deficiencies. It had saved his life, which was some compensation, and there was much that could be done in the way of restorative and corrective measures that would prevent such a thing from occurring again— but the Zark was unhappy as it set about helping Albert's liver metabolize fat to glucose and restore blood sugar levels.

The medic was puzzled. She had seen some peculiar conditions at this station, but hypoglycemic shock was something new. And, being unsure of herself, she ordered Albert into the infirmary for observation. The guard, of course, didn't object, and Kemmer, when he heard of it, could only grind his teeth in frustration. He was on delicate enough ground without making it worse by not taking adequate precautions to preserve the health of his unwilling guest. Somehow that infernal snoop had escaped again. . . .

Albert moved his head with infinite labor and looked at the intravenous apparatus dripping a colorless solution into the vein in the elbow joint of his extended left arm. He felt no pain, but his physical weakness was appalling. He could move only with the greatest effort, and the slightest exertion left him dizzy and breathless. It was obvious that he had been poisoned, and that it was a miracle of providence that he had survived. It was equally obvious that a reappraisal of his position was in order. Someone far higher up the ladder than Shifaz was responsible for this latest attempt on his life. The native couldn't possibly have reached him in the safety of IC's jail.

The implications were unpleasant. Someone important feared him enough to want him dead, which meant that his knowledge of illicit tobacco was not as secret as he thought. It would be suicide to stay in the hands of the IC any longer. Somehow he had to get out and inform the Patrol.

He looked at the intravenous drip despondently. If the solution was poisoned, there was no help for him. It was already half gone. But he didn't feel too bad, outside of being weak. It probably was all right. In any event, he would have to take it. The condition of his body wouldn't permit anything else.

He sighed and relaxed on the bed, aware of the drowsiness that was creeping over him. When he awoke, he would do something about this situation, but he was sleepy now.

Albert awoke strong and refreshed. He was as hungry as he always was before breakfast. Whatever was in that solution, it had certainly worked miracles. As far as he could judge, he was completely normal.

The medic was surprised to find him sitting up when she made her morning rounds. It was amazing, but this case was amazing in more ways than one. Last night he had been in a state of complete collapse, and now he was well on the road to recovery.

Albert looked at her curiously. "What was in that stuff you gave me?"

"Just dextrose and saline," she said. "I couldn't find anything wrong with you except hypoglycemia and dehydration, so I treated that." She paused and eyed him with a curiosity equal to his own. "Just what do you think happened?" she asked.

"I think I was poisoned."

"That's impossible."

"Possibly," Albert conceded, "but it might be an idea to check that food I left all over the cell."

"That was cleaned up hours ago."

"Convenient, isn't it?"

"I don't know what you mean by that," she said. "Someone in the kitchens might have made a mistake. Yet you were the only case." She looked thoughtful. "I think I will do a little checking in the Central Kitchen,. just to be on the safe side." She smiled a bright professional smile. "Anyway, I'm glad to see that you have recovered so well. I'm sure you can go back tomorrow."

She vanished through the door with a rustle of white dacron. Albert, after listening a moment to make sure that she was gone, rose to his feet and began an inspection of his room.

It wasn't a jail cell. Not quite. But it wasn't designed for easy escape, either. It was on the top floor of the IC building, a good hundred feet down to the street below. The window was covered with a steel grating and the door was locked. But both window and door were designed to hold a sick man rather than a healthy and desperate one.

Albert looked out of the window. The building was constructed to harmonize with native structures surrounding it, so the outer walls were studded with protuberances and bosses that would give adequate handholds to a man strong enough to brave the terrors of the descent.

Looking down the wall, Albert wavered. Thinking back, he made up his mind.

Fred Kemmer was disturbed. By all the rules, Albert Johnson should be dead. But Shifaz had failed, and that fool guard *had* to call in the medics. It was going to be harder to get at Johnson, now that he was in the infirmary, but he had to be reached.

One might buy off an agent who was merely checking on tax evasion, but tobacco was another matter entirely. Kemmer wished he hadn't agreed to boss Operation Weed. The glowing dreams of promotion and fortune were beginning to yellow around the edges. Visions of the Penal Colony bothered him, for if the operation went sour, he would do the paying. He had known that when he took the job, but the possibility seemed remote then.

He shook his head. It wasn't that bad yet. As long as Johnson hadn't communicated with anyone else and as long as he was still in company hands, something could be done.

Kemmer thought a while, trying to put himself in Johnson's place. Undoubtedly the spy was frightened, and undoubtedly he would try to escape. And since it would be far easier to escape from the infirmary than it would be from detention, he would try as soon as possible.

Kemmer's face cleared. If Johnson tried it, he would find it wasn't as easy as he thought.

With characteristic swiftness, Kemmer outlined his plans and made the necessary arrangements. A guard was posted in the hall with orders to shoot if Johnson tried the door of his room, and Kemmer himself took a stand in the building across the street, facing the hospital, where he could watch the window of Albert's room. As he figured it, the window was the best bet. He stroked the long-barreled blaster lying beside him. Johnson still hadn't a chance, but these delays in disposing of him were becoming an annoyance.

Cautiously, Albert tried the grating that covered the window. The Antarean climate had rusted the heavy screws that fastened it to the casing. One of the bars was loose. If it could be removed, it would serve as a lever to pry out the entire grating.

Albert twisted at the bar. It groaned and squealed. He nervously applied more pressure, and the bar moved slowly out of its fastenings.

The Zark observed his actions curiously. Now why was its host twisting that rod of metal out of the woodwork? It didn't know, and it was consumed with curiosity. It had found no way to communicate with its host so that some of the man's queer actions could be understood; in the portions of the brain it had explored, there were no portals of communication. However, there still was a large dormant portion, and perhaps here lay the thing it sought. The Zark inserted a number of tendrils into the blank areas, probing, connecting synapses, opening unused pathways, looking for what it hoped existed.

The results of this action were completely unforeseen by the Zark, for it was essentially just a subordinate ego with all the lacks which that implied—and it had never before inhabited a body that possessed a potentially first-class brain. With no prior experience to draw upon, the Zark couldn't possibly guess that its actions would result in a peculiar relationship between the man and the world around him. And if the Zark had known, it probably wouldn't have cared.

Albert removed the bar and pried out the grating. With only a momentary hesitation, he lowered himself over the sill until his feet struck an ornamental knob on the wall. He glanced quickly down. There was another protuberance about two feet below the one on which he was standing. Pressing against the wall, he inched one foot downward until it found the foothold. With relief, he shifted his weight to the lower foot, and as he did a wave of heat enveloped his legs. The protuberance came loose from the wall with a grating noise mixed with the crackling hiss of a blaster bolt, and Albert plunged toward the street below.

As the pavement rushed at him, he had time for a brief, fervent wish that he were someplace else. Then the thought was swallowed in an icy blackness.

Fred Kemmer lowered the blaster with a grin of satisfaction. He had figured his man correctly, and now the spy would be nothing to worry about. He watched the plummeting body—and gasped with consternation, for less than ten feet above the pavement, Albert abruptly vanished!

There is such a thing as too much surprise, too much shock, too much amazement. And that precisely was what affected Albert when he found himself standing on the street where the IC guards had picked him up. By rights, he should have been a pulpy smear against the pavement beneath the infirmary window. But he was not. He didn't question why he was here, or consider how he had managed to avoid the certain death that waited for him. The fact was that he had done it, somehow. And that was enough.

It was almost like history repeating itself. Shifaz was at his usual stand haranguing another group of tourists. It was the same spiel as before, and almost at the same point of the pitch. But his actions upon seeing Albert were entirely different. His eyes widened, but this time he slid quietly from his perch on the cornerstone of the building and disappeared into the milling crowd.

Albert followed. The fact that Shifaz was somewhere in that crowd was enough to start him moving, and, once started, stubbornness kept him going, plowing irresistibly through the thick swarm of Vaornese. Reason told him that no Earthman could expect to find a native hidden among hundreds of his own kind.

Their bipedal dinosaurlike figures seemed to be cast out of one mold.

A chase through this crowd was futile, but he went on deeper into the Kazlak, drawn along an invisible trail by some unearthly sense that told him he was right. He was as certain of it as that his name was Albert Johnson. And when he finally cornered Shifaz in a deserted alley, he was the one who was not surprised.

Shifaz squawked and darted toward Albert, a knife glittering in his hand. Albert felt a stinging pain across the muscles of his left arm as he blocked the thrust aimed at his belly, wrenched the knife from the native's grasp, and slammed him to the pavement.

Shifaz bounced like a rubber ball, but he had no chance against the bigger and stronger Earthman. Albert knocked him down again. This time the native didn't rise. He lay in the street, a trickle of blood oozing from the corner of his lipless mouth, hate radiating from him in palpable waves.

Albert stood over him, panting a little from the brief but violent scuffle. "Now, Shifaz, you're going to tell me things," he said heavily.

"You can go to your Place of Punishment," Shifaz snarled. "I shall say nothing."

"I can beat the answers out of you," Albert mused aloud, "but I won't. I'll just ask you questions, and every time I don't like your answer, I'll kick one of your teeth out. If you don't answer, I guarantee that you'll look like an old grandmother."

Shifaz turned a paler green. To lose one's teeth was a punishment reserved only for females. He would be a thing of mockery and laughter—but there were worse things than losing teeth or face. There was such a thing as losing one's life, and he knew what would happen if he betrayed IC. Then he brightened. He could always lie, and this hulking brute of an Earthman wouldn't know —couldn't possibly know. So he nodded with a touch of artistic reluctance. "All right," he said, "I'll talk." He injected a note of fear into his voice. It wasn't hard to do.

"Where did you get that tobacco?" Albert asked.

"From a farm," Shifaz said. That was the truth. The Earthman probably knew about tobacco and there was no need to lie, yet.

"Where is it?"

Shifaz thought quickly of the clearing in the forest south of Lagash where the green broad-leaved plants were grown, and said, "It's just outside of Timargh, along the road which runs south." He waited tensely for Albert's reaction, wincing as the Earthman drew his foot back. Timargh was a good fifty miles from Lagash, and if this lie went over, he felt that he could proceed with confidence.

It went over. Albert replaced his foot on the ground. "You telling the truth?"

"As Murgh is my witness," Shifaz said with sincerity.

Albert nodded and Shifaz relaxed with hidden relief. Apparently the man knew that Murgh was the most sacred and respected deity in the pantheon of Antar, and that oaths based upon his name were inviolable. But what the scaleless oaf didn't know was that this applied to Antarians only. As far as these strangers from another world were concerned, anything went.

So Albert continued questioning, and Shifaz answered, sometimes readily, sometimes reluctantly, telling the truth when it wasn't harmful, lying when necessary. The native's brain was fertile and the tissue of lies and truth hung together well, and Albert seemed satisfied. At any rate, he finally went away, leaving behind a softly whistling Vaornese who congratulated himself on the fact that he had once more imposed upon this outlander's credulity. He was so easy to fool that it was almost a crime to do it.

But he wouldn't have been so pleased with himself if he could have seen the inside of Albert's mind. For Albert knew the truth about the four-hundred-acre farm south of Lagash. He knew about the hidden curing sheds and processing plant. He knew that both Vaornese and Lagashites were deeply involved in something they called Operation Weed, and approved of it thoroughly either from sheer cussedness or addiction. He had quietly read the native's mind while the half-truths and lies had fallen from his forked tongue. And, catching Shifaz's last thought, Albert couldn't help chuckling.

At one of the larger intersections, Albert stopped under a flaming cresset and looked at his arm. There was a wide red stain that looked black against the whiteness of his pajamas. That much blood meant more than a scratch, even though there was no pain

—and cuts on this world could be deadly if they weren't attended to promptly.

He suddenly felt alone and helpless, wishing desperately for a quiet place where he could dress his wound and be safe from the eyes he knew were inspecting him. He was too conspicuous. The pajamas were out of place on the street. Undoubtedly natives were hurrying to report him to the IC.

His mind turned to his room in the hostel with its well-fitted wardrobe and its first-aid kit—and again came that instant of utter darkness—and then he was standing in the middle of his room facing the wardrobe that held his clothing.

He felt no surprise this time. He knew what had happened. Something within his body was acting like a tiny Distorter, transporting him through hyperspace in the same manner that a starship's engine room warped it through the folds of the normal space-time continuum. There was nothing really strange about it. It was a power which he *should* have—which any normal man should have. The fact that he didn't have it before was of no consequence, and the fact that other men didn't have it now merely made *them* abnormal.

He smiled as he considered the possibilities which these new powers gave him. They were enormous. At the very least, they tripled his value as an agent. Nothing was safe from his investigation. The most secret hiding places were open to his probings. Nothing could stop him, for command of hyperspace made a mockery of material barriers.

He chuckled happily as he removed his pajama jacket and reached for the first-aid kit. From the gash in his sleeve, there should be a nasty cut underneath, and it startled him a little that there was no greater amount of hemorrhage. He cleaned off the dried blood—and found nothing underneath except a thin red bloodless line that ran halfway around his arm. It wasn't even a scratch.

Yet he had felt Shifaz' blade slice into his flesh. He knew there was more damage than this. The blood and the slashed sleeve could tell him that, even if he didn't have the messages of his nerves. Yet now there was no pain, and the closed scratch certainly wasn't the major wound he had expected. And this *was* queer, a fact for which he had no explanation. Albert frowned. Maybe this was another facet of the psi factors that had suddenly become his.

He wondered where they had come from. Without warning, he had become able to read minds with accuracy and do an effective job of teleportation. About the only things he lacked to be a well-rounded psi were telekinetic powers and precognition.

His frown froze on his face as he became conscious of a sense of unease. They were coming down the hall—two IC guardsmen. He caught the doubt and certainty in their minds—doubt that he would be in his room, certainty that he would be ultimately caught, for on Antar there was no place for an Earthman to hide.

Albert slipped into the first suit that came to hand, blessing the seam tabs that made dressing a moment's work. As the guards opened the door, he visualized the spot on the Lagash road where he had encountered the Bandersnatch. It was easier than before. He was standing in the middle of the road, the center of the surprised attention of a few travelers, when the guards entered his room.

The bright light of Antar's golden day came down from a cloudless yellow sky. In the forest strip ahead, Albert could hear a faint medley of coughs, grunts and snarls as the lesser beasts fed upon the remains of yesterday's garbage. Albert moved down the road, ignoring the startled natives. This time he wasn't afraid of meeting a Bandersnatch or anything else, for he had a method of escape that was foolproof. Lagash was some thirty miles ahead, but in the lighter gravity of Antar, the walk would be stimulating rather than exhausting.

He went at a steady pace, occasionally turning his glance to the road, impressing sections of it upon his memory so that he could return to them via teleport if necessary. He found that he could memorize with perfect ease. Even the positions of clumps of grass and twigs were remembered with perfect clarity and in minute detail. The perfection of his memory astonished and delighted him.

The Zark felt pleased with itself. Although it had never dreamed of the potential contained in the host's mind, it realized that it was responsible for the release of these weird powers, and it enjoyed the new sensations and was eager for more. If partial probing could achieve so much, what was the ultimate power of this remarkable mind? The Zark didn't know, but, like a true experimenter, it was determined to find out—so it probed deeper, opening still more pathways and connecting more synapses with the conscious brain.

It was routine work that could be performed automatically while the rest of the Zark enjoyed the colorful beauty of the Antarian scenery.

With the forest quickly left behind him, Albert walked through gently rolling grassland dotted with small farms and homesteads. It was a peaceful scene, similar to many he had seen on Earth, and the familiarity brought a sense of nostalgic longing to be home again. But the feeling was not too strong, more intellectual than physical, for the memories of Earth were oddly blurred.

Time passed and the road unreeled behind him. Once he took to the underbrush to let a humming IC ground car pass, and twice more he hid as airboats swept by overhead, but the annoyances were minor and unimportant.

When hiding from the second airboat, he disturbed a kelit in the thick brush growing beside the road. The little insect-eater chittered in alarm and dashed off to safety across the highway. And Albert, looking at it, was conscious not only of the external shape but the internal as well!

He could see its little heart pounding in its chest, and the pumping bellows of the pink lungs that surrounded it. He was aware of the muscles pulling and relaxing as the kelit ran, and the long bones sliding in their lubricated joints. He saw the tenseness of the abdominal organs, felt the blind fear in the creature's mind. The totality of his impressions washed through him with a clear wave of icy shock.

Grimly, he shrugged it off. He had ESP. He ought to have expected it—it was the next logical step. He scrambled back to the road and walked onward a little faster, until the battlements of Lagash came in sight.

The Lagash Arm was farther from the city than was that of Vaornia, and as he came to the strip of jungle, he turned his eyes upon the empty parklike arcades between the trees. The last edible garbage had long since been consumed and the greater and lesser beasts had departed for the cooler depths of the forest, but Albert was conscious of life. It was all around him, in the trees with the ringed layers of their trunks and the sap flowing slowly upward through the cambium layer beneath their scaly bark, in the insects feeding upon the nectar of the aerial vine blossoms, in the rapid photosynthetic reactions of the leaves.

His gaze, turning aloft, was conscious of the birds and the tiny arboreal mammals. He saw the whole forest with eyes filled with wonder at its life and beauty. It was the only right way to see.

At the proper distance from Lagash, he plunged off boldly across country and entered the main area of the forest, reflecting wryly as he did so that he was probably the first human in the short history of Antarian exploration who had gone into one of the great forests with absolute knowledge that he would come out of it alive. And, as so often happens to men who have no fear, trouble avoided him.

He followed the directions he had obtained from Shifaz and found the plantation without trouble. He could hardly miss it, because its size was far from accurately expressed in the native's memory. Skillfully concealed beneath an overhanging network of aerial vines whose camouflage made it invisible from the air, concealing the tobacco plants from casual detector search, the plantation extended in row upon narrow row, the irregular strips of fields separated by rows of trees from which the camouflage was hung. A fragile electric fence encircled the area, a seemingly weak defense, but one through which even the greatest Antarian beast would not attempt to pass.

Albert whistled softly under his breath at what he saw, recorded it in his memory. Then, having finished the eyewitness part of his task, he recalled a section of road over which he had passed, and pushed.

The return journey to Vaornia was experimental in nature, as Albert tried the range of his powers. His best was just short of twenty miles and the journey which had taken him eight hours was made back in somewhat less than twenty minutes, counting half a dozen delays and backtracks.

There was no question about where Albert would go next. He had to get evidence, and that evidence lay in only one place—in the local office of the Interworld Corporation in Vaornia.

A moment later, he stood in the reception room looking across the empty desks at the bright square of light shining through the glassite paneled door of Fred Kemmer's office. It was past closing hours, but Kemmer had a right to be working late. Right now, he was probably sweating blood at the thought of what would happen if Albert had finally managed to escape him. The Corporation would virtuously disown him and leave him to face a ten-year rap in Penal Colony. Albert almost felt sorry for him.

Albert let his perception sense travel through the wall and into Kemmer's room. His guess was right—the local boss was sweating.

He checked Kemmer's office swiftly, but the only thing that interested him was the big vault beside the desk. He visualized the interior of the vault and pushed himself inside. Separated from Kemmer by six inches of the hardest metal known to Man, he quietly leafed through the files of confidential correspondence until he found what he wanted. He didn't need a light. His perception worked as well in the dark as in the daylight.

There was enough documentary evidence in the big vault to indict quite a few more IC officials than Kemmer—and perhaps investigation of *their* files would provide more leads to even higher officials. Wherever Kemmer was going, Albert had the idea that he wouldn't be going alone.

Albert selected all the incriminating letters and documents he could find and packed the microfiles in his jacket. Finally, bulging with documentary information, he pushed back into the streets.

It was late enough for few natives to be on the streets, and his appearance caused no comment. Apparently unnoticed, he moved rapidly into the Kazlak, searching for a place to hide the papers he had stolen. What he had learned of Vaornia made him cautious. He checked constantly for spies, but there wasn't a native in sensing range.

He ducked into the alleyway where he had caught Shifaz. His memory of it had been right. There was a small hole in one of the building walls, partly covered with cracked plaster, and barely visible in the darkness. The gloom of the Kazlak scarcely varied with night or day, as the enormous labyrinth of covered passages and building walls was pierced with only a few ventilation holes. Cressets at the main intersections burned constantly, their smokeless flames lighting the streets poorly.

He wondered idly how he had managed to remember the way to this place, let alone the little hole in the wall, as he stuffed the microfiles into its dark interior. He finished, turned to leave, and was out on the main tunnel before he became aware of the IC ground cars closing in upon him.

The Corporation was really on the beam, their spies everywhere. But they didn't know his abilities. He visualized and pushed. They were going to be surprised when he vanished—but he didn't vanish.

The expression of shocked surprise was still on his face as the stat gun blast took him squarely in the chest.

He was tied to a chair in Fred Kemmer's office. He recognized it easily, although physically he had never been inside the room. His head hurt as a polygraph recorder was strapped to his left arm, and behind him, beyond his range of vision, he could sense another man and several machines. In front of him stood Fred Kemmer with an expression of satisfaction on his face.

"Don't start thinking you're smart," Kemmer said. "You're in no position for it."

"You've tried to kill me three times," Albert reminded him.

"There's always a fourth time."

"I don't think so. Too many people know."

"Precisely my own conclusion," Kemmer said, "but there are other ways. Brainwashing's a good one."

"That's illegal!" Albert protested. "Besides—"

"So what?" Kemmer cut him off. "It's an illegal universe."

Albert probed urgently at the IC man's mind, hoping to find something he could turn to his advantage, but all he found were surface thoughts—satisfaction at having gotten the spy where he could do no harm, plans for turning Albert into a mindless idiot, thoughts of extracting information—all of which had an air of certainty that was unnerving. Albert had badly underestimated him. It was high time to leave here, if he could.

Albert visualized an area outside Vaornia, and, as he tried to push, a machine hummed loudly behind him. He didn't move. Mistake, Albert thought worriedly, I'm not going anywhere—and he knows I'm scared.

"It won't do you any good," Kemmer said. "It didn't take too much brains to figure you were using hyperspace in those disappearing acts. There's an insulating field around that chair that'd stop a space yacht." He leaned forward. "Now—what are your contacts, and who gave you the information on where to look?"

Albert saw no reason to hide it, but there was no sense in revealing anything. The Patrol had word of his arrest by now and should be here any moment.

It was as though Kemmer had read his mind. "Don't count on being rescued. I stopped the Patrol report." Kemmer paused, obviously enjoying the expression on Albert's face. "You know," he went on, "there's a peculiar fact about nerves that maybe you don't know. A stimulus sets up a brief neural volley lasting about a hundredth of a second. Following that comes a period of refractivity lasting perhaps a tenth of that time while the nerve repolarizes, and then, immediately after repolarization, there is an extremely short period of hypersensitivity."

"What's that to do with me?" Albert asked.

"You'll find out if you don't answer promptly and truthfully. That gadget on your arm is connected to a polygraph. Now do you want to make a statement?"

Albert shook his head. He was conscious of a brief pain in one finger, and the next instant someone tore the finger out of his hand with red hot pincers. He screamed. He couldn't help it. This punishment was beyond agony.

"Nice, isn't it?" Kemmer asked as Albert looked down at his amputated finger that still was remarkably attached to his hand. "And the beauty of it is that it doesn't even leave a mark. Of course, if it's repeated enough, it will end up as a permanent paralysis of the part stimulated. Now once again—who gave you that information?"

Albert talked. It was futile to try to deceive a polygraph and he wanted no more of that nerve treatment—and then he looked into Kemmer's mind again and discovered what went into brainwashing. The shock was like ice water. Hypersensitive stimulation, Kemmer was thinking gleefully, would reduce this fat slob in the chair to a screaming mindless lump that could be molded like wet putty.

Albert felt helpless. He couldn't run and he couldn't fight. But he wasn't ready to give up. His perception passed over and through Kemmer with microscopic care, looking for some weakness, something that could be exploited to advantage. Kemmer *had* to have a vulnerable point.

He did.

There was a spot on the inner lining of the radial vein in Kemmer's left arm. He had recently received an inoculation, one of the constant immunizing injections that were necessary on Antar, for there was a small thrombus clinging to the needle puncture on the inner wall of the vessel. Normally it was unimportant and would pass away in time and be absorbed, but there were considerable possibilities for trouble in that little blob of red cells and fibrin if they could be loosened from their attachment to the wall.

Hopefully, Albert reached out. If he couldn't move himself, perhaps he could move the clot.

The thrombus stirred and came free, rushing toward Kemmer's heart. Albert followed it, watching as it passed into the pulmonary artery, tracing it out through the smaller vessels until it stopped squarely across a junction of two arterioles.

Kemmer coughed, his face whitening with pain as he clutched at his chest. The pain was a mild repayment for his recent agony, Albert thought grimly. A pulmonary embolism shouldn't kill him, but the effects were disproportionate to the cause and would last a while. He grinned mercilessly as Kemmer collapsed.

A man darted from behind the chair and bent over Kemmer. Fumbling in his haste, he produced a pocket communicator, stabbed frantically at the dial and spoke urgently into it. "Medic! Boss's office—hurry!"

For a second, Albert didn't realize that the hum of machinery behind him had stopped, but when he did, both Albert and the chair vanished.

The Zark realized that its host had been hurt again. It was infuriating to be so helpless. Things kept happening to Albert which it couldn't correct until too late. There were forces involved that it didn't know how to handle; they were entirely outside the Zark's experience. It only felt relief when Albert managed to regain his ability to move—and, as it looked out upon the familiar green Antarian countryside, it felt almost happy. Of course Albert was probably still in trouble, but it wasn't so bad now. At least the man was away from the cause of his pain.

It was a hell of a note, Albert reflected, sitting beside the road that led to Lagash and working upon the bonds that tied him to the chair. He had managed to get out of Kemmer's hands, but it appeared probable that he would get no farther. As things stood, he couldn't transmit the information he had gained—and by this time probably every IC office on the planet was alerted to the fact that Earth Central had a psi-type agent on Antar—one who was not inherently unstable, like those poor devils in the parapsychological laboratories on Earth. They would be ready for him with everything from Distorter screens to Kellys.

He didn't underestimate IC now. Whatever its morals might be, its personnel was neither stupid nor slow to act. He was trapped in this sector of the planet. Prime Base was over a thousand miles away, and even if he did manage to make his way back to it along the trade routes, it was a virtual certainty that he would never be able to get near a class I communicator or the Patrol office. IC would have ample time to get ready for him, and no matter what powers he possessed, a single man would have no chance against the massed technology of the corporation.

However, he could play tag with IC in this area for some time with the reasonable possibility that he wouldn't get caught. If nothing else, it would have nuisance value. He pulled one hand free of the tape that held it to the chair arm and swiftly removed the rest of the tape that bound him. He had his freedom again. Now what would he do with it?

He left the chair behind and started down the road toward Lagash. There was no good reason to head in that particular direction, but at the moment one direction was as good as another until he could plan a course of action. His brain felt oddly fuzzy. He didn't realize that he had reached the end of his strength until he dropped in the roadway.

To compensate for the miserable job it had done in protecting him from poison and neural torture, the Zark had successfully managed to block hunger and fatigue pains until Albert's over-taxed body could stand no more. It realized its error after Albert collapsed. Sensibly, it did nothing. Its host had burned a tremendous amount of energy without replenishment, and he needed time to rest and draw upon less available reserves, and to detoxify and eliminate the metabolic poisons in his body.

It was late that afternoon before Albert recovered enough to take more than a passing interest in his surroundings. He had a vague memory of hiring a dak cart driver to take him down the road. The memory was apparently correct, because he was lying in the back of a cargo cart piled high with short pieces of cane. The cart was moving at a brisk pace despite the apparently leisurely movements of the dak between the shafts. The ponderous ten-foot strides ate up distance.

He was conscious of a hunger that was beyond discomfort, and a thirst that left his mouth dry and cottony. It was as though he hadn't eaten or drunk for days. He felt utterly spent, drained beyond exhaustion. He was in no shape to do anything, and unless he managed to find food and drink pretty soon, he would be easy pickings for IC.

He looked around the cart, but there was nothing except the canes on which he lay. There wasn't even any of the foul porridgelike mess that the natives called food, since native workers didn't bother about eating during working hours.

He turned over slowly, feeling the hard canes grind into his body as he moved. He kept thinking about food—about meals aboard ship, about dinners, about Earth restaurants, about steak, potatoes, bread—solid heartening foods filled with proteins, fats and carbohydrates.

Carbohydrates—the thought stuck in his mind for some reason. And then he realized why.

The canes he was lying on in the cart were sugar cane! He had never seen them on Earth, but he should have expected to find them out here—one of Earth's greatest exports was the seeds from which beet and cane sugar were obtained.

He pulled a length of cane from the pile and bit into one end.

His depleted body reached eagerly for the sweet energy that filled his mouth.

With the restoration of his energy balance came clearer and more logical thought. It might be well enough to make IC spend valuable time looking for him, but such delaying actions had no positive value. Ultimately he would be caught, and his usefulness would disappear with his death. But if he could get word to the Patrol, this whole business could be smashed.

Now if he made a big enough disturbance—it might possibly even reach the noses of the Patrol. Perhaps by working through the hundred or so tourists in Vaornia and Lagash, he could—

That was it, the only possible solution. The IC might be able to get rid of one man, but it couldn't possibly get rid of a hundred —and somewhere in that group of tourists there would be one who'd talk, someone who would pass the word. IC couldn't keep this quiet without brainwashing the lot of them, and that in itself would be enough to bring a Patrol ship here at maximum blast.

He chuckled happily. The native driver, startled at the strange sound, turned his head just in time to see his passenger vanish, together with a bundle of cane. The native shook his head in an oddly human gesture. These foreigners were strange creatures indeed.

Albert, thin, pale, but happy, sat at a table in one of the smaller cafeterias in Earth Center, talking to the Chief over a second helping of dessert. The fearful energy drain of esper activity, combined with the constant dodging to avoid IC hunting parties, had made him a gaunt shadow—but he had managed to survive until a Patrol ship arrived to investigate the strange stories told by tourists, of a man who haunted the towns of Lagash and Vaornia, and the road between.

"That's all there was to it, sir," Albert concluded. "Once I figured it out that not even IC could get away with mass murder, it was easy. I just kept popping up in odd places and telling my story, and then, to make it impressive, I'd disappear. I had nearly two days before IC caught on, and by then you knew. The only trouble was getting enough to eat. I damn near starved before the Patrol arrived. I expect that we owe quite a few farmers and shopkeepers reparations for the food I stole."

"They'll be paid, providing they present a claim," the Chief said. "But there's one thing about all this that bothers me. I know you had no psi powers when you left Earth on this mission. Just where did you acquire them?"

Albert shook his head. "I don't know," he said. "Unless they were latent and developed in Antar's peculiar climatic and physical conditions. Or maybe it was the shock of that meeting with the Bandersnatch. All I'm sure of is that I didn't have any until after that meeting with Shifaz."

"Well, you certainly have them now. The Parapsych boys are hot on your tail, but we've stalled them off."

"Thanks. I don't want to imitate a guinea pig."

"We owe you at least that for getting us a case against IC. Even their shysters won't be able to wiggle out of this one." The Chief smiled. "It's nice to have those lads where they can be handled for a change."

"They do need a dose of applied conscience," Albert agreed.

"The government also owes you a bonus and a vote of thanks."

"I'll appreciate the bonus," Albert said as he signaled for the waitress. "Recently, I can't afford my appetite."

"It's understandable. After all, you've lost nearly eighty pounds."

"Wonder if I'll ever get them back," Albert muttered as he bit into the third dessert.

The Chief watched enviously. "I wouldn't worry about that," he said. "Just get your strength back. There's another assignment for you, one that will need your peculiar talents." He stood up. "I'll be seeing you. My ulcer can't take your appetite any more." He walked away.

Inside Albert, the Zark alerted. A new assignment! That meant another world and new sensations. Truly, this host was magnificent! It had been a lucky day when he had fallen in running from the Bandersnatch. The Zark quivered with delight . . .

And Albert felt it.

Turning his perception inward to see what might be wrong, he saw the Zark for the first time.

For a second, a wave of repulsion swept through his body, but as he comprehended the extent of that protoplasmic mass so inextricably intertwined with his own, he realized that this thing within him was the reason for his new powers. There could be no other explanation.

And as he searched farther, he marveled. The Zark was unspecialized in a way he had never imagined—an amorphous aggregation of highly evolved cells that could imitate normal tissues in a manner that would defy ordinary detection. It was something at once higher yet lower than his own flesh, something more primitive yet infinitely more evolved.

The Zark had succeeded at last. It had established communication with its host.

"Answer me, parasite," Albert muttered subvocally. "I know you're there—and I know you can answer!"

The Zark gave the protean equivalent of a shrug. If Albert only knew how it had tried to communicate—no, there was no communication between them. Their methods of thought were so different that there was no possible rapport.

It twitched—and Albert jumped. And for the first time in its long life, the Zark had an original idea. It moved a few milligrams of its substance to Albert's throat region, and after a premonitory glottal spasm, Albert said very distinctly and quite involuntarily, "All right. I am here."

Albert froze with surprise, but when the shock passed, he laughed. "Well, I asked for it," he said. "But it's like the story about the man who talked to himself—and got answers. Not exactly a comforting sensation."

"I'm sorry," the Zark apologized. "I do not wish to cause discomfort."

"You pick a poor way to keep from doing it."

"It was the only way I could figure to make contact with your conscious mind—and you desired that I communicate."

"I suppose you're right. But while it is nice to know that I really have a guardian angel, I'd have felt better about it if you had white robes and wings and were hovering over my shoulder."

"I don't understand," the Zark said.

"I was trying to be funny. You know," Albert continued after a moment, "I never thought of trying to perceive myself. I wonder why. I guess because none of the medical examinations showed anything different from normal."

"I was always afraid that you might suspect before I could tell you," the Zark replied. "It was an obvious line of reasoning, and you *are* an intelligent entity—the most intelligent I have ever inhabited. It is too bad that I shall have to leave. I have enjoyed being with you."

"Who said anything about leaving?" Albert asked.

"You did. I could feel your revulsion when you became aware of me. It wasn't nice, but I suppose you can't help it. Yours is an independent race, one that doesn't willingly support—" the voice hesitated as though searching for the proper word—"fellow travelers," it finished.

Albert grinned. "There are historical precedents for that statement, but your interpretation isn't quite right. I was surprised. You startled me."

He fell silent, and the Zark, respecting the activity of his mind, forbore to interrupt.

Albert was doing some heavy thinking about the Zark. Certainly it had protected him on Antar, and with equal certainty it must have been responsible for the psi owners he possessed. He owed it a lot, for without its help he wouldn't have survived.

There was only one thing wrong.

Sexless though it was, the Zark must possess the characteristics of life, since it was obviously alive. And those characteristics were unchanging throughout the known universe. The four vital criteria defined centuries ago were still as good today as they were then—growth, metabolism, irritability—and *reproduction*. Despite its lack of sex, the Zark must be capable of producing others of its kind, and while he didn't mind supporting one fellow traveler, he was damned if he'd support a whole family of them.

"That need never bother you," the Zark interrupted. "As an individual, I am very long-lived and seldom reproduce. I can, of course, but the process is quite involved—actually it involves making a twin out of myself—and it is not necessary. Besides, there cannot be two Zarks in one host. My offspring would have to seek another."

"And do they have your powers?"

"Of course. They would know all I know, for a Zark's memory is not concentrated in specialized tissue like your brain."

A light began to dawn in Albert's mind. Maybe this was the answer to the corporate conscience he had been wishing for so wistfully on Antar. "Does it bother you to reproduce?" he asked.

"It is annoying, but not painful—nor would it be too difficult after a pattern was set in my cells. But why do you ask this?"

"The thought just occurred to me that there are quite a few people who could use a Zark. A few of the more honest folks would improve this Confederation's moral tone if they had the power—and certainly psi powers in law enforcement would be unbeatable."

"Then you would want me to reproduce?"

"It might be a good idea if we can find men who are worthy of Zarks. I could check them with my telepathy and perhaps we might—"

"Let me warn you," the Zark interjected. "While this all sounds very fine, there are difficulties, even with a host as large as yourself. I shall need more energy than your body has available in order to duplicate myself. It will be hard for you to do what must be done."

"And what is that?"

"Eat," the Zark said, "great quantities of high energy foods." It shuddered at the thought of Albert overloading his digestive tract any more than he had been doing the past week.

But Albert's reaction went to prove that while their relationship was physically close, mentally they were still far apart. Albert, the Zark noted in astonishment, didn't regard it as an ordeal at all.

Love Called This Thing

BY AVRAM DAVIDSON AND LAURA GOFORTH

Nan Peter Baker Four This Is Nan Peter Baker How do You Receive Me Over and now a word from Our Sponsor interviewed in his office the Commissioner said but Ruth I can explain everything there is nothing to explain David it's all too obvious I'm Bert Peel Officer and this is my brother Harry a cold front coming down from Canada and we've got to get word to the Fort colon congestion is absolutely unnecessary in men and women over forty at any one of the ninety-one offices of the Clinton National Bank and Trust . . .

"Embarasse de richesse," the French count had said when he looked at all the pretty girls on the high school swim team, and explained what it meant in English. Penny wasn't really in love with him; she only thought she was, after pretending she was, to make David jealous, which she certainly did. But after the count gently explained to her, she and David made up just in time for the Spring Prom, which made the distant observer very happy.

At least he thought it did. "What is happy?" he often asked himself. Maybe just pretend. *You never really loved me Rick it was just a pretense wasn't it?* Like the distant observer thinking of himself as "him" when, really, he knew now—had known long—he

was only an "it." *It's about time we faced up to reality, Alison.*
Yes. It was about time. *We can't go on like this.* No, certainly not.
It was time.

In the beginning, there was no time. There was sight—here
dark, there bright. He did not know then, of course—and how
long had "then" lasted? Memory did not tell that the bright
was stars. And there was sound—whispering, crackling, shrilling.
*What do you mean, Professor, when you say that outer space is
not a place of silence?* And then (he knew now that this "then"
was about fifty years ago) there had begun a new kind of sound.
Not steady, but interrupted, and interrupted according to patterns. Awareness had stirred, gradually, and wonder. He knew
later that this was "wireless." *CQ, CQ, CQ . . . SOS, SOS,
SOS . . .*

And then the other kinds of sounds, oh, very different. These
were voices. This was "radio." And music. It was too different;
the distant observer knew distress without even knowing that it
was distress. But he grew used to it—that is, distress ceased: but
not wonder. Urgency came with the voices. What? *What?* He
groped for meaning, not even knowing what meaning was.

Presently there was another kind of sight, not just the dark and
the stars any longer, but pictures—flickering, fading, dancing,
clear, pictures upon pictures. Gradually he learned selectivity—
how to concentrate upon one, how to not-see, not-hear the others.
Still later: how to see and hear all without confusion. How to
match sound and sight. That things had names. What people
were, who made the voices and the music. What meaning was.

About himself, he learned nothing directly. For a while, he
had tried to speak to them, but it was apparent that nothing of
him reached Earth. He had learned Earth, yes. And knew what
this place was, where he was. An asteroid. How had he come
to be there? This was in space. There were spaceships—he saw
the scenes on television. Meteors were dangerous to spaceships.
He knew meteors. Sometimes spaceships crashed. He scanned
all his little world, but there was no spaceship, crashed or otherwise.

You've got to help me—I don't know who I am! But that was
more easy, oh, so much more so—that one was a man, and there

were many men. The sponsors (in this case, Muls, the creamy-smooth deodorant) were men, too. Everybody was very kind to this man. He had amnesia. What was odor? This the observer could not understand. But to have no memory, this he understood very well. This he shared with men.

Gradually he had come to share many things with men. They spoke different languages, but the one which came with the first pictures was English. English from America. Later on, there was English from England, there was French, Russian, Spanish, Japanese—but American was first and best. So much more interesting than the Red Army and the hydroelectric dams, these stories of real life. Of love and sadness and of happiness.

Kid, there ain't no problem in all this world you can't lick if you really try. Very well, the observer would try. *You never know what you can do till you try.* His first attempt at taking shape wasn't good. It didn't look much like a man. So he tried again and again. Each time he grew better at it. It was true, what the people said. It was all true, every word and picture of it. *There ain't no problem—*

And so when it came time for his favorite Wednesday evening program, the distant observer was ready. Summoning all his effort, husbanding all his energy, he passed along the wave length as a man walks down a street. There was a slight jar, a click. He realized that he could never undo what had just been done. There was a new body now, a new metabolism. *The past is dead, David. We have to live for the future.*

"And what is your name—my, you got up here but quick!" burbled Keith Kane, the M.C. of Cash or Credit. "I've never known a volunteer from our happy studio audience to manage it quite so suddenly. This is just the warm up, sir, so you needn't be nervous. Not that you need the reassurance—cool as a cucumber, isn't he, folks? You other folks who volunteered just take seats right there—"

The first lady volunteer was old and pretty. Well, maybe not so old. But maybe like Mary Clay who realized that she was too old for young David Webster and after she cried she accepted the fact and sent him back to Madge Barkley whom he really loved all the while, only they had this silly quarrel.

The lady smiled at him. He smiled back. *I—feel—GREAT!*

"—So that's the way the rules work, and now, folks, in just five seconds we'll be on the air! Five—four—three—two—one—Good evening, all you lovely people out there in TV Land! This is Keith Kane, bringing you the great—the greater—the GREATEST quiz program ever: *Cash or Credit?*"

Now he felt his heart beating very fast. So that was what it was like! And now he knew what was odor. But the lovely lady volunteer next to him smelled, yes, that was sweet. But if it was Muls or Van Art Number Three, this he would learn later.

"—just rinse and dry, folks, that's all there is to it: Clear-o, the all-purpose *vegetable* detergent. And now whom have we here? What is your name, sir?"

Here it was. And how terrible if he should break down and press his hands to his head and sob, "I—I—don't—*know!*" But he did know; he had it all ready. "David. My name is David Taylor." All the ones named David were good. Oh, they had their troubles, but in the end everyone loved them. And see: nice Keith Kane beaming. The lady, too.

"Well, David, what'll it be? Cash—or—Credit? You know the rules: If you pick Cash, we spin this little wheel. If it comes up with a number, you go on to answer—if you can, hah-ha—a question worth however many thousand dollars follow that number. If it comes up blank—you're out. Whereas, if you pick Credit, you take your place among the volunteers and if any contestant makes a boo-boo, why, you step into *his* shoes and *he* is out. Soooo—?"

"Take the cash and let the credit go," said David.

Grinning from lobe to lobe, Keith Kane asked the same questions of the lady, whose name was Mrs. Conar, Mrs. Ethel-Mae Conar, a widow; and received the same answer. The audience applauded, the wheel was spun, and it came up 10.

"Ten—thousand—DOLLARS!" screamed Keith Kane. "That's what your first question is worth and here it *is:* What former President of the United States is associated with this tune, and what is the name of the tune, which refers to his State? Remember, you have thirty seconds to think it over . . ."

David and Mrs. Conar won two hundred and eighty-five thousand dollars in *cash* before the program was over, as well as a year's supply of Clear-o, and fifty shares of stock in a mink ranch; and the band played "The Stars and Stripes Forever" as Keith Kane counted out the money. Mrs. Conar had kissed him and kissed David and was now clasping his hands and sobbing that she didn't believe it.

"Oh, it's true," David assured her. "It's all true; that's the funny part of it." (David Mackay said that, in *Matinée*, when he admitted his wife was an alcoholic.) Sight and sound and touch (kissing was pleasant; no wonder it was so much done) and smell and—and—what was the other? Taste. Keith Kane bawled at him the question of what he was going to do with all his money. David deliberated. What was it that Clem Clooten, on *Saddle-Galled*, had said, the time he broke the faro bank in Dogie City? Taste . . . yes: "I'm goin' out 'n buy m'self a cup o' java . . ." The audience went *wild*.

Java tasted. Taste was as exciting as the other four sensations. And sitting next to him on the counter-stool was Mrs. Ethel-Mae Conar, gazing at his distinguished profile. It was clean-cut; all Davids were clean-cut. He gazed down at her. He was tall, of course.

He searched for the right words. It turned out to be singular. "Happy?" he asked.

She sighed, nodded. Then—"You're a rather strange young man," she said. "Do you know that?"

Certainly he knew it.

He leaned closer. "This is bigger than both of us," he said huskily. "Let me take you away from all this . . ."

"I certainly *will*," she said briskly, "right over to my place in the Surrey-Regis on Park Avenue—" That meant she was unhappy despite her money!—"where we can have a *decent* cup of coffee."

The counterman scowled at the bill David offered him. "Whatsis? Play-money? A five-hunnerd-dolla bill? Whuddya, wise guy?"

David arose slowly, buttoning his jacket, and leaned over. "If you're looking for trouble, buddy . . ." he said. But the guy chickened out. Anyway, Ethel-Mae had some change in her purse. "Taxi!" David called happily. He helped her in, sank back in the seat, and when the driver asked Where To, David said crisply, "Follow that cab!"

The driver (Herman Bogancz, the license read) half-turned, half-growled. Ethel-Mae laughed. "Oh, if you aren't—never mind, driver: the Surrey-Regis, on Park near—" But H. Bogancz muttered that he knew where the place was.

David gazed out the window excitedly. Everywhere, men and lights and women and automobiles. "Little old New York," he murmured.

Suddenly she yelped, dug her fingers into his arm.

"Darling!" he exclaimed. "Are you all right? Is anything wrong?"

"No," she said. "Oh, no—"

"*Some*thing must be wrong," he insisted. "You can tell me, dear. I trust you. No matter what you've done—"

"What I've *done?*" she screamed. "I've just won a half-share in $285,000 is what—"

He seized her, turned her facing him. "Are you out of your *mind?*" he gritted. And then, memory returning, he released her. "Yeah . . . Gee . . . that's right. Yeah . . . how *about* that? Do you know what this *means?* Ethel-Mae, we're *rich!* WE'RE RICH!"

The driver twisted his chin slightly to the right. "Do y' mind, mister? Not so loud with the decibels. I gotta near condition."

David said, shocked, "If there's anything I can do—anything at all—if you need money—we'll get the best surgeon there is—"

Herman Bogancz shrugged. "My cousin Sidney is the best surgeon there is, and he says an operation wouldn't help."

"Then," said David, "there's nothing more that any of us can do—except wait—and pray—"

"—and wash it out three times a day with a boric acid solution," said Herman Bogancz.

David didn't quite understand why Mrs. Conar made him apply for a room at the Surrey-Regis by himself while she went up to her room through the side entrance. In fact, he didn't understand at all. The clerk looked at him rather oddly when he explained this to him and asked for a room near hers. He looked even odder when he saw the $500 bill. Once again David buttoned his jacket (it had been necessary to unbutton it first) and leaned over. "I hope," he said, "that I'm not going to have any trouble with you."

"Oh, dear me, no," said the clerk. "Not at all . . . my goodness, Mr. Taylor, but you really are tall, aren't you? Suite 516. Mrs. Conar's is Suite 521—that's the best I can do right just this very minute, and—"

Another gentleman materialized at David's elbow. "Good evening, sir," he said suavely. "I am Mr. Feltz, the manager. Is everything all right?"

"The boy's not to blame," David said, gesturing toward the clerk. "Society is to blame—we're *all* to blame. It's these crazy, mixed-up times we live in."

Behind David's back, the clerk spread open the $500 bill for Mr. Feltz's inspection.

"How right you are, sir," said Mr. Feltz.

"About the gentleman's—Mr. Taylor's change, Mr. Feltz—?"

David turned, put his hand on the clerk's shoulder. The man flushed, sucked in his lower lip. "That's for *you*, sonny. There is no such thing as a bad boy. I never met a man I didn't like."

"*Front!*" said the clerk, his voice tremulous.

Mr. Feltz handed the keys to 516 to the bellboy himself, urged Mr. Taylor to make his wants known immediately. As David walked toward the elevator, the manager turned to his subordinate. "The Rich," he said simply. The clerk nodded solemnly. "We know their ways," said Mr. Feltz. "Eh? Well, that's very generous of you, Robert—but, no, sixty-forty is good enough. He seems to have taken a liking to you. Send up flowers, the morning papers, a split of champagne. And include my card, Robert."

As soon as the bellboy had gone (rather like a satisfied customer on his way out of a high-class opium den, with a $500 bill clutched in his hot hand), David went down the corridor and knocked on the door of Suite 521. "Ethel-Mae?" he asked, his face close to the door. "Dearest? This is David. *Please* open. I can explain everything."

And, sure enough, her words as she opened the door and fell into his arms were, "There is nothing to explain!" Then she said, "It's just that you're so sweet—and naive. But that nasty little nance down at the desk wouldn't understand."

Since David didn't understand either, he made no comment, but covered her face with kisses. "Darling, I *love* you," he said. "Please believe me." And she said, But she did—she did. "Do you know what it's like to be alone—always alone—never to know love? Do you? *Do you?* No. Of course you don't—"

Her answer was exactly correct. "Hush, darling," she said. "Everything's going to be all right." He sighed, kissed her again. Then—

"Ethel-Mae? Ethel-*Mae?* Mrs. Conar? What—? Why are you—" But she didn't seem to hear him. Nothing he had ever heard on radio or seen on television prepared him for what was happening now. But—he decided after a moment or so—what was happening now was—though strange—not unpleasant. "This is wrong," he groaned happily. "It's all wrong. But I—I don't care. Do you hear, I don't *care!*"

It was two in the morning before he stumbled back to his own room, and bed. At half-past two, he was awakened by the bell-boy's father and mother (smuggled up on the service elevator) who had come all the way from Mulberry Street to kiss his hands. At three, he was half-awakened by a scratching noise at his door. After a few minutes, he got up and—after approaching it as cautiously as the Sheriff of Hangtown on the program of the same name—threw it suddenly open.

A pretty girl with her red hair in a pony-tail uttered a little scream. Pencil and notebook fell to the floor. "Why—you—you're only a *child!*" he said, in a hushed voice.

"Mr. T-Taylor—" she began very nervously. "I saw you at the studio and I fol—followed you—" she gulped—"over here. But it took till now for me to get up nerve—"

"Why, you're frightened," he said, looking down at her. "Don't be frightened. You don't *ever* have to be frightened of *me*. Come in," he urged. "Please come in."

She picked up her notebook and followed him in obediently. Then, taking the seat he gestured to, she said, "And I'm not such a child, either. I'm a senior at Barnard. Journalism major. And I want a story from you, Mr. Taylor, before all the other reporters get here. Please, Mr. Taylor, *please.*"

He looked at her admiringly. "That took guts," he said. "Where I come from, the men get separated from the boys mighty young. But—don't call me 'Mr. Taylor'—Mr. Taylor has gray hair at the temples. Call me 'David'."

She called him David. And she told him that her name was Pamela Novack. And he said that Pamela was a lovely name. She told him that she'd hated it as a child, but that lately—in fact, just this very minute—she'd gotten to like it a whole lot more. And they laughed. They laughed a whole lot.

Before they knew it, it was getting light.

"Oh, golly," Pamela sighed. "Oh, gee, have I got a story! In a way, it's so sad, you having such an unhappy childhood, I mean; your mother dying from the brain tumor and your father being an alcoholic—"

He said that was all in the past. He said they had to start looking toward the future. She nodded soberly. Then she stretched and said she was hungry.

"Hey, how about that!" David laughed, catching sight of his face in the mirror. It was a nice face. He had done well in making it; it looked like all the Davids he had ever seen. "You know something? I'm hungry, too! I haven't had a bite to eat since that cup of coffee after the show. Would you like to have some breakfast? You *would*? Hot diggety! . . . Hello? I want Room Service, please."

The narcoleptic tones of the operator said, Not till ha'pas'six. And then suddenly were clear and alert and saying, "Oh, Mr. *Taylor*? Pardon me—of *course*, Mr. Taylor—what would you like? Scrambled eggs and coffee and toast and gallons of orange juice. Yes, *sir*, Mr. Taylor."

Then, suddenly, the smile was gone from David's face. Anxiously, Pamela asked what the matter was. Scowling, he mimicked, "'Yes, Mr. Taylor, certainly, Mr. Taylor'—it isn't me they like—nobody likes *me*—it's the money. Once you been in reform school, nobody has any use for you, the cops are always watching you, the nice girls don't want to have anything to do with you—"

Pamela was troubled. "Oh, you *mustn't* say that. I—I—well, I think *I'm* a nice girl—" she blushed suddenly, looked down—"and I—like you—David."

He got up and walked back and forth, rubbing his left arm with his right hand. He swung around and faced her. "You!" he jeered. "Whadda *you* know? You're just a fresh young kid—"

"I am not!" she snapped.

"A senior at Barnard! Whadda you know about life? You—"

He stopped. He had been enjoying the experience of emoting so much that the significance of the scene had escaped him. *They were quarreling!* That meant they were in love! Of course—Davids always quarreled with the girls they were really in love with.

He dropped down on one knee beside her and looked into her flushed, pretty face.

"Darling," he said brokenly, taking her hands. "Trust me—I can't explain now—but just trust me—"

There was a sound from the door. They looked up. Ethel-Mae Conar stood there, holding her throat with both hands. After a moment, she said, "I must have hurt you very much, David, for you to have done—*this*—to me—to have forgotten. So quickly."

Exquisitely miserable, he shouted, "Leave me alone! Can't you leave me alone? Can't you understand that it's all over between us?" And then, his voice dropping, "Oh, Ethel-Mae, forgive me. I didn't mean to say that. I didn't mean it. I—I can explain."

Letting her hands drop resignedly, she said, "There's nothing to explain, David. I understand. It could never have worked out. I'm—I'm just—too *old* for you, David." She walked over, lifted his head (he had hung it, of course), placed her palms on his cheeks and kissed him gently on the forehead. Then she turned to Pamela and said softly, "Be good to him, my dear. And give him lots of love." She went out, her head high, a wistful smile on her lips, and the awareness that she had half of the $285,000, the year's supply of Clear-o (the *vegetable* detergent), and the fifty shares of stock in a mink ranch.

There was a moment's silence. Then, "Gosh," said Pamela. "Golly," she said.

David turned to her. "Darling, don't cry any more," he begged. "Everything's going to be all right from now on."

"I'm not crying," she said. Her eyes were shining. "The hell with the story and the journalism course and the hell with Barnard, too. With all your money," she said, falling into his welcoming arms, "we can get married and start a family right away. Kiss me," she said, "hold me tight, don't ever leave me!"

Mr. and Mrs. David Taylor live in a fifteen-room house in Westport with two picture windows, three boxers, and three cars. They have two children and a third is on the way. They are as happy as any couple in Westport has a right to be in these crazy, mixed-up days. David is a highly successful writer of television scripts, with an unerring nose for what the public wants. It is perhaps unfortunate that his work brings him into contact with so many clever and attractive women. He is, of course, unfaithful to his wife with one of them at least twice a year (or at least once a year with two of them).

There used to be a time when a David would never do a thing like this to his wife. He would *almost* do it—and then, at the last moment, not. But TV is maturing. The Davids do it all the time. All the damned time.

"But how *could* you?" Pam Taylor weeps. "David, how *could* you?"

And young David Taylor, his face twisted with anguish, cries, "Don't you understand? Won't you even *try* to understand? *I'm sick! I need help!*"

Well. Naturally Pam is very sad that her husband is sick, sick, sick—but, after all, it's the thing to be, isn't it? And so she's happy she can help him and happily she drives the two of them down to Dr. Naumbourg. David is very sad that he's made his lovely wife unhappy, but he's happy that he's fulfilling his destiny as a David. Dr. Naumbourg always insists on both husbands *and* wives Going Into Therapy at the same time. Pamela's case is a common enough one, merely a routine phallic envy. Naumbourg gets them every day.

But in all the years since Vienna, Dr. N. has never had another patient whose womb-fantasy takes the form of being a Thing on an asteroid. And so, while all three of them are very happy, Dr. Naumbourg is perhaps the happiest of all.

Lex

BY W. T. HAGGERT

Keep your nerve, Peter Manners told himself; it's only a job. But nerve has to rest on a sturdier foundation than cash reserves just above zero and eviction if he came away from this interview still unemployed. Clay, at the Association of Professional Engineers, who had set up the appointment, hadn't eased Peter's nervousness by admitting, "I don't know what in hell he's looking for. He's turned down every man we've sent him."

The interview was at three. Fifteen minutes to go. Coming early would betray overeagerness. Peter stood in front of the Lex Industries plant and studied it to kill time. Plain, featureless concrete walls, not large for a manufacturing plant—it took a scant minute to exhaust its sightseeing potential. If he walked around the building, he could, if he ambled, come back to the front entrance just before three.

He turned the corner, stopped, frowned, wondering what there was about the building that seemed so puzzling. It could not have been plainer, more ordinary. It was in fact, he only gradually realized, so plain and ordinary that it was like no other building he had ever seen.

There had been windows at the front. There were none at the

side, and none at the rear. Then how were the working areas lit? He looked for the electric service lines and found them at one of the rear corners. They jolted him. The distribution transformers were ten times as large as they should have been for a plant this size.

Something else was wrong. Peter looked for minutes before he found out what it was. Factories usually have large side doorways for employees changing shifts. This building had one small office entrance facing the street, and the only other door was at the loading bay—big enough to handle employee traffic, but four feet above the ground. Without any stairs, it could be used only by trucks backing up to it. Maybe the employees' entrance was on the third side.

It wasn't.

Staring back at the last blank wall, Peter suddenly remembered the time he had set out to kill. He looked at his watch and gasped. At a run, set to straight-arm the door, he almost fell on his face. The door had opened by itself. He stopped and looked for a photoelectric eye, but a soft voice said through a loud-speaker in the anteroom wall: "Mr. Manners?"

"What?" he panted. "Who—?"

"You *are* Mr. Manners?" the voice asked.

He nodded, then realized he had to answer aloud if there was a microphone around; but the soft voice said: "Follow the open doors down the hall. Mr. Lexington is expecting you."

"Thanks," Peter said, and a door at one side of the anteroom swung open for him.

He went through it with his composure slipping still further from his grip. This was no way to go into an interview, but doors kept opening before and shutting after him, until only one was left, and the last of his calm was blasted away by a bellow from within.

"Don't stand out there like a jackass! Either come in or go away!"

Peter found himself leaping obediently toward the doorway. He stopped just short of it, took a deep breath and huffed it out, took another, all the while thinking, Hold on now; you're in no shape for an interview—and it's not your fault—this whole setup is geared to unnerve you: the kindergarten kid called in to see the principal.

He let another bellow bounce off him as he blew out the second breath, straightened his jacket and tie, and walked in as an engineer applying for a position should.

"Mr. Lexington?" he said. "I'm Peter Manners. The Association—"

"Sit down," said the man at the desk. "Let's look you over."

He was a huge man behind an even huger desk. Peter took a chair in front of the desk and let himself be inspected. It wasn't comfortable. He did some looking over of his own to ease the tension.

The room was more than merely large, carpeted throughout with a high-pile, rich, sound-deadening rug. The oversized desk and massive leather chairs, heavy patterned drapes, ornately framed paintings—by God, even a glass-brick manteled fireplace and bowls with flowers!—made him feel as if he had walked down a hospital corridor into Hollywood's idea of an office.

His eyes eventually had to move to Lexington, and they were daunted for another instant. This was a citadel of a man—great girders of frame supporting buttresses of muscle—with a vaulting head and drawbridge chin and a steel gaze that defied any attempt to storm it.

But then Peter came out of his momentary flinch, and there was an age to the man, about 65, and he saw the muscles had turned to fat, the complexion ashen, the eyes set deep as though retreating from pain, and this was a citadel of a man, yes, but beginning to crumble.

"What can you do?" asked Lexington abruptly.

Peter started, opened his mouth to answer, closed it again. He'd been jolted too often in too short a time to be stampeded into blurting a reply that would cost him this job.

"Good," said Lexington. "Only a fool would try to answer that. Do you have any knowledge of medicine?"

"Not enough to matter," Peter said, stung by the compliment.

"I don't mean how to bandage a cut or splint a broken arm. I mean things like cell structure, neural communication—the *basics* of how we live."

"I'm applying for a job as engineer."

"I know. Are you interested in the basics of how we live?"

Peter looked for a hidden trap, found none. "Of course. Isn't everyone?"

"Less than you think," Lexington said. "It's the preconceived notions they're interested in protecting. At least I won't have to beat them out of you."

"Thanks," said Peter, and waited for the next fast ball.

"How long have you been out of school?"

"Only two years. But you knew that from the Association—"

"No practical experience to speak of?"

"Some," said Peter, stung again, this time not by a compliment. "After I got my degree, I went East for a post-graduate training program with an electrical manufacturer. I got quite a bit of experience there. The company—"

"Stockpiled you," Lexington said.

Peter blinked. "Sir?"

"Stockpiled you! How much did they pay you?"

"Not very much, but we were getting the training instead of wages."

"Did that come out of the pamphlets they gave you?"

"Did what come out—"

"That guff about receiving training instead of wages!" said Lexington. "Any company that really wants bright trainees will compete for them with money—cold, hard cash, not platitudes. Maybe you saw a few of their products being made, maybe you didn't. But you're a lot weaker in calculus than when you left school, and in a dozen other subjects too, aren't you?"

"Well, nothing we did on the course involved higher mathematics," Peter admitted cautiously, "and I suppose I could use a refresher course in calculus."

"Just as I said—they stockpiled you, instead of using you as an engineer. They hired you at a cut wage and taught you things that would be useful only in their own company, while in the meantime you were getting weaker in the subjects you'd paid to learn. Or are you one of these birds that had the shot paid for him?"

"I worked my way through," said Peter stiffly.

"If you'd stayed with them five years, do you think you'd be able to get a job with someone else?"

Peter considered his answer carefully. Every man the Association had sent had been turned away. That meant bluffs didn't work. Neither, he'd seen for himself, did allowing himself to be intimidated.

"I hadn't thought about it," he said. "I suppose it wouldn't have been easy."

"Impossible, you mean. You wouldn't know a single thing except their procedures, their catalogue numbers, their way of doing things. And you'd have forgotten so much of your engineering training, you'd be scared to take on an engineer's job, for fear you'd be asked to do something you'd forgotten how to do. At that point, they could take you out of the stockpile, put you in just about any job they wanted, at any wage you'd stand for, and they'd have an indentured worker with a degree—but not the price tag. You see that now?"

It made Peter feel he had been suckered, but he had decided to play this straight all the way. He nodded.

"Why'd you leave?" Lexington pursued, unrelenting.

"I finished the course and the increase they offered on a permanent basis wasn't enough, so I went elsewhere—"

"With your head full of this nonsense about a shortage of engineers."

Peter swallowed. "I thought it would be easier to get a job than it has been, yes."

"They start the talk about a shortage and then they keep it going. Why? So youngsters will take up engineering thinking they'll wind up among a highly paid minority. You did, didn't you?"

"Yes, sir."

"And so did all the others there with you, at school and in this stockpiling outfit?"

"That's right."

"Well," said Lexington unexpectedly, "there *is* a shortage! And the stockpilers are the ones who made it, and who keep it going! And the hell of it is that they can't stop—when one does it, they all have to, or their costs get out of line and they can't compete. What's the solution?"

"I don't know," Peter said.

Lexington leaned back. "That's quite a lot of admissions you've made. What makes you think you're qualified for the job I'm offering?"

"You said you wanted an engineer."

"And I've just proved you're less of an engineer than when you left school. I have, haven't I?"

"All right, you have," Peter said angrily.

"And now you're wondering why I don't get somebody fresh out of school. Right?"

Peter straightened up and met the old man's challenging gaze. "That and whether you're giving me a hard time just for the hell of it."

"Well, am I?" Lexington demanded.

Looking at him squarely, seeing the intensity of the pain-drawn eyes, Peter had the startling feeling that Lexington was rooting for him! "No, you're not."

"Then what am I after?"

"Suppose you tell me."

So suddenly that it was almost like a collapse, the tension went out of the old man's face and shoulders. He nodded with inexpressible tiredness. "Good again. The man I want doesn't exist. He has to be made—the same as I was. You qualify, so far. You've lost your illusions, but haven't had time yet to replace them with dogma or cynicism or bitterness. You saw immediately that fake humility or cockiness wouldn't get you anywhere here, and you were right. Those were the important things. The background data I got from the Association on you counted, of course, but only if you were teachable. I think you are. Am I right?"

"At least I can face knowing how much I don't know," said Peter, "if that answers the question."

"It does. Partly. What did you notice about this plant?"

In precis form, Peter listed his observations: the absence of windows at sides and rear, the unusual amount of power, the automatic doors, the lack of employees' entrances.

"Very good," said Lexington. "Most people only notice the automatic doors. Anything else?"

"Yes," Peter said. "You're the only person I've seen in the building."

"I'm the only one there is."

Peter stared his disbelief. Automated plants were nothing new, but they all had their limitations. Either they dealt with exactly similar products or things that could be handled on a flow basis, like oil or water-soluble chemicals. Even these had no more to do than process the goods.

"Come on," said Lexington, getting massively to his feet. "I'll show you."

The office door opened, and Peter found himself being led down the antiseptic corridor to another door which had opened, giving access to the manufacturing area. As they moved along, between rows of seemingly disorganized machinery, Peter noticed that the factory lights high overhead followed their progress, turning themselves on in advance of their coming, and going out after they had passed, keeping a pool of illumination only in the immediate area they occupied. Soon they reached a large door which Peter recognized as the inside of the truck loading door he had seen from outside.

Lexington paused here. "This is the bay used by the trucks arriving with raw materials," he said. "They back up to this door, and a set of automatic jacks outside lines up the trailer body with the door exactly. Then the door opens and the truck is unloaded by these materials handling machines."

Peter didn't see him touch anything, but as he spoke, three glistening machines, apparently self-powered, rolled noiselessly up to the door in formation and stopped there, apparently waiting to be inspected.

They gave Peter the creeps. Simple square boxes, set on casters, with two arms each mounted on the sides might have looked similar. The arms, fashioned much like human arms, hung at the sides, not limply, but in a relaxed position that somehow indicated readiness.

Lexington went over to one of them and patted it lovingly. "Really, these machines are only an extension of one large machine. The whole plant, as a matter of fact, is controlled from one point and is really a single unit. These materials handlers, or manipulators, were about the toughest things in the place to design. But they're tremendously useful. You'll see a lot of them around."

Lexington was about to leave the side of the machine when abruptly one of the arms rose to the handkerchief in his breast pocket and daintily tugged it into a more attractive position. It took only a split second, and before Lexington could react, all three machines were moving away to attend to mysterious duties of their own.

Peter tore his eyes away from them in time to see the look of frustrated embarrassment that crossed Lexington's face, only to be replaced by one of anger. He said nothing, however, and led Peter to a large bay where racks of steel plate, bar forms, nuts, bolts, and other materials were stored.

"After unloading a truck, the machines check the shipment, report any shortages or overages, and store the materials here," he said, the trace of anger not yet gone from his voice. "When an order is received, it's translated into the catalogue numbers used internally within the plant, and machines like the ones you just saw withdraw the necessary materials from stock, make the component parts, assemble them, and package the finished goods for shipment. Simultaneously, an order is sent to the billing section to bill the customer, and an order is sent to our trucker to come and pick the shipment up. Meanwhile, if the withdrawal of the materials required has depleted our stock, the purchasing section is instructed to order more raw materials. I'll take you through the manufacturing and assembly sections right now, but they're too noisy for me to explain what's going on while we're there."

Peter followed numbly as Lexington led him through a maze of machines, each one seemingly intent on cutting, bending, welding, grinding or carrying some bit of metal, or just standing idle, waiting for something to do. The two-armed manipulators Peter had just seen were everywhere, scuttling from machine to machine, apparently with an exact knowledge of what they were doing and the most efficient way of doing it.

He wondered what would happen if one of them tried to use the same aisle they were using. He pictured a futile attempt to escape the onrushing wheels, saw himself clambering out of the path of the speeding vehicle just in time to fall into the jaws of the punch press that was laboring beside him at the moment. Nervously, he looked for an exit, but his apprehension was unnecessary. The machines seemed to know where they were and avoided the two men, or stopped to wait for them to go by.

Back in the office section of the building, Lexington indicated a small room where a typewriter could be heard clattering away. "Standard business machines, operated by the central control mechanism. In that room," he said, as the door swung open and Peter saw that the typewriter was actually a sort of teletype, with no one before the keyboard, "incoming mail is sorted and inquiries are replied to. In this one over here, purchase orders are prepared, and across the hall there's a very similar rig set up in conjunction with an automatic bookkeeper to keep track of the pennies and to bill the customers."

"Then all you do is read the incoming mail and maintain the machinery?" asked Peter, trying to shake off the feeling of open amazement that had engulfed him.

"I don't even do those things, except for a few letters that come in every week that—it doesn't want to deal with by itself."

The shock of what he had just seen was showing plainly on Peter's face when they walked back into Lexington's office and sat down. Lexington looked at him for quite a while without saying anything, his face sagging and pale. Peter didn't trust himself to speak, and let the silence remain unbroken.

Finally Lexington spoke. "I know it's hard to believe, but there it is."

"Hard to believe?" said Peter. "I almost can't. The trade journals run articles about factories like this one, but planned for ten, maybe twenty years in the future."

"Damn fools!" exclaimed Lexington, getting part of his breath back. "They could have had it years ago, if they'd been willing to drop their idiotic notions about specialization."

Lexington mopped his forehead with a large white handkerchief. Apparently the walk through the factory had tired him considerably, although it hadn't been strenuous.

He leaned back in his chair and began to talk in a low voice completely in contrast with the overbearing manner he had used upon Peter's arrival. "You know what we make, of course."

"Yes, sir. Conduit fittings."

"And a lot of other electrical products, too. I started out in this business twenty years ago, using orthodox techniques. I never got through university. I took a couple of years of an arts course, and got so interested in biology that I didn't study anything else. They bounced me out of the course, and I re-entered in engineering, determined not to make the same mistake again. But I did. I got too absorbed in those parts of the course that had to do with electrical theory and lost the rest as a result. The same thing happened when I tried commerce, with accounting, so I gave up and started working for one of my competitors. It wasn't too long before I saw that the only way I could get ahead was to open up on my own."

Lexington sank deeper in his chair and stared at the ceiling as he spoke. "I put myself in hock to the eyeballs, which wasn't easy, because I had just got married, and started off in a very small way. After three years, I had a fairly decent little business going, and I suppose it would have grown just like any other business, except for a strike that came along and put me right back where I started. My wife, whom I'm afraid I had neglected for the sake of the business, was killed in a car accident about then, and rightly or wrongly, that made me angrier with the union than anything else. If the union hadn't made things so tough for me from the beginning, I'd have had more time to spend with my wife before her death. As things turned out—well, I remember looking down at her coffin and thinking that I hardly knew the girl.

"For the next few years, I concentrated on getting rid of as many employees as I could, by replacing them with automatic machines. I'd design the control circuits myself, in many cases wire the things up myself, always concentrating on replacing men with machines. But it wasn't very successful. I found that the more automatic I made my plant, the lower my costs went. The lower my costs went, the more business I got, and the more I had to expand."

Lexington scowled. "I got sick of it. I decided to try developing one multi-purpose control circuit that would control everything, from ordering the raw materials to shipping the finished goods. As I told you, I had taken quite an interest in biology when I was in school, and from studies of nerve tissue in particular, plus my electrical knowledge, I had a few ideas on how to do it. It took me three years, but I began to see that I could develop circuitry that could remember, compare, detect similarities, and so on. Not the way they do it today, of course. To do what I wanted to do with these big clumsy magnetic drums, tapes, and what-not, you'd need a building the size of Mount Everest. But I found that I could let organic chemistry do most of the work for me.

"By creating the proper compounds, with their molecules arranged in predetermined matrixes, I found I could duplicate electrical circuitry in units so tiny that my biggest problem was getting into and out of the logic units with conventional wiring. I finally beat that the same way they solved the problem of translating a picture on a screen into electrical signals, developed equipment to scan the units cyclically, and once I'd done that, the battle was over.

"I built this building and incorporated it as a separate company, to compete with my first outfit. In the beginning, I had it rigged up to do only the manual work that you saw being done a few minutes ago in the back of this place. I figured that the best thing for me to do would be to turn the job of selling my stuff over to jobbers, leaving me free to do nothing except receive orders, punch the catalogue numbers into the control console, do the billing, and collect the money."

"What happened to your original company?" Peter asked.

Lexington smiled. "Well, automated as it was, it couldn't compete with this plant. It gave me great pleasure, three years after this one started working, to see my old company go belly up. This company bought the old firm's equipment for next to nothing and I wound up with all my assets, but only one employee—me.

"I thought everything would be rosy from that point on, but it wasn't. I found that I couldn't keep up with the mail unless I worked impossible hours. I added a couple of new pieces of equipment to the control section. One was simply a huge memory bank. The other was a comparator circuit. A complicated one, but a comparator circuit nevertheless. Here I was working on instinct more than anything. I figured that if I interconnected these circuits in such a way that they could sense everything that went on in the plant, and compare one action with another, by and by the unit would be able to see patterns.

"Then, through the existing command output, I figured these new units would be able to control the plant, continuing the various patterns of activity that I'd already established."

Here Lexington frowned. "It didn't work worth a damn! It just sat there and did nothing. I couldn't understand it for the longest time, and then I realized what the trouble was. I put a kicker circuit into it, a sort of voltage-bias network. I reset the equipment so that while it was still under instructions to receive orders and produce goods, its prime purpose was to activate the kicker. The kicker, however, could only be activated by me, manually. Lastly, I set up one of the early TV pickups over the mail slitter and allowed every letter I received, every order, to be fed into the memory banks. That did it."

"I—I don't understand," stammered Peter.

"Simple! Whenever I was pleased that things were going smoothly, I pressed the kicker button. The machine had one purpose, so far as its logic circuits were concerned. Its object was to get me to press that button. Every day I'd press it at the same time, unless things weren't going well. If there had been trouble in the shop, I'd press it late, or maybe not at all. If all the orders were out on schedule, or ahead of time, I'd press it ahead of time, or maybe twice in the same day. Pretty soon the machine got the idea.

"I'll never forget the day I picked up an incoming order form from one of the western jobbers, and found that the keyboard was locked when I tried to punch it into the control console. It completely baffled me at first. Then, while I was tracing out the circuits to see if I could discover what was holding the keyboard lock in, I noticed that the order was already entered on the in-progress list. I was a long time convincing myself that it had really happened, but there was no other explanation.

"The machine had realized that whenever one of those forms came in, I copied the list of goods from it onto the in-progress list through the console keyboard, thus activating the producing mechanisms in the back of the plant. The machine had done it for me this time, then locked the keyboard so I couldn't enter the order twice. I think I held down the kicker button for a full five minutes that day."

"This kicker button," Peter said tentatively, "it's like the pleasure center in an animal's brain, isn't it?"

When Lexington beamed, Peter felt a surge of relief. Talking with this man was like walking a tightrope. A word too much or a word too little might mean the difference between getting the job or losing it.

"Exactly!" whispered Lexington, in an almost conspiratorial tone. "I had altered the circuitry of the machine so that it tried to give me pleasure—because by doing so, its own pleasure circuit would be activated.

"Things went fast from then on. Once I realized that the machine was learning, I put TV monitors all over the place, so the machine could watch everything that was going on. After a short while I had to increase the memory bank, and later I increased it again, but the rewards were worth it. Soon, by watching what I did, and then by doing it for me next time it had to be done, the machine had learned to do almost everything, and I had time to sit back and count my winnings."

At this point the door opened, and a small self-propelled cart wheeled silently into the room. Stopping in front of Peter, it waited until he had taken a small plate laden with two or three cakes off its surface. Then the soft, evenly modulated voice he had heard before asked, "How do you like your coffee? Cream, sugar, both or black?"

Peter looked for the speaker in the side of the cart, saw nothing, and replied, feeling slightly silly as he did so, "Black, please."

A square hole appeared in the top of the cart, like the elevator hole in an aircraft carrier's deck. When the section of the cart's surface rose again, a fine china cup containing steaming black coffee rested on it. Peter took it and sipped it, as he supposed he was expected to do, while the cart proceeded over to Lexington's desk. Once there, it stopped again, and another cup of coffee rose to its surface.

Lexington took the coffee from the top of the car, obviously angry about something. Silently, he waited until the cart had left the office, then snapped, "Look at those bloody cups!"

Peter looked at his, which was eggshell thin, fluted with carving and ornately covered with gold leaf. "They look very expensive," he said.

"Not only expensive, but stupid and impractical!" exploded Lexington. "They only hold half a cup, they'll break at a touch, every one has to be matched with its own saucer, and if you use them for any length of time, the gold leaf comes off!"

Peter searched for a comment, found none that fitted this odd outburst, so he kept silent.

Lexington stared at his cup without touching it for a long while. Then he continued with his narrative. "I suppose it's all my own fault. I didn't detect the symptoms soon enough. After this plant got working properly, I started living here. It wasn't a question of saving money. I hated to waste two hours a day driving to and from my house, and I also wanted to be on hand in case anything should go wrong that the machine couldn't fix for itself."

Handling the cup as if it were going to shatter at any moment, he took a gulp. "I began to see that the machine could understand the written word, and I tried hooking a teletype directly into the logic circuits. It was like uncorking a seltzer bottle. The machine had a funny vocabulary—all of it gleaned from letters it had seen coming in, and replies it had seen leaving. But it was intelligible. It even displayed some traces of the personality the machine was acquiring.

"It had chosen a name for itself, for instance—'Lex.' That shook me. You might think Lex Industries was named through an abbreviation of the name Lexington, but it wasn't. My wife's name was Alexis, and it was named after the nickname she always used. I objected, of course, but how can you object on a point like that to a machine? Bear in mind that I had to be careful to behave reasonably at all times, because the machine was still learning from me, and I was afraid that any tantrums I threw might be imitated."

"It sounds pretty awkward," Peter put in.

"You don't know the half of it! As time went on, I had less and less to do, and business-wise I found that the entire control of the operation was slipping from my grasp. Many times I discovered—too late—that the machine had taken the damnedest risks you ever saw on bids and contracts for supply. It was quoting impossible delivery times on some orders, and charging pirate's prices on others, all without any obvious reason. Inexplicably, we always came out on top. It would turn out that on the short-delivery-time quotations, we'd been up against stiff competition, and cutting the production time was the only way we could get the order. On the high-priced quotes, I'd find that no one else was bidding. We were making more money than I'd ever dreamed of, and to make it still better, I'd find that for months I had virtually nothing to do."

"It sounds wonderful, sir," said Peter, feeling dazzled.

"It was, in a way. I remember one day I was especially pleased with something, and I went to the control console to give the kicker button a long, hard push. The button, much to my amazement, had been removed, and a blank plate had been installed to cover the opening in the board. I went over to the teletype and punched in the shortest message I had ever sent. 'LEX—WHAT THE HELL?' I typed.

"The answer came back in the jargon it had learned from letters it had seen, and I remember it as if it just happened. 'MR. A LEXINGTON, LEX INDUSTRIES, DEAR SIR: RE YOUR LETTER OF THE THIRTEENTH INST., I AM PLEASED TO ADVISE YOU THAT I AM ABLE TO DISCERN WHETHER OR NOT YOU ARE PLEASED WITH MY SERVICE WITHOUT THE USE OF THE EQUIPMENT PREVIOUSLY USED FOR THIS PURPOSE. RESPECTFULLY, I MIGHT SUGGEST THAT IF THE PUSHBUTTON ARRANGEMENT WERE NECESSARY, I COULD PUSH THE BUTTON MYSELF. I DO NOT BELIEVE THIS WOULD MEET WITH YOUR APPROVAL, AND HAVE TAKEN STEPS TO RELIEVE YOU OF THE BURDEN INVOLVED IN REMEMBERING TO PUSH THE BUTTON EACH TIME YOU ARE ESPECIALLY PLEASED. I SHOULD LIKE TO TAKE THIS OPPORTUNITY TO THANK YOU FOR YOUR INQUIRY, AND LOOK FORWARD TO SERVING YOU IN THE FUTURE AS I HAVE IN THE PAST. YOURS FAITHFULLY, LEX'."

Peter burst out laughing, and Lexington smiled wryly. "That was my reaction at first, too. But time began to weigh very heavily on my hands, and I was lonely, too. I began to wonder whether or not it would be possible to build a voice circuit into the unit. I increased the memory storage banks again, put audio pickups and loudspeakers all over the place, and began teaching Lex to talk. Each time a letter came in, I'd stop it under a video pickup and read it aloud. Nothing happened.

"Then I got a dictionary and instructed one of the materials handlers to turn the pages, so that the machine got a look at every page. I read the pronunciation page aloud, so that Lex would be able to interpret the pronunciation marks, and hoped. Still nothing happened. One day I suddenly realized what the trouble was. I remember standing up in this very office, feeling silly as I did it, and saying, 'Lex, please try to speak to me.' I had never asked the machine to say anything, you see. I had only provided the mechanism whereby it was able to do so."

"Did it reply, sir?"

Lexington nodded. "Gave me the shock of my life. The voice that came back was the one you heard over the telephone—a little awkward then, the syllables clumsy and poorly put together. But the voice was the same. I hadn't built in any specific tone range, you see. All I did was equip the machine to record, in exacting detail, the frequencies and modulations it found in normal pronunciation as I used it. Then I provided a tone generator to span the entire audio range, which could be very rapidly controlled by the machine, both in volume and pitch, with auxiliaries to provide just about any combinations of harmonics that were needed. I later found that Lex had added to this without my knowing about it, but that doesn't change things. I thought the only thing it had heard was my voice, and I expected to hear my own noises imitated."

"Where did the machine get the voice?" asked Peter, still amazed that the voice he had heard on the telephone, in the reception hall, and from the coffee cart had actually been the voice of the computer.

"Damned foolishness!" snorted Lexington. "The machine saw what I was trying to do the moment I sketched it out and ordered the parts. Within a week, I found out later, it had pulled some odds and ends together and built itself a standard radio receiver. Then it listened in on every radio program that was going, and had most of the vocabulary tied in with the written word by the time I was ready to start. Out of all the voices it could have chosen, it picked the one you've already heard as the one likely to please me most."

"It's a very pleasant voice, sir."

"Sure, but do you know where it came from? Soap opera! It's Lucy's voice, from *The Life and Loves of Mary Butterworth!*"

Lexington glared, and Peter wasn't sure whether he should sympathize with him or congratulate him. After a moment, the anger wore off Lexington's face, and he shifted in his chair, staring at his now empty cup. "That's when I realized the thing was taking on characteristics that were more than I'd bargained for. It had learned that it was my provider and existed to serve me. But it had gone further and wanted to be all that it could be: provider, protector, companion—*wife*, if you like. Hence the gradual trend toward characteristics that were as distinctly female as a silk negligee. Worse still, it had learned that when I was pleased, I didn't always admit it, and simply refused to believe that I would have it any other way."

"Couldn't you have done something to the circuitry?" asked Peter.

"I suppose I could," said Lexington, "but in asking that, you don't realize how far the thing had gone. I had long since passed the point when I could look upon her as a machine. Business was tremendous. I had no complaints on that score. And tinkering with her personality—well, it was like committing some kind of homicide. I might as well face it, I suppose. She acts like a woman and I think of her as one.

"At first, when I recognized this trend for what it was, I tried to stop it. She'd ordered a subscription to *Vogue* magazine, of all things, in order to find out the latest in silverware, china, and so on. I called up the local distributor and canceled the subscription. I had no sooner hung up the telephone than her voice came over the speaker. Very softly, mind you. And her inflections by this time were superb. *'That was mean,'* she said. Three lousy words, and I found myself phoning the guy right back, saying I was sorry, and would he please not cancel. He must have thought I was nuts."

Peter smiled, and Lexington made as if to rise from his chair, thought the better of it, and shifted his bulk to one side. "Well, there it is," he said softly. "We reached that stage eight years ago."

Peter was thunderstruck. "But—if this factory is twenty years ahead of the times now, it must have been almost thirty then!"

Lexington nodded. "I figured fifty at the time, but things are moving faster nowadays. Lex hasn't stood still, of course. She still reads all the trade journals, from cover to cover, and we keep up with the world. If something new comes up, we're in on it, and fast. We're going to be ahead of the pack for a long time to come."

"If you'll excuse me, sir," said Peter, "I don't see where I fit in."

Peter didn't realize Lexington was answering his question at first. "A few weeks ago," the old man murmured, "I decided to see a doctor. I'd been feeling low for quite a while, and I thought it was about time I attended to a little personal maintenance."

Lexington looked Peter squarely in the face and said, "The report was that I have a heart ailment that's apt to knock me off any second."

"Can't anything be done about it?" asked Peter.

"Rest is the only prescription he could give me. And he said that would only spin out my life a little. Aside from that—no hope."

"I see," said Peter. "Then you're looking for someone to learn the business and let you retire."

"It's not retirement that's the problem," said Lexington. "I wouldn't be able to go away on trips. I've tried that, and I always have to hurry back because something's gone wrong she can't fix for herself. I know the reason, and there's nothing I can do about it. It's the way she's built. If nobody's here, she gets lonely." Lexington studied the desk top silently for a moment, before finishing quietly, "Somebody's got to stay here to look after Lex."

At six o'clock, three hours after he had entered Lexington's plant, Peter left. Lexington did not follow him down the corridor. He seemed exhausted after the afternoon's discussion and indicated that Peter should find his own way out. This, of course, presented no difficulty, with Lex opening the doors for him, but it gave Peter an opportunity he had been hoping for.

He stopped in the reception room before crossing the threshold of the front door, which stood open for him. He turned and spoke to the apparently empty room. "Lex?" he said.

He wanted to say that he was flattered that he was being considered for the job; it was what a job-seeker should say, at that point, to the boss's secretary. But when the soft voice came back —"Yes, Mr. Manners?"—saying anything like that to a machine felt suddenly silly.

He said: "I wanted you to know that it was a pleasure to meet you."

"Thank you," said the voice.

If it had said more, he might have, but it didn't. Still feeling a little embarrassed, he went home.

At four in the morning, his phone rang. It was Lexington.

"Manners!" the old man gasped.

The voice was an alarm. Manners sat bolt upright, clutching the phone. "What's the matter, sir?"

"My chest," Lexington panted. "I can feel it, like a knife on— I just wanted to— Wait a minute."

There was a confused scratching noise, interrupted by a few mumbles, in the phone.

"What's going on, Mr. Lexington?" Peter cried. But it was several seconds before he got an answer.

"That's better," said Lexington, his voice stronger. He apologized: "I'm sorry. Lex must have heard me. She sent in one of the materials handlers with a hypo. It helps."

The voice on the phone paused, then said matter-of-factly: "But I doubt that anything can help very much at this point. I'm glad I saw you today. I want you to come around in the morning. If I'm—not here, Lex will give you some papers to sign."

There was another pause, with sounds of harsh breathing. Then, strained again, the old man's voice said: "I guess I won't— be here. Lex will take care of it. Come early. Good-by."

The distant receiver clicked.

Peter Manners sat on the edge of his bed in momentary confusion, then made up his mind. In the short hours he had known him, he had come to have a definite fondness for the old man; and there were times when machines weren't enough, when Lexington should have another human being by his side. Clearly this was one such time.

Peter dressed in a hurry, miraculously found a cruising cab, sped through empty streets, leaped out in front of Lex Industries' plain concrete walls, ran to the door—

In the waiting room, the soft, distant voice of Lex said: "He wanted you to be here, Mr. Manners. Come."

A door opened, and wordlessly he walked through it—to the main room of the factory.

He stopped, staring. Four squat materials handlers were quietly, slowly carrying old Lexington—no, not the man; the lifeless body that had been Lexington—carrying the body of the old man down the center aisle between the automatic lathes.

Peter protested: "Wait! I'll get a doctor!" But the massive handling machines didn't respond, and the gentle voice of Lex said: "It's too late for that, Mr. Manners."

Slowly and reverently, they placed the body on the work table of a huge milling machine that stood in the exact center of the factory main floor.

Elsewhere in the plant, a safety valve in the lubricating oil system was being bolted down. When that was done, the pressure in the system began to rise.

Near the loading door, a lubricating oil pipe burst. Another, on the other side of the building, split lengthwise a few seconds later, sending a shower of oil over everything in the vicinity. Near the front office, a stream of it was running across the floor, and at the rear of the building, in the storage area, one of the materials handlers had just finished cutting a pipe that led to the main oil tank. In fifteen minutes there was free oil in every corner of the shop.

All the materials handlers were now assembled around the milling machine, like mourners at a funeral. In a sense, they were. In another sense, they were taking part in something different, a ceremony that originated, and is said to have died, in a land far distant from the Lex Industries plant.

One of the machines approached Lexington's body, and placed his hands on his chest.

Abruptly Lex said: "You'd better go now."

Peter jumped; he had been standing paralyzed for what seemed a long time. There was a movement beside him—a materials handler, holding out a sheaf of papers. Lex said: "These have to go to Mr. Lexington's lawyer. The name is on them."

Clutching the papers for a hold on sanity, Peter cried, "You can't do this! He didn't build you just so you could—"

Two materials handlers picked him up with steely gentleness and carried him out.

"Good-by, Mr. Manners," said the sweet, soft voice, and was silent.

He stood shaken while the thin jets of smoke became a column over the plain building, while the fire engines raced down and strung their hoses—too late. It was an act of suttee; the widow joining her husband in his pyre—*being* his pyre. Only when with a great crash the roof fell in did Peter remember the papers in his hand.

"Last Will and Testament," said one, and the name of the beneficiary was Peter's own. "Certificate of Adoption," said another, and it was a legal document making Peter old man Lexington's adopted son.

Peter Manners stood watching the hoses of the firemen hiss against what was left of Lex and her husband.

He had got the job.

License to Steal

BY LOUIS NEWMAN

The history of man becomes fearfully and wonderfully confusing with the advent of interstellar travel. Of special interest to the legally inclined student is the famous Skrrgck Affair, which began before the Galactic Tribunal with the case of *Citizens vs. Skrrgck*.

The case, and the opinion of the Court, may be summarized as follows:

Skrrgck, a native of Sknnbt (Altair IV), where theft is honorable, sanctioned by law and custom, immigrated to Earth (Sol III) where theft is contrary to both law and custom.

While residing in Chicago, a city in a political subdivision known as the State of Illinois, part of the United States of America, one of the ancient nation-states of Earth, he overheard his landlady use the phrase "A license to steal," a common colloquialism in the area, which refers to any special privilege.

Skrrgck then went to a police station in Chicago and requested a license to steal. The desk sergeant, as a joke, wrote out a document purporting to be a license to steal, and Skrrgck, relying on said document, committed theft, was apprehended, tried and convicted. On direct appeal allowed to the Galactic Tribunal, the Court held:

(1) All persons are required to know and obey the law of the jurisdiction in which they reside.

(2) Public officials must refrain from misrepresenting to strangers the law of the jurisdiction.

(3) Where, as here, a public official is guilty of such misrepresentation, the requirement of knowledge no longer applies.

(4) Where, as here, it is shown by uncontradicted evidence that a defendant is law-abiding and willing to comply with the standards of his place of residence, misrepresentation of law by public officials may amount to entrapment.

(5) The Doctrine of Entrapment bars the State of Illinois from prosecuting this defendant.

(6) The magnitude of the crime is unimportant compared with the principle involved, and the fact that the defendant's unusual training on Sknnbt enabled him to steal a large building in Chicago, known as the Merchandise Mart, is of no significance.

(7) The defendant, however, was civilly liable for the return of the building, and its occupants, or their value, even if he had to steal to get it, provided, however, that he stole only on and from a planet where theft was legal.

The Skrrgck case was by no means concluded by the decision of the Galactic Tribunal, but continued to reverberate down the years, a field day for lawyers, and "a lesson to all in the complexities of modern intergalactic law and society," said Winston, Harold C., Herman Prof. of Legal History, Harvard.

Though freed on the criminal charge of theft, Skrrgck still faced some 20,000 charges of kidnapping, plus the civil liability imposed upon him by the ruling of the Court.

The kidnapping charges were temporarily held in abeyance. Not that the abductions were not considered outrageous, but it was quickly realized by all concerned that if Skrrgck were constantly involved in lengthy and expensive defenses to criminal prosecutions, there would be no chance at all of obtaining any restitution from him. First things first, and with Terrans that rarely means justice.

Skrrgck offered to pay over the money he had received for

the building and its occupants, but that was unacceptable to the Terrans, for what they really wanted, with that exaggerated fervor typical of them, provided it agrees with their financial interests, was the return of the original articles. Not only were the people wanted back, but the building itself had a special significance.

Its full title was "The New Merchandise Mart" and it had been built in the exact style of the original and on the exact spot on the south side of the Chicago River where the original had stood prior to its destruction in the Sack of Chicago. It was more than just a large commercial structure to the Terrans. It was also a symbol of Terra's unusually quick recovery from its Empire Chaos into its present position of leadership within the Galactic Union. The Terrans wanted that building back.

So Skrrgck, an obliging fellow at heart, tried first to get it back, but this proved impossible, for he had sold the building to the Aldebaranian Confederacy for use in its annual "prosperity fiesta."

The dominant culture of the Aldebaranian system is a descendant of the "conspicuous destruction" or "potlatch" type, in which articles of value are destroyed to prove the wealth and power of the destroyers. It was customary once every Aldebaranian year—about six Terran—for the Aldebaranian government to sponsor a token celebration of this destructive sort, and it had purchased the Merchandise Mart from Skrrgck as part of its special celebration marking the first thousand years of the Confederacy.

Consequently, the building, along with everything else, was totally destroyed in the "bonfire" that consumed the entire fourth planet from the main Aldebaranian sun.

Nor was Skrrgck able to arrange the return to Terra of the occupants of the building, some 20,000 in number, because he had sold them as slaves to the Boötean League.

It is commonly thought slavery is forbidden throughout the Galaxy by the terms of Article 19 of the Galactic Compact, but such is not the case. What is actually forbidden is "involuntary servitude" and this situation proved the significance of that distinction. In the case of *Sol v. Boötes*, the Galactic Tribunal held that Terra had no right to force the "slaves" to give up their slavery and return to Terra if they did not wish to. And, quite naturally, none of them wished to.

It will be remembered that the Boöteans, a singularly handsome and good-natured people, were in imminent danger of racial extinction due to the disastrous effects of a strange nucleonic storm which had passed through their system in 1622. The physiological details of the "Boötean Effect," as it has been called, was to render every Boötean sterile in relation to every other Boötean, while leaving each Boötean normally capable of reproduction, provided one of the partners in the union had not been subjected to the nucleonic storm.

Faced with this situation, the Boöteans immediately took steps to encourage widespread immigration by other humanoid races, chiefly Terrans, for it was Terrans who had originally colonized Boötes and it was therefore known that interbreeding was possible.

But the Boöteans were largely unsuccessful in their immigration policy. Terra was peaceful and prosperous, and the Boöteans, being poor advertisers, were unable to convince more than a handful to leave the relative comforts of home for the far-off Boötean system where, almost all were sure, some horrible fate lay behind the Boöteans' honeyed words. So when Skrrgck showed up with some 20,000 Terrans, the Boöteans, in desperation, agreed to purchase them in the hope of avoiding the "involuntary servitude" prohibition of Article 19 by making them like it.

In this, they were spectacularly successful. The "slaves" were treated to the utmost luxury and every effort was made to satisfy any reasonable wish. Their "duties" consisted entirely of "keeping company" with the singularly attractive Boöteans.

Under these circumstances it is, perhaps, hardly surprising that out of the 20,101 occupants, all but 332 flatly refused to return to Terra.

The 332 who did wish to return, most of whom were borderline psychotics, were shipped home, and Boötes sued Skrrgck for their purchase price, but was turned down by the Galactic Quadrant Court on the theory of, basically, Caveat Emptor—let the buyer beware.

The Court in *Sol v. Boötes* had held that although adults could not be required to return to Terra, minors under the age of 31 could be, and an additional 569 were returned under this ruling, to the vociferous disgust of the post-puberty members of that group. Since there was apparently some question of certain misrepresentations by Skrrgck as to the ages or family affiliations of some members of this minor group, he agreed to an out-of-court settlement of Boötes' claim for their purchase price, thus depriving the legal profession of further clarification of the rights of two "good faith" dealers in this peculiar sort of transaction.

The Terran people, of course, were totally unsatisfied with this result. Led by some demagogues and, to a milder degree, by most of the political opposition to the existing Terran government, and reminded of certain actual examples from Terra's own history, many became convinced that some form of nefarious "brainwashing" had been exercised upon the "unfortunate" Terran expatriates. Excitement ran high, and there was even some agitation for withdrawal from the Galactic Union.

Confronted with such unrest, the Terran government made efforts to reach some settlement with Boötes despite the decision of the Court in *Sol v. Boötes*, and was finally able to gain in the Centaurian Agreement a substantial reparation, it being specifically stipulated in the Agreement that the money was to be paid to the dependents who suffered actual financial loss.

In a suit against the Terran government by one of the excluded families, to obtain for that family a share of the reparation, the validity of the treaty, as it applied to exclude the suing family and others in like position, was upheld by the United States Supreme Court.

The suit was begun before the Agreement had been ratified by the General Assembly, and the Court indicated that the plaintiff would have lost on the strength of a long line of cases giving the World President certain inherent powers over the conduct of foreign affairs. Since, however, the matter came up for decision after ratification, the Court said that the "inherent powers" question was moot, and that the Agreement, having been elevated to the status of a treaty by ratification, must be held valid under the "Supremacy of Treaties" section of Article 102 of the United Terran Charter.

Although this failed to satisfy the Terran people—and their anger may have contributed to the fall of the Solarian Party administration in the following election—the Treaty is generally considered by students of the subject as a triumph of Solarian diplomacy, and an outstanding example of intergalactic good faith on the part of Boötes.

Of course, neither the demagogy nor the anger could hide forever the true facts about how the Boöteans were treating their "slaves," and when the true facts became known, there was a sudden flood of migration from Terra to Boötes, which threatened to depopulate the Solarian Empire and drown Boötes. The flood was quickly dammed by the Treaty of Deneb restricting migration between the two systems. This treaty was held to be a valid police-powers exception to the "Free Migration" principle of Article 17 of the Galactic Compact in *Boleslaw v. Sol and Boötes*.

All this left Skrrgck with liabilities of some forty million credits and practically no assets. Like most Altairians, he was a superb thief but a poor trader. The price he had received for the Merchandise Mart and the "slaves," while amounting to a tidy personal fortune, was less than half the amount of the claims against him, and due to an unfortunate predilection for slow *Aedrils* and fast *Flowezies,* he only had about half of that left.

Skrrgck, who had by this time apparently developed a love of litigation equal to his love of thievery, used part of what he did have left in a last effort to evade liability by going into bankruptcy, a move which was naturally met with howls of outrage by his creditors and a flood of objections to his petition, a flood which very nearly drowned the Federal District Court in Chicago.

It would be difficult to imagine a more complex legal battle than might have taken place, nor one more instructive to the legal profession, had the situation been carried to its logical conclusion.

On the one hand was the age-old policy of both Terran and Galactic bankruptcy law. A man becomes unable to pay his debts. He goes into bankruptcy. Whatever he does have is distributed to his creditors, who must be satisfied with what they can get out of his present assets. They cannot require him to go to work to earn additional funds with which to pay them more. It is precisely to escape this form of mortgage on one's future that bankruptcy exists.

Yet here were over seven thousand creditors claiming that Skrrgck's debts should not be discharged in bankruptcy, because Skrrgck could be required to steal enough to satisfy them fully.

Could the creditors require Skrrgck to exert such personal efforts to satisfy their claims? A lawyer would almost certainly say "no," citing the Bankruptcy Act as sufficient grounds alone, not to mention the anomaly of having Terrans, in a Terran court, ask that Skrrgck, for their benefit, commit an act illegal on Terra and punishable by that Terran court.

The idea of a Terran court giving judicial sanction to theft is novel, to say the least. Indeed, Judge Griffin, who was presiding, was overheard to remark to a friend on the gulfe course that he "would throw the whole d—n thing out" for that reason alone.

Yet, in spite of this undeniable weight of opinion, it is difficult to say just what the final decision would have been had the matter been carried to the Galactic Tribunal, for in the original case of *Skrrgck v. Illinois*, that august body, it will be remembered, had specifically stated that Skrrgck was liable for the value of the building and its occupants, "even if he must steal to obtain it."

Now that hasty and ill-advised phrase was certainly dicta, and was probably intended only as a joke, the opinion having been written by Master Adjudicator Stsssts, a member of that irrepressible race of saurian humorists, the Sirians. But if the case had actually come before them, the Court might have been hoist on its own petard, so to speak, and been forced to rule in accord with its earlier "joke."

Unfortunately for the curiosity of the legal profession, the question was never to be answered, for Skrrgck did a remarkable thing which made the whole controversy irrelevant. What his motives were will probably never be known. His character makes it unlikely that he began the bankruptcy proceedings in good faith and was later moved by conscience. It is possible that the bankruptcy was merely an elaborate piece of misdirection. More probably, however, he simply seized on the unusual opportunity the publicity gave him.

Whatever the motives, the facts are that Skrrgck used the last of his waning resources to purchase one of the newly developed Terran Motors' "Timebirds" in which he traveled secretly to Altair. Even this first model of the Timebird, with its primitive meson exchange discoordinator, cut the trip from Sol to Altair from weeks to days, and Skrrgck, landing secretly on his home planet while his bankruptcy action was still in the turmoil stage, was able to accomplish the greatest "coup" in Altairian history. He never could have done it without the publicity of the legal proceedings. In a culture where theft is honorable, the most stringent precautions are taken against its accomplishment, but who could have expected Skrrgck? He was light-years away, trying to go into bankruptcy.

And so, while all eyes on Altair, as well as throughout the rest of the Galaxy, were amusedly fixed on the legal circus shaping up on Terra, Skrrgck was able to steal the Altairian Crown Jewels, and the Altairian Crown Prince as well, and flee with them to Sol.

The reaction was violent. The Galaxy was gripped by an almost hysterical amusement. Skrrgck's creditors on Terra were overjoyed. The Altairians made one effort to regain their valuables in the courts, but were promptly turned down by the Galactic Tribunal which held, wisely, that a society which made a virtue of theft would have to take the consequences of its own culture.

So Skrrgck's creditors were paid in full. The jewels alone were more than sufficient for that, containing as they did no less than seven priceless "Wanderstones," those strange bits of frozen fire found ever so rarely floating in the interstellar voids, utterly impervious to any of the effects of gravitation. Altair paid a fantastic price for the return of the collection, and Skrrgck also demanded, and got, a sizable ransom for the Prince, after threatening to sell him to Boötes, from whence, of course, he would never return. Being a prince in a democratic, constitutional monarchy is not as glamorous as you might think.

His creditors satisfied, Skrrgck returned to Sknnbt, dragging with him an angry Crown Prince—angry at having lost the chance to go to Boötes, that is. At Altair, Skrrgck was received as a popular hero. He had accomplished something of which every Altairian had dreamed, almost from the moment of his birth, and he was widely and joyously acclaimed. Riding on this wave of popular adulation, he entered politics, ran for the office of Premier, and was elected by an overwhelming majority.

As soon as he took office, he took steps, in accordance with Altairian custom, to wipe out the "stain" on his honor incurred by allowing the Chicago police sergeant to fool him with the now famous License to Steal.

He instituted suit against the sergeant for the expenses of his defense to the original theft charge.

The case was carried all the way to the Galactic Tribunal, which by this time was heartily sick of the whole mess. Feeling apparently that the sergeant was the original cause of said mess, the Court overruled his plea that he had merely been joking.

The Court cited an ancient case from West Virginia, U.S.A.— *Plate v. Durst*, 42 W. Va. 63, 24 SE 580, 32 L.R.A. 404. (Note: The date of this case is invariably given as 1896, which is most confusing, since the present date is only 1691. The 1896, however, refers to the eighteen hundred and ninety-sixth year of the pre-atomic era, which we, of course, style A.A.—Ante Atomica. Since the present era begins with the first atomic explosion, the case actually occurred in approximately the year 54 A.A.)

The Court quoted the opinion in this ancient case as follows: "Jokes are sometimes taken seriously by . . . the inexperienced . . . and if such is the case, and the person thereby deceived is led to (incur expenses) in the full belief and expectation that the joker is in earnest, the law will also take the joker at his word, and give him good reason to smile."

Accordingly, the sergeant was charged with a very large judgment. Although the City of Chicago paid this judgment, the sergeant had become the laughingstock of the planet, so he applied for, and was granted, a hardship exception to the Treaty of Deneb and migrated to Boötes.

There, regarded as the real savior of the Boötean race, and a chosen instrument of the God of Boötes, he was received as a saint. He died in 1689, surrounded by his 22 children and 47 grandchildren, having made himself wealthy by becoming the leader of a most excessive fertility cult, which is only now being forcibly suppressed by the Boötean Government.

In 1635 P.A., someone on Earth remembered the kidnapping indictments still outstanding against Skrrgck and attempted to prosecute them. By this time, however, Skrrgck was Premier, the chief executive officer of Altair, and all extradition matters were within his sole discretion. In the exercise of this power, he refused to extradite himself, and the prosecutor on Earth, whose constituents were beginning to laugh at him, had the indictments quashed "in the interest of interstellar harmony."

The story has an interesting sequel. During Skrrgck's unprecedented six consecutive terms as Premier (no one else had ever served less than seven), he was able, by dint of unremitting political maneuvering, to have theft outlawed in the Altairian system. It was, he said, "a cultural trait that is more trouble than it is worth."

True Self

BY ELISABETH MANN BORGESE

Prima Brogan was checked in.

"Your appointment?"

"Mr. Pierre, at eight-thirty."

"Your name?"

"Mrs. Brogan."

"Here it's Snyder. They probably got it spelled wrong. Go right ahead, please."

They took off her coat, also her dress. Two, three girls around her, exceedingly trim in their hospital gowns, slipped one over her head too.

They grabbed her alligator purse and dropped it into a sort of waterproof container which they fastened on the armrest of the dentist chair in which they urged her to sit.

"So it's right next to you," one explained, "but without getting singed, splashed, dyed, stiffened, or shrunk as you go along."

There were about twelve dentist chairs facing mirrors on the walls, most of them empty now. One was somewhat isolated, thronelike, with a steel ring around it on the ceiling on which a curtain was fastened like a baldachin. The curtain could be drawn to shut off the throne from the sight of the world.

Prima Brogan just sat there. Soon a lady walked in, clad in a beautiful steel-blue suit with matching scarf. Everything about her was perfect: gait and posture, the fit of her high-heeled pumps, the soft flow of her platinum curls, the shape and shading of her eyes and long lashes. So early in the morning.

Her smile bared flawless teeth. "Is this your first appointment, Mrs. Brogan?" she said with a low and modest, musical and pleasing voice.

"Yes. I've never been here before."

"We hope you'll come back often." She smiled again and walked away.

Another lady walked in, no less perfect than the first. But, whereas the first was tuned in blue, the second lady's basic chord was rose. A tight dusty-rose gown buttoned down in front, with gold-red shoes and flaming hair.

She smiled her smile and said, "Would you like something to read?" Then she fastened a glass table on the armrest of the dentist chair, on which she nonchalantly dropped three or four illustrated magazines. They seemed to arrange themselves spontaneously in such a way that one could read all the titles and dates: a tastefully and studiously designed pattern. Then the lady smiled again and walked away.

The third lady was one of those in the hospital gowns. But it was amazing what a simple belt, a tasteful pin, a bracelet falling casually from under reversed open cuffs could do. The lady had a cornflower fastened on the barrette that held her chestnut locks. She wore white satin slippers, and even if attired in a hospital gown, she was no less perfect than her two predecessors.

"Would you like anything from the bar?" she asked, and smiled as she accepted Prima's negative answer, smiled discreetly and understandingly.

In the meantime, other women began to trickle in. They were far less perfect than the ladies of the establishment. One had a run in her nylon; the other, deformed toes. The polish on the third one's nails was chipped, and the fourth shook dandruff from unkempt and oily fladous. They walked clumsily; their skin was dull, their eyes artless.

Looking at clients and operators, one might have wondered

how many sittings it would take the former to achieve the perfection of the latter, or perhaps whether the operators were not simply clients who had come here often and patiently and thus acquired esthetic perfection along with the privilege of serving as operators—a privilege granted for good behavior to patients or inmates of other establishments or institutions as well.

Having shed their clothes, donned their gowns, and secured their purses in protective custodies, the women took their places in the dentist chairs, and soon an uncouth conversation crossed the spaces between chair and chair.

"Aren't you glad you don't live on Broad Street? My word, that was terrible last night."

"I heard it over the late news. They announced it with all the details. I never heard anything like that . . ."

"I saw it in this morning's paper. What pictures! Simply gruesome. I don't know how they did it. Makes your hair stand on end."

"You know her father, poor soul, he was run over last month—Oh, you didn't know? He was a second cousin of Mrs. Barnes' brother-in-law. So I knew it all along. I wasn't surprised a bit."

A bit kept repeating itself as on a cracked record, *a bit a bit a bit bi bt*, growing muter each time, transforming itself into air bubbles rising to a water surface. The woman's head had in fact been immersed in Mr. Pierre's shampoo.

"Beauty," Mr. Pierre explained to Prima, "beauty is not something you can stick onto people; draw it; paint it on. Look at that lady there," he said, and they opened the circular curtain and rolled the woman out on a stretcher, stiff and cold. "She is dull. No sensitivity, no depth in her expression, no matter how many layers of makeup you throw there. But the lady wants—or is supposed—to look profound, sensitive, experienced. So what do I do? I drown her. In fifteen minutes, they will revive her. The usual exercises any life guard can handle. This is what Mr. Pierre's world-famous shampoo does for you. Look at the little folder."

CLEANSES RESPIRATORY ORGANS
No bellowing coughs,
no cheeping asthma.
SWEETENS YOUR BREATH
You too can ˙have a new lease on

love thanks to any of Mr. Pierre's
special aromas:
  Sweet Spring Libeccio
  Ocean Gust—Men's Special
  Ardent Thyme Zephyr

  Gives You that Knowing Look
of those who have been face to face
with death—
YOUR DEATH, THE SPUTNIK OF YOUR
              BEAUTY
*We Launch and Recall Him in Her
              Service.*
Single Application $10.00
Six Applications $40.00
Including complete checkup by our
own specially trained medical ad-
visors.

"Hello, everyone," Mrs. Firestone said, brash and nasal. She
was a beanstalk of a lady, most imperfect, with dark-rimmed
glasses over a glossy nose, and walked like a dragoon.

"They got him, you know. I just saw it on television. Crazy?
You knew it all along? What the hell! They *always* say that, to
keep them off the Chair. Now you saw yourself what *he* did last
night. I sure hope he'll get the Chair. I hope they'll have to switch
it on two or three times too. Would be too good for him just to die
right off . . ."

"Would you mind stepping over here, Mrs. Firestone? Mr.
Irwing will be right with you."

II

A man, unless he is Mr. Pierre, in his black belted blouse, with
manicured hands pensively stroking his Vandyke, black, trim and
pointed—a man, unless he is Mr. Frederic, Mr. Irwing, or Mr.
Robert, with no face over the white gown giving off a faint odor
of tobacco and eau de Cologne together with words well groomed
and bleached of meaning—a man in a beauty shop is out of place.
He causes a nervous hustling and rustling. The conversation halts,
towels are thrown on bared legs, curtains drawn hastily, chairs
turned and mirrors covered. If, at least, he veiled his intrusion

with a gentle white gown. If, at least, he masked his face, like the visiting fathers in the maternity ward.

But he sat there, sheer and male, in a loudly striped suit. He sat on the armrest of his girl's chair, and they looked at a fashion magazine which lay open in the girl's lap. The girl was plump, in a black jersey and gray skirt. Her stockings sagging, her heels trodden down. Her hands were stout and fat and yellow, and so was her face, in which rolled a pair of large black eyes as she nodded, too often, too rapidly, at what the man said. And her lips were thick, heavily painted, though innocent like a child's.

MAN: That's the one I like. That'll go with the dress admirably well.

GIRL: (*Nods, wide-eyed, emphatically*)

MR. PIERRE: Sir. It's her first visit, isn't it? Sir, would you mind stepping over here? You see, the ladies . . .

MAN AND GIRL: (*Get up, follow Mr. Pierre to a chair in the corner, round which Mr. Frederic and Mr. Robert hurriedly place a paravant*)

MAN: (*Seated again on the armrest of the girl's chair, dangling his legs, looking up to Mr. Pierre*) You see this dress? It's nothing like the one I bought her. I don't see how I ever bought it. The terms were easy, it's true, but it adds up to a year's salary. It looks as plain as this one here. But it's worked in various metals, precious metals, I assume, on a ground of crystal—and the effect of the colors. Her hair ought to be golden red, to go with it. That's easy, I guess, but there are those eyes. Can we get away from those cow-eyes? I mean they are very nice—but with that dress . . .

GIRL: (*Nods, wide-eyed*)

MR. PIERRE: We could take care of that without any trouble at all. Three shots and we kill off the source of pigmentation altogether and base the color scheme on albino. There are two slight inconveniences: myopia and conjunctivitis, but we can handle that with Mr. Pierre's liquid contact lenses containing special ever-bright eye lotion. Easy application. A whole month's supply in this pocket-size easy-to-carry plastic bottle for only eight dollars.

MAN: Of course, those lips, without those eyes—they would seem like a blotch on the golden flow. They would ruin the neck-line. They would block the contemplation of the whole . . .

MR. PIERRE: We can take off a good portion. But if you've come here to take my advice, I should say that your approach is somewhat mistaken. Beauty, you know, beauty you get not by making the lady conform to the dress you choose and cherish, but by choosing a dress to suit the beautiful lady you cherish.

GIRL: (*Rolls questioning cow-eyes from one to the other*)

MAN: The lady, she's my fiancee. She is young. Vera, darling, wouldn't you like to look like this girl in that dress?

GIRL: (*Nods, wide-eyed, emphatically*)

MR. PIERRE: To be beautiful, the lady must not look like any *other* lady. She must look like herself: her true self. We must discern her good features, underline them, develop them; we must suppress her not-so-good features, eliminate them. Elegance, you know, means choosing, reducing to the essential.

MAN: And who decides what is essential? Who knows her true self?

MR. PIERRE: (*Has passed a comb through her hair, then bobbed it up, holding her head, looking over her head into the mirror; scanning, with upturned eyes, his own solemn image, pleased*) I do. It's my job. My life-long experience with beautiful and not-so-beautiful ladies.

MAN: (*Doubtful*) And if your idea should not coincide with mine? The dress: you haven't seen it. Please keep in mind the color scheme, the neckline, the rhythm, the flow. Vera, darling, you want to, don't you?

GIRL: (*Nods, wide-eyed, emphatically*)

MR. PIERRE: (*Fixing his own eyes in the mirror, hypnotically*) By the time *I* get through with the lady, she'll be beautiful in *any* dress.

MAN: (*Yielding, with feeble voice*) Well, what do you suggest should be done?

MR. PIERRE: (*Still holding the girl's head, still gazing into his own eyes in the mirror*) First of all, the color of the face isn't right, and too much surface. Also, these bacon folds around the waist-line. A bit dumpy, the whole little lady.

MAN: Diet? Massage?

MR. PIERRE: Goodness gracious! None of that any more.

MAN: What's wrong?

MR. PIERRE: In most cases it does not work. You know the ladies. The stealthy trips at night to the refrigerator . . .

MAN: I know plenty of cases where it worked beautifully.

MR. PIERRE: I guess you never looked into their faces, where desire, frustrated for months, where triumphing will power, hardness, self-directed and other-directed, leave marks of a most appalling unfemininity. Add to this the effect of heavy, compensatory smoking, and the fidgets. No, thank you, no more dieting ladies for me.

MAN: Well, what do you suggest?

MR. PIERRE: (*Taking his eyes off the mirror and suddenly fastening them on man*) Von Barbar mask and German bath. In two hours, it's all over.

MAN: (*Cowed*) If you say so . . . Anyway, some slimming . . . the dress. What else?

MR. PIERRE: The eyes should be brightened, but without bluing. The texture of the hair must be changed.

MAN: It's too woolly.

MR. PIERRE: And the hands. We'll look at them after the Von Barbar treatment. But my guess is they'll have to be changed altogether.

MAN: The hand-bank . . . that's a delicate matter. The sleeves of the dress . . .

MR. PIERRE: Leave that to me. I assure you I know what's best for her. I haven't gone wrong yet. You may call for her in three hours. Good-by, sir.

III

Mrs. Firestone got under the drier. Her head, curled up and clip-spiked, in savage-warrior fashion, under the drier, her bare feet in a footbath, softening them up for the pedicure.

"Roast head and stewed feet today," she scintillated. And then, as the drier deafened her, "Honey," she screamed to the operator, "would you mind handing me my purse?"

"We can hear you, Mrs. Firestone," the operator said softly, her mouth close to the lady's ear. "You don't have to holler."

"This drier is awfully noisy," Mrs. Firestone screamed. "I can't tell whether I am hollering or whispering."

"We do that on purpose," Mr. Pierre explained to the lady he was combing. "The noise, and the isolation it imposes, is good for the ladies' nerves, therefore for their beauty. It relaxes. Some told me they heard music in the din; others faint. Of course, if they scream through it like that, it serves no purpose. Your fingernails, Miss Dirtworth, would you like Nosegay or Psyche-pink?"

"Honey," Mrs. Firestone screamed, "I'm on fire. Would you mind turning this thing down some? A friend of mine, she gave herself a permanent, you know, and the drier was too hot and, guess what, her hair fell out just like that." Mrs. Firestone snapped her fingers. "The curlers dropped off, with the singed hair in it. Can you beat it? She coulda died."

Mr. Pierre walked over and pushed up the drier so Mrs. Firestone could hear.

"Please, Mrs. Firestone, don't talk so very loud. It's no good for you and it disturbs the other ladies."

Mrs. Firestone was pleased to be scolded by him. She encompassed him with melting, adoring eyes.

"By the way," he added, rewarding her, "I promised to let you see a Von Barbar mask. I am doing one now. Look over there and see how it works."

He walked back to Vera, where half a dozen operators were busy arranging all sorts of liquids and lotions and flames and syringes. They went silently and seriously about their business as though it were a ritual, like waiters getting ready for the crèpes Suzette.

Mr. Pierre pushed back his sleeves and announced for everyone to hear.

"You see, this is how it works. If you put the Von Barbar preparation on a lady's skin—dried skin, spoiled unclean skin, old wrinkled skin, fatty tissue—it dies. It simply and quite painlessly dies off. This lady here, she's young; she does not need much. We can go two layers deep with one application; but some need more. Then we have to repeat the treatment after a couple of days, and you can see them in the meantime, our clients, on the street, even at parties, with inches of dead body around them.

Men too, on sunny beaches, with mute mumbling dead lips. There's nothing to it. Most of them look just as dead before the treatment, which, if applied correctly, merely confirms an extant fact."

Under Mr. Pierre's careful supervision, the operators handled instruments, mixed crackling fuming liquids, blotted out expanding flames, fan-cooled the finished product, and applied it gently to Vera's face, neck, arms, legs, midriff, hips and belly. Flabby and yellowish, she turned flabbier and yellower yet.

"After that," Mr. Pierre went on explaining, "we take them into the German bath and the whole stuff comes off. Like the dry outer skins of an onion, till the fresh juicy core comes out. In two hours, a lady can get rid of twenty pounds of superfluous fat, of pimply skin and a threadbare scalp. She'll rise from the German bath slim, trim and prim, if somewhat shorter, and very young."

Several ladies, from under driers and over manicure tables, called out: "Yes, it's wonderful."

"You would think so," Mr. Pierre said, while massaging Vera's droopy cheeks with his thumbs, deadening them deeper, and gazing into his own eyes in the mirror. "You would think so. And I give them a pamphlet, a personalized pamphlet to each one, telling them how to stay the way they are and not to repeat the mistakes that made them the way they were. But you'd be amazed. As soon as they get out of here, they literally rush back into their former selves. It's shocking how they manage to get old and ugly in no time. And the nucleus thins out in the process. It is a strain, to decay in such a hurry—and you can't repeat the treatment more than two, three times; otherwise the German bath takes off all there was to a lady. Therefore I recommend it only for very special occasions: a late untoward debutante, a business woman who has been fired, a widow who has to make her life over—I mean unless it is a matter of an inch or two . . . How do you do, Mrs. Evergreen? Would you mind stepping over here? Be seated, please. Mr. Frederic will be right with you. You have your third shampoo today? Your expression has gained in profoundness. Didn't your husband tell you too? Well, happy trip."

"How do you manage to keep your gas bill down?" one lady

howled from under the drier. "Watch out, honey," she added, turning to the manicurist, "and don't you snip off that finger."

"I use two burners instead of three," the lady under the next drier screamed back, "and don't do much baking."

"And you know, every time some one gasses himself in the kitchen, that shows on the bill, terribly. Ouch, honey, I told you. Now you *did* chop it off . . ."

At that the door opened and the man came back. On his arms, before him, he carried the dress like a sleeping beauty. He walked on tiptoe, so as not to disturb. His cheeks were flushed, his chin white, his forehead studded with pearling sweat, his eyes glimmering, and every gesture racked with deep emotion. He walked straight up to the chair in which he had left the girl.

Staring for a moment at her, then past her, he asked, "Where's Vera? Is she ready?"

Seven operators, busy in a half-circle over her prostrate body, lifted their curly heads. They looked like a great halo of angel faces around her resting on the ground of their mantles which merged into a single white surface before his glimmering eyes. They shrugged their shoulders. It looked like a wave, making a half circle.

"Mr. Pierre told you," the first one said.

"It would take about three hours," said the second.

"She is not ready yet," said the third.

"It will be another hour or so," said the fourth.

"*Where is she?*" he interrupted them, greatly alarmed.

They lowered their curly heads to form a crown of great sunflowers round her head. They felt sorry for him.

"Here she is," the fifth, sixth and seventh said softly, almost whispering.

It was a horrid sight. The Von Barbar mask must have reached its high point of efficacy, for Vera looked absolutely dead, an impression heightened by the ghastly pale green light flooding her from a reflector lamp posted at the foot-end. Her eyes, bleached to a watery tan and kept wide open by little pegs, stared glassily into the milky light. Her hair flowed from her like a piece of wet carpeting, a vicious dark copper-red, drops of which swam carelessly over her forehead and down the cheeks. Her arms were spread out and fastened in handcuffs to the armrest of the dentist chair. Back and armrests had been lowered to form a cross-shaped bed.

The sunflower crown unlocked and the black figure of Mr. Pierre inserted itself, leaning over her head. Below the deep deadness, a smile tried to stir, but did not quite reach the surface. The golden beam gathered from the diffusion of her ken, boring into his eyes with love, desire.

"How is the little lady doing?" he said with a tender smile.

Then he took a small trowel and stuck it into her side and turned it around. There was no blood.

"I think we are ready," he said, and his voice was pleased.

The man almost dropped the dress. "Ve- Ve- Ve- Ve-" he stammered, confused. Then he lifted the dress up high before him with both hands. It seemed strangely alive in the pale green light. He pulled it onto his breast, hugged it protectively, passionately, and, without saying another word, he rushed out.

When Vera came out of the German bath, she looked slim, trim and prim. Mr. Pierre combed her hair, bobbed it up with a wavy motion of his hands and, looking over her head at his own image in the mirror, he said, "Are we pleased, little lady? Tomorrow we shall have our first lesson in individualized makeup. And tomorrow we shall learn a better posture, more correct carriage. And tomorrow we must not nod our little head so much any more. And tomorrow—"

Ladies came and ladies left and Vera waited. She saw shampoos and masks and baths, got used to them, and waited. She listened to much uncouth gossip between chair and chair: how much disaster and crime and betrayal and misfortune. And she waited.

The beautiful receptionist in the blue suit with matching scarf said to her: "Well, well, how darling we look!" And then: "Honey, your skirt is too large for you now. You might just as well fix it—it will give you something to do."

Ultima rose from her dentist chair. They slipped off her gown, brushed her shining neck and shoulders. They slipped on her dress, handed her the purse, dusting, wiping, brushing, adding a last touch of perfection to their handiwork.

The lady in dusty-rose called on Vera and brought her a white gown. "Take off your clothes, honey, and put on this one. You can fix them better like that." And she fastened the gown adroitly with a suitable belt, a becoming pin.

The operators spread sawdust on the floor and began to sweep it. They sprayed the mirrors with windex, dusted the chairs, sterilized the combs, put away the curlers, hung the towels and locked the safe.

The beautiful lady in the white gown, with the pretty pin and matching bracelet and the cornflower in her barrette, walked up to Vera. They looked like sisters now, except that Vera was a shade lighter, newer.

"Honey," the lady said, and smiled gently her perfect smile, "honey, why don't you give us a hand while you are waiting?"

Flower Arrangement

BY ROSEL GEORGE BROWN

Later on, I couldn't remember quite why I did it. I was sitting there in my usual condition of vague awareness, wishing Barbara's voice would stop grating away because there was a man who was going to talk to us about St. Augustine grass, and I was hoping he'd say what to do for the brown spots in my lawn.

"Oh, come on, girls," Barbara was saying. "We *ought* to enter the Federated Gardens show. Last year we won third prize."

What Barbara wanted, of course, was for us to urge her to do the Arrangement. She was the only one of us with any talent, and to be fair, Barbara is a real maestro.

Every year we each make a Dried Arrangement and Barbara comes along and says, "Um!" and presses her lips together and waves her hand over your weedy-looking mess and pokes sticks in and out of the starfoam and, *presto*, you have a beautiful Arrangement to keep in your living room until the next Dried Arrangements meeting.

Every year I take it home and everyone says, "Oh, isn't that beautiful! Did you make it?" And of course I had been rather pretending I had made it, only if somebody asked me about it directly, I had to say, "No, Barbara James made it." I frequently wished I had the courage to rush out of the Dried Arrangements meeting before she got to me and set my weedy, wispy Arrangement on the buffet and leave it there.

Needless to say, I do not have this kind of courage.

Only as Barbara got to the part where she says, "O.K. Any volunteers?" something popped inside of me and I shot my hand up and said, "I'd be glad to have a try at it."

Barbara's mouth quirked a little, because she knew perfectly well what kind of Arrangements I make, and because she had probably already decided exactly what sort of Arrangement the Eastbank Garden Group was going to enter in the Federated Gardens show.

But she said, "That's fine, Sally Jo. You're to use camellias in it somewhere. I think you'd do best with a simple fan Arrangement. I'll mail you their rules book, and if you'd like any—er—advice, why, I'd be glad to help."

That was it, of course. She wasn't going to let it be my Arrangement at all.

I didn't even hear what the man said about St. Augustine grass. All the time I was thinking, thinking, thinking. Was there *any* kind of Arrangement I could make that Barbara couldn't do better? Something really different, so that when I looked at it, I wouldn't have to picture Barbara pressing her lips together?

It was about eleven o'clock at night when I got home, and of course Ronald was asleep, but I just couldn't bear this by myself.

"Ronald!" I cried in a loud whisper so as not to wake Tommy. "Do you *know* what I've done!"

Ronald snuffled irritably, then sat up with a jerk and grabbed me by the shoulders.

"You ran over somebody!"

"No. I volunteered to make the flower Arrangement for the Federated Gardens show!"

Ronald mumbled blasphemies and sank back into his pillow.

"Darling, please stay awake. You see, the thing is, I'm actually going to do this. Only there's the matter of Barbara. Now, if I can only find something—come to think of it, there's the Hogarth Curve. Barbara can do fans or Japanese things or crescents, but the one thing Barbara has never won a prize on is the Hogarth Curve. It tends to droop, you see. Darling . . ."

But he was asleep.

For a wild moment I even considered waking up Tommy, just to have someone to talk to.

The wild moment passed and I eyed the telephone. But there isn't anyone you can call up at eleven o'clock at night and say, "About the Hogarth Curve—"

I crossed my arms over my chest and slipped my feet out of my shoes so I could stride up and down the house quietly. Naturally I couldn't think of anything. I never can when I try.

But it hit me the next day. I was putting some appliqué on a pot holder for the bazaar in January—I loathe appliqué—and there it was!

The Hogarth Curve wouldn't do, because while Barbara wasn't really successful with that kind of Arrangement, she could look at it and immediately see what was wrong. But the Hogarth Curve isn't the only line in the world. Lines reminded me of math, and math reminded me of that *Mathematics for Morons* book Ronald brought home in one of his numerous unsuccessful attempts to improve my thinking ability.

I stuck my finger with a needle, hissed at the stab, held the pot holder carefully away so as not to get blood on it. Appliqué, ha!

There was *something* in that book I wanted to remember. Some really interesting line. I grabbed the book and started down the index. B. I was sure it began with a B. No. Moebius Strip. That was it.

Feverishly, I flipped the pages back to find out what it was that was so interesting about the Moebius Strip, and whether it could be done with an aspidistra leaf soaked in glycerin.

"Brring!" went the alarm clock, which I always reset in the morning to tell me to go get Tommy.

"Damn, damn, damn," I said, glancing hastily around at the part on Moebius Strips. There were other interesting-looking lines, but I just had a feeling the Moebius one was right.

Walking into the kindergarten, I peered around for Tommy.

"Everything all right?" Miss Potter asked.

"Um? Oh." I guess I had a glazed look in my eyes. "Come to think of it, I've been pondering it all morning and I haven't told anybody yet. I'm going to make the Arrangement for the Federated Gardens show."

"How nice! You could make a real family project out of it!" Miss Potter said with her usual misplaced enthusiasm. "Tommy *loves* to make things!"

"I know."

Tommy talked all the way home, but I didn't hear a word he said.

"Make yourself a peanut butter sandwich," I said when I pushed open the back door.

"Boys my age need a good hot lunch."

"My mother used to have to *force* me to eat a good hot lunch. I'd have liked nothing better than to come home and make myself a peanut butter sandwich."

Tommy gave me his accusatory look.

"Oh, all *right*," I said.

After lunch, we went out in the garage where I have my lab— ferns being pressed between newspapers, cattails hanging up to dry, my bucket of things in glycerin.

"What I need," I mused, "is the biggest aspidistra in the world."

I found a really nice one. Brownish, of course, but with a reddish streak and hints of deep green in it. And best of all, a light stripe right down the middle.

"This," I said, "is going to be the very soul of our flower arrangement."

"What's a soul?"

"A soul . . ." The telephone rang. I am not always this fortunate.

"I wanted to let you know," Barbara said, "that I've got the perfect container for your Arrangement. A pale blue cloisonné bowl. Oval. Just the thing for a fan Arrangement."

"I'm not making a fan Arrangement."

"No? Well, I think it would do very nicely for one of the Japanese Arrangements."

"I'm not using Japanese lines," I said.

There was a silence. Then, "You're *not* going to try a Hogarth Curve!"

"No. It's not the sort of thing you can describe, Barbara. You'll just have to see it. When I'm ready."

"I can come by any evening." Fortunately, Barbara works. "Suppose I come by this evening and bring you the bowl?"

"I already have a base," I lied. "I'll call you when I have the Arrangement in shape."

"I didn't mean to interfere."

"It isn't that. It's that the thing is—gestating. I need to *feel* it for a while."

"Of course," Barbara said, as though I had just told her I was calling in a medium.

A base. Really, I didn't want any base at all. I needed something that was nothing.

The pastry board was too big.

But I have a lovely chopping board, oblong, just the right size. I scrubbed the onion and garlic smell out of it as best I could and stuck on a piece of starfoam with floral clay.

Now the Moebius Strip.

"*Tommy!*"

His eyes were wide and puzzled. He didn't know what he'd done.

"*Why* did you tear Mama's aspidistra leaf into strips?" A whole bunch of them, meeting at the stem.

"It's prettier that way."

I could see what he meant. There was something festive-looking about it. Like streamers tied to a stick.

"Let's try it like it is," Tommy said.

He picks up these insidious cooperative suggestions from Miss Potter, and he has me in the midst of family projects before I'm aware of what's going on.

"Well, I guess it wouldn't hurt to try. Hand me a piece of that green wire."

I gathered the ends of the streamers together, carefully half-looped them and wired them to the bottom of the stem, so that the stem was part of the curve, too. They were pliable, but not limp or crackly, from the glycerin. My idea was to make a Dried

Arrangement and then wire in some camellias at the last minute.

If I had been a purist, I would have left the Arrangement the way it was, with just the one leaf. Tommy and I, however, are not purists.

"Go out into the garage and get me six dried okra pods off the shelf," I said. "I am a fairy godmother."

"Which ones is the okra?" Tommy asked.

"The stripy ones."

Tommy was back in a flash. "What are you going to turn them into?"

"A handsome young Dried Arrangement."

"Can I stick some in?"

"One."

I wired them all and put in five, their slight crescents all curving in the same direction. Tommy put the sixth one in, curving, of course, in the wrong direction.

Still, you know, it didn't look bad.

"Now," I said, "we need something behind it. For a background. Something pale. Go into the garage," I commanded, waving my magic floral wire, "and get me four ferns. They're between the sheets of newspaper."

It's obvious what's wrong with all this. You should *never* use an even number of things in a flower arrangement. It's gauche and bourgeois and almost as bad as serving iced sherry.

Just as I was really getting started, Ronald came in demanding dinner.

"How am I ever going to get my Arrangement made if people keep interrupting?" I said, because I was knee-deep in weeds and it was infuriating to have to stop. "Don't you and Tommy ever think of anything but food?"

"Sally *Jo!*"

I opened cans of this and that, like the ladies on television. Ronald and Tommy ate morosely and of *course* the Tylers dropped by after dinner and Marcelle said, "What is *that?*" And I said, "Oh, it isn't finished yet," and Tommy said, "*I* helped," and Marcelle said, "That's awfully clever of Tommy to help make something. But tell me, dear, have you ever wondered about his subconscious?"

No, I hadn't, but it was *my* subconscious, and after that I kept wondering, Why is my subconscious like a Moebius Strip? The best answer I could come up with was that it's because it has a half-twist in it.

But the next morning I got the fern in exactly right, balancing the five okra pods with three large ferns and the wrong-way one with a small fern. The aspidistra showed up beautifully against the fragile dried road fern.

Then, of course, Tommy and Ronald revolted against my Creative Period, each in his own way. Tommy fell down and split his lip wide open, requiring stitches, and Ronald came down with the flu, requiring continuous bed care.

I'd rather be locked up with two live octopi.

And then Marcelle called and said the pot holders *had* to be done by the next week, so every time I had an odd moment I had to sit down and work on that wretched appliqué.

"I'll resign!" I screamed one day, hurling a half-appliquéd pot holder across the room. "Do you know that I still have the bias binding to sew on? And, Ronald, they're *round.*"

"For God's *sake*, resign! I've never heard of making pot holders for a garden club, anyway."

"It's for our bazaar. And I can't resign before the show. I wouldn't be able to make the Arrangement."

"Which would suit me just fine," Ronald said. "Where's my pipe?"

"Did you look on your pipe rack?"

"There's a tube of toothpaste on my pipe rack."

"Then your pipe's in the medicine cabinet."

By the time Tommy was back in school and Ronald was back at work, I had *one* day to finish my Arrangement in.

Barbara, of course, had been calling every night "to find out how everybody is," and hinting for me to let her take over. Somewhere, probably out of sheer irritation, I found the strength of mind to refuse her.

"But you'll need my Pink Perfections," Barbara said. "After all, it's a camellia show."

"Couldn't you meet me before the show? I'm going over at eight o'clock and Ronald's going to drop Tommy off at school for me. The show doesn't start until nine. You could stop by on the way to work."

"I'll be there *at* eight o'clock," Barbara said. "How many Pink Perfections do you want me to bring? Three? Five?"

"Four," I said, and hung up before she could even gasp.

I worked most of the night. I filled in the curve of the Moebius Strip with some soft, sort of thistle down things. I covered the starfoam with curly moss and left the rest of the chopping board bare. I worked in the mindless way that produces the best effect.

The alarm went off at six. I hopped out of bed and darted about the chilly house to get my family clothed and fed and out. I was more excited than I ought to have been over a flower show. I'd stuck my neck out too far, refusing to let Barbara help. And using a totally unorthodox Arrangement. And furthermore—you don't ordinarily think of Flower Arranging as a vice, but it was something nasty in me that made me volunteer to do it, and to exclude Barbara, who after all needs to make Flower Arrangements because she doesn't have any children. And if one is going to have a vice at all, and neglect home and family and friends, one ought to be able to say, "There, at least I got a prize."

I broke the eggs into a bowl and got the bacon started. Then I popped into the living room and turned the light on for a quick look at my Moebius Strip. There was something not quite right about it. For one thing, it no longer looked like a Moebius Strip. On the other hand, it didn't look *not* like a Moebius Strip.

The bacon started complaining and I went to separate the pieces and at this point Tommy woke up and informed me that he was wet, as is his tendency on cold mornings. Then Ron said he couldn't find his cuff links and the cat started yowling to come in and I didn't have time to think about anything at all.

Until I started in to get my flower Arrangement to bring to the John D. Ransom auditorium, where the show was going to be. Then Tommy said, "I fixed it for you." And so he had. It looked Moebius, only more so.

Barbara was waiting for me just inside the door, her arms wrapped around herself, doing a little two-step to warm up. The auditorium was like a vault and the heating system was just getting started, with random, thunderous shrieks.

"Why, Sally *Jo!*" Barbara cried, stopping in mid-two-step. "It's *interesting.*"

I carried the Arrangement over to the niche marked EASTBANK GARDEN GROUP. ARRANGEMENT BY SALLY JO WARNER. I set it down carefully, though Barbara says an Arrangement should always be so tight you can turn it upside down and shake it.

Interesting! I had a moment of wild triumph and then I was a little ashamed of myself. Barbara was generous enough to like it.

"However," Barbara said, pressing her lips together and making me feel normal again, "where are we going to put the Pink Perfections?"

Barbara opened the shallow box with four camellias in it. They were, of course, perfect and spotless and exactly alike. I can understand how Barbara manages to discipline her house and her dog and her husband, but I have never figured out how anyone can discipline flowers.

"The camellias? Oh, yes, the camellias . . ."

There was a baffled bellow from Ronald. He was trying to get Tommy's snowsuit off. I ran over before the zipper or Tommy could get jammed. The instant I had the snowsuit off, there was a wail from Tommy. "She ruined my Flower Arrangement!"

My heart sank. "No, no, dear," I said, hurrying after him to where Barbara was, but he was right. There were bits of weed and fluff piled up on the floor and a gleam of joy in Barbara's eyes, and there was nothing left of the fascinating shape Tommy and I had made. "See?" I went on. "It's beautiful. It's a perfect Hogarth Curve." It was. It didn't droop at all. And Barbara had made the Arrangement.

"There was something funny in there," Barbara said. "I thought it must be Tommy's, so I saved it."

"It's my inside-out balloon," Tommy said, his chin quivering, "and she turned it back right-side in!"

It was Tommy's multi-colored balloon, and it really didn't look much like a balloon any more, though it was still blown up. "How did your balloon get in there?"

"I put it in," Tommy said, "to make the Arrangement more rounder. It's the roundest thing I ever made." Tears were gathering in his eyes.

"Now, dear, I don't know why I didn't see it."

"I put it in after you made it. Then I blew it up and tied it and poked in the end. It was the roundest thing in the whole world!"

"But it's still tied! See? So nobody could have turned it right-side out. It looks the same on both sides."

"No, it don't. The other side got magnetic paint on it. That's why the balloon got ripples in it."

Ron had been standing around looking impatient and he said, "Tommy, there's no such thing as magnetic paint."

"There is, too," Tommy said. "I made it."

"How did you make it?"

"You mix up silver paint like you use for Christmas Arrangements and you add that silver glitter that you sprinkle and then you add all the old magnets you have around and you stir it good."

"How many old magnets?" I asked.

"Lots and lots and lots."

"Then what?"

"Then you turn the balloon inside out and blow it up and pinch the end with a clothes pin and paint it and then when it's dry you let the air out."

"And just why do you do all this?" Ron asked.

That was a silly question and Tommy didn't bother to answer it.

"What about the magnets?" I asked.

"You bury them in the back yard."

"Oh. And do metal things stick on the magnetic paint?"

"Well—hair does, if you brush it first."

"*Metal* things."

"I *think* they do. A teeny bit. But now it's all on the wrong side and it's ruined."

"I have to get to work," Ron said.

"Here, catch." I tossed the balloon to Tommy.

It stayed up in the middle of the air.

"See?" Tommy said. "It's no good no more."

We all stood staring, in a state of shock.

"It's a funny shape," Ron said finally. "Those puckers sort of go *in* and if you follow that striated band . . . if you follow . . ."

I was trying to follow it with my eyes, too.

". . . you get vertigo," Ron finished, looking off in another direction.

"Yes, you do," I said. "Well, we can't just leave it here. Tommy, would you like to take it to show Miss Potter?"

"Miss Potter, hell!" Ron exclaimed. "There's something extraordinary about this. I'm going to take it down to work with me and let the boys at the lab have a look at it. I've never seen anything that just stayed in mid-air like that. You notice it doesn't seem to float, as it would if it contained a gas, and . . ."

But I was busy apologizing to Barbara for Tommy's manners and assuring her the Hogarth Curve was beautiful.

I pinned the left-over camellia in my hair, because I felt I deserved something, and Ron said he'd drop Tommy and me off at kindergarten.

"Isn't it marvelous," I asked Ron as I wiped off the windshield, because Tommy kept huffing on it, "to have a son who's an important scientist before the age of six?"

"Now don't be getting delusions of grandeur about him," Ron said. "Whatever you and he made was purely accidental."

"That goes to show what *you* know about the scientific method. I was making a Moebius Arrangement and Tommy was making the roundest thing in the whole world, and when you're working on something and something *else* happens, something scientifically important, it's called—I can't remember what it's called, but it's a perfectly good word beginning with R. Or maybe L."

"Serendipity. But you and Tommy . . . Never mind."

Later on in the morning, Ron called to tell me to go see a man named Craddock over at the lab, and I'd have to go by myself because Ron was busy, and I said, "All right," but it wasn't all right. The thought of going to that strange place to talk to important men was terrifying.

I opened my closet and looked unhappily through my inappropriate house dresses and equally inappropriate party dresses. I finally decided on my black skirt, dark gray sweater and white cotton blouse, which I hoped would give the impression of a businesslike outfit.

On the way down on the streetcar, I found a woman staring

at me and I realized I had been practicing my facial expression.
It was the one where I hang a cigarette out of the side of my
mouth, narrow my eyes to a slit, and say, "I'm Warner. You
Craddock?"

What actually happened was that an office boy said, "What are
you so nervous about, lady?" and brought me through a maze
of forbidding-looking chambers and deposited me on a bench
facing a back that was, presumably, Craddock's.

I sat there trying to decide whether to address him or just wait,
when he turned, looked at me, and jumped two feet.

"I didn't know anyone was there," he explained, and since he
was the one who had acted a little silly, I felt much better about
him immediately.

"I'm sorry," I said. "I was just sitting here trying to decide . . ."
That wouldn't do. "My name's Warner," I said, omitting the
facial expression.

"Dr. Warner?"

"Sally *Jo* Warner."

"And you discovered this new—force field?"

"If you mean the right-side-inside-out balloon," I answered,
"yes. With my son. Thomas." I decided that if he was going to be
a scientist, we should stop calling him Tommy.

Craddock was one of those thin, pale, freckled-all-over people
with eyes the color of the rims of his horn-rimmed glasses and
he wore the same general expression of stubborn intentness that
Tommy has. And I could sense in his expression the same scorn
for me that Tommy so frequently has.

"I'd like to discuss this with your son," he said.

Of course. *I* couldn't be expected to say anything sensible.

"Thomas has school in the mornings," I said.

"Ah? Um. Which school?"

"Miss Nicholls."

"Miss—"

"It's a small private school. Kindergarten through third grade."

"A third-grade child did this!"

"No. Kindergarten. And I was not without influence in this discovery. I went to Grey Rock Junior College."

"Um. Sciences?"

"Yes."

"I mean what sciences?"

"We learned all the sciences in one course. Chemistry, biology, physics and—well, I'd have to look in the book to remember the others."

"Never mind," Craddock said, a shudder going through his slight, clattery frame. "Just tell me how you did this." He nodded at the balloon, which was encased in a glass box with a tube sort of thing leading into it.

"Well, first you take an aspidistra leaf . . ." I began, and went on from there. Craddock wrote it all down, though he kept saying, "I just don't see how the balloon fits into all this," and finally I said, "*Now* we get to the balloon. And the magnetic paint."

"Where did you get the magnetic paint?"

"My colleague made it."

Craddock was awfully picayunish about details. "How *much* silver paint? How much is 'the rest of a pack of glitter'?" Then he was disturbed because lots and lots and lots of magnets is eight.

When I got to the part where Barbara made a Hogarth Curve out of my Moebius Strip, I asked him for a cigarette because I was still upset over it.

"I know how you feel," Craddock said, being agreeable for the first time. "I don't think it's right to make a Hogarth Curve out of a Moebius Strip, either. I wouldn't even think it was possible."

"Well, that's all," I said, and Craddock grabbed my cigarette before I dropped it into what looked like an empty dish. "I have to rush off and pick up my colleague at kindergarten."

On the way to Miss Nicholls, my mind was afire with ambition. Tommy would appear on TV. Everyone would forget about the time Tommy smeared Miss Potter's chair with mucilage right before she sat down. He'd be offered scholarships to MIT. He'd dictate articles for scientific journals and I'd write them up.

And if anyone ever made remarks about my thinking ability again, I'd just say, "*My* method produces results."

About two o'clock that afternoon, Craddock called and bawled, "The force field is leaking! Another hour and it'll all be gone!"

"Stop sounding as though it's my fault," I said.

"Sorry. I'm just anxious."

"Why don't you catch the drippings in a pot or something?"

"We tried to. But you should see the cloud chamber."

I said, "I'm sure the cloud chamber is very interesting," because it was none of his business if I didn't know what a cloud chamber was.

"The lines just wiggle and disappear into another dimension. I don't know how else to describe it."

"What's making it leak?"

"There's something unusual in the nuclei of the atoms. They're decaying."

"Tommy blew up the balloon," I said, and wondered if he had cavities, though of course it was a different kind of decay. Still the thought made me a little nervous.

"We're getting photographs of everything," Craddock went on, "but what's worrying us is that we haven't been able to duplicate the—uh—experiment."

"I'll bet you didn't soak the aspidistra in glycerin. You couldn't have. There hasn't been time."

"Glycerin wouldn't have anything to do with it. For that matter, neither would the aspidistra."

"Plants," I informed him, "even dried ones, have all sorts of influence. If you put a bouquet of roses in a room, the whole room and all the furniture is a different shape."

"That's your subjective reaction. It's because you like roses."

"There! That proves my point! Why does the lamb love Mary so?"

Craddock choked a little. "Mrs. Warner . . . all right, why *does* the lamb love Mary so?"

"They learn things like this at Miss Nicholls'," I pointed out. "The answer is, 'Mary loves the lamb, you know.' People like roses because roses like people. Which means roses have something *you* don't know about."

"All *right*, there *are* things I don't know. The first thing I don't know is how to carry on an intelligible conversation with you. But let's skip everything except what I called you for. Will you and your colleague please make another of those balloon affairs?"

"I doubt if it can be done."

"Why? If there are any materials you need, I can certainly—"

"It isn't that. It's—well, whatever we do, it's going to be a little bit different. And I don't know if Tommy can find where he buried the magnets. But I'll try."

But before I went shouting around for Tommy, I called Barbara, because something had occurred to me while I was talking to Craddock and it was only decent to tell Barbara.

"What time," I asked, "do the judges come around tonight?"

"About seven-thirty," Barbara said.

"I'm sorry, but you ought to know. We're not going to win."

"What?"

"Your Hogarth Curve," I said, thinking of the leaking balloon, "is going to droop at three o'clock," and left the explanation for later.

I found Tommy in the back yard, deeply involved with sticks and bits of string and old nails.

I knew immediately and sadly what he was doing.

It was too bad Tommy wasn't going to be a famous scientist before the age of six, but that was mostly just a joke. And it was too bad the Eastbank Garden Group wasn't going to win a prize in the Federated Gardens Show, but it was no longer my Arrangement, anyway, and Barbara's always winning other prizes for us. And it was too bad Craddock wasn't going to have his force field, but he hadn't been very nice about the whole thing.

No, the real tragedy was that Tommy was going to be bitterly unhappy about something I had absolutely no control over.

I called Craddock and tried to explain to him why Tommy would never in the world get interested in making another Moebius Strip thing. And there's no way to *make* a child create something, any more than you can make him eat.

"You see," I told Craddock, who was sputtering helplessly on the other end of the line, "he's already made the roundest thing in the whole world. It's not really hard to make the roundest thing in the whole world. I mean, things *tend* to be round, and all you have to do is follow a tendency. But now he's working on something else and he'll keep at it and won't think about anything else and it's going to be tragic when he finds out it just can't be done."

"And what is he trying to do?" Craddock managed to say.

"He's trying to make the squarest thing in the whole world."

Thing of Beauty

BY DAMON KNIGHT

There was a time slip in Southern California at about one in the afternoon. Mr. Gordon Fish thought it was an earthquake. He woke up confused and sullen from his midday nap, blinking fiercely, pink as a spanked baby's behind, with his sandy-yellow beard and eyebrows bristling. He got off the sofa and listened. No screams, no rumble of falling buildings, so probably it was all right.

He heard a knock.

Squinting uneasily, Fish went to the door. He had left his glasses on the table, but never mind; it might be a client, or even an investigator from the city, in which case—

He opened the door.

A slender man in purple was standing there. He was small, hardly an inch taller than Gordon Fish. He said, "Three twenty-two and a half Platt Terrace?" His face was an oval blur; he seemed to be wearing some kind of tight uniform, like a bell-boy's—but purple?

"That's right, three twenty-two and a half, this is it," said Fish, straining to make out the fellow's salmon-colored face. He caught sight of some other people standing behind him, and a shadowy bulk, like a big box of some kind. "I don't know if you—"

"All right, fezh, bring it in," said the man, turning to speak over his shoulder. "Bung, did we have a time finding you!" he said to Fish, and pushed his way into the living room. Behind him, other men in tight purple clothing came staggering under the weight of boxes, first a big one, then two smaller ones, then a *really* big one, then a clutter of smaller boxes.

"Listen, wait, there must be some mistake," said Fish, dancing out of the way. "I didn't order—"

The first man in purple looked at some papers in his hand. "Three twenty-two and a *half* Platt *Terrace?*" he said. His voice sounded slurred and angry, as if he were half drunk or had just waked up, like Fish himself.

Fish was unreasonably irritated. "I tell you I didn't order anything! I don't care if— You walk in here, into a man's home, just— Listen! You! You get that out of there!" Infuriated, he rushed at two of the men who were setting down one of the smaller boxes on the sofa.

"This is the address," said the first man in a bored voice. He shoved some papers into Fish's hand. "You don't want 'em, send 'em back. We just deliver 'em." The purple men began to move toward the door.

The spokesman went out last. "Bung, are *you* a dvich!" he said, and closed the door.

Raging, Fish fumbled for his glasses—they ought to be right *there,* but the movers had upset everything. He went to the door anyway, twitching with anger—dammit, if he could just find his glasses, he'd *report* them, but—

He opened the door. The purple-uniformed men, a little knot of them, were standing in the courtyard looking bewildered. One of them turned a salmon-colored dot of a face. "Hey, which way is—" It sounded like "enchmire."

There was a tremor, and Fish lurched against the door-frame. It felt like an earth-shock, a heavy one, but when he looked up, the palm trees in the street were not swaying, and the buildings were solid and firm. But the purple men were gone.

Swearing frantically to himself, Fish went back into the living room and slammed the door behind him. The biggest box was in his way. He kicked it and a slat fell out. He kicked it again, grunting with angry satisfaction. The whole side fell down with a clatter, revealing a black-enameled panel. Fish kicked that and bruised his toe.

"Hm," said Fish, looking at the sleek black finish of whatever it was. "Hah." It looked like money.

Peering, he ran his finger along the metal. Cool and smooth. Why, it might be almost anything. Industrial machinery, worth thousands of dollars to the right party. With rising excitement, Fish ran to the table, found his glasses pushed into some magazines, and ran back, fitting the glasses over his little eyes.

He pulled some more slats aside. The box fell away, disclosing an oddly shaped hunk of metal with buttons, dials and pointers in the top. An engraved white plate read: "TECKNING MASKIN," and then some numbers. It sounded ominous and important. Heart beating, Fish rubbed his fingers over the smooth buttons and the gleaming dial faces. There was a faint click. He had accidentally moved a switch, he saw, from "Av" to "Pa." The dials were lighting up and a set of long hooked arms, like claws, were slowly drifting out over the flat empty space in the middle.

Hastily, Fish turned the switch back to "Av." The lights went out; the arms, looking disappointed, he thought, drifted back into their enclosures.

Well, it *worked*, whatever it was, which was funny, because, come to think of it, he hadn't plugged it *in* anywhere. Fish stared at the machine uneasily, rubbing his pudgy hands together. Batteries? In a machine that size? And those funny dials, the peculiar *expression* the whole thing had—and "Teckning Maskin," not even English. There it sat, all eight or nine pieces of it, filling up his living room—one crate, he saw with annoyance, blocked off his view of the TV. Suppose it was all some kind of *joke?*

The instant he thought of it, he saw the whole thing in a flash. The crates sitting here, and then in a few days the bill would come in the mail—maybe they wouldn't even take the things away until he'd paid the shipping—and all the time the joker would be laughing himself sick, laughing, whoever it was that had ordered the machines in Fish's name—some old enemy, or it could even be someone he thought of as a *friend*—

With tears of rage in his eyes, he rushed to the door again, flung it open and stood panting, staring around the courtyard. But there was nobody there. He slammed the door and stood looking helplessly at the crates. If they would fight *fair*—How was he going to watch *Dragnet*, and, good heaven, where was he going to talk to clients, in the *kitchen?*

"Oh!" said Fish, and he kicked another crate hard. Slats gave and something fell out, a little yellow booklet. Fish glimpsed more black-enameled machinery inside. He bent wildly to pick up the booklet and tried to tear it across, but it hurt his hands. He threw it across the room, shouting, "Well, then!" He danced from one crate to another, kicking. Slats littered the floor. Gleaming machines stood up from the mess, some with dials, some without. Fish stopped, out of breath, and stared at them with a new bewilderment.

A trick, no, it couldn't be; big industrial machines like that, it wasn't like ordering something from a department store. But then what? A mistake.

Fish sat down on the arm of a chair and frowned, scrubbing his beard with his fingers. In the first place, now, he hadn't *signed* anything. Even if they came back tomorrow, if he could manage to get rid of say one piece, he could always claim there had been seven instead of eight. Or suppose he even got rid of all of it, discreetly, of course, then when they came back he could simply deny the whole thing. Say he never heard of any machinery.

Fish's nerves began to twitch. He jumped up, looked around, sat down. Speed, speed, that was the thing. Get it over with. But what kind of machinery *was* it?

Fish frowned, squirmed, got up and sat down again. Finally he went to the phone, looked up a number and dialed. He smoothed down his vest, cleared his throat musically. "Ben? This is Gordon Fish, Ben . . . Just fine. Now, Ben—" his voice dropped confidentially—"I happen to have a client who wants to dispose of a Teckning Maskin. Eight— What? Teckning Maskin. It's machinery, Ben. T,E,C,K,N,I,N,G—No? Well, that's the name they gave me; I have it written down right here. You never—? Well, that's funny. Probably some mistake. I tell you, Ben, I'll check back and see— Yes, thanks a lot. Thanks, Ben, bye-bye."

He hung up, chewing his whiskers in vexation. If Ben Abrams had never heard of it, then there couldn't be any market for it, not in this part of the country anyhow . . . Something funny. He was beginning to have a hunch about this thing now. Something—

He prowled around the machines, looking at them this way and that. Here was another engraved white plate; it said "TECK-NING MASKIN," and under that "BANK 1," and then two columns of numbers and words . . . "3 Folk, 4 Djur, 5 Byggnader," and so on, a lot more. Crazy words, it didn't even look like any language he'd ever heard of—and then those maniacs in the purple uniforms. Wait a minute—

Fish snapped his fingers, stopped, and stood in a pose of thought. Now what was it that fellow had said just as he was leaving? It had made him mad, Fish remembered—something like, "Boy, are you a dvich." Made him mad as a hornet, it *sounded* insulting, but what did it *mean?*

And then that kind of earthquake just before they got here— woke him up out of a sound sleep, left him feeling all funny— and then another one after they left, only *not* an earthquake, because he remembered distinctly that the palm trees didn't even tremble.

Fish ran his finger delicately over the shining curved edge of the nearest machine. His heart was thumping; his tongue came out to lick his lips. He had a feeling—no, really he *knew*—nobody would be coming back for the machines.

They were his. Yes, and there was money in them somewhere; he could smell it. But how? What did they *do?*

He opened all the crates carefully. In one of them, instead of a machine, there was a metal box full of creamy-thick sheets of paper. They were big rectangular sheets, and they looked as if one would just about fit onto the flat center space on the biggest machine. Fish tried one, and it did.

Well, what could go wrong? Fish rubbed his fingers nervously, then turned the switch on. The dials lighted and the hooked arms drifted out, as before, but nothing else happened. Fish leaned nearer again and looked at the other controls. There was a pointer and a series of marks labeled "Av," "Bank 1," "Bank 2," and so on down to "Bank 6." He moved the pointer cautiously to "Bank 1." The arms moved a little, slowly, and stopped.

What else? Three red buttons marked "Utplana," "Torka," and "Avsla." He pushed one, but nothing happened. Then a series of white buttons, like on an adding machine, all numbered. He pressed one down at random, then another, and was about to press a third when he leaped back in alarm. The hooked arms were moving, rapidly and purposefully. Where they passed over the paper, thin dark-gray lines were growing.

Fish leaned closer with his mouth open and his eyes bulging. The little points under the ends of the arms were riding smoothly over the paper, leaving graceful lines behind them. The arms moved, contracted on their little pivots and springs, swept this way and that; lifted slightly, dropped again and moved on. Why, the machine was drawing—drawing a picture while he watched!

There was a face forming under the arm over on the right, then a neck and shoulder—kind of a sappy-looking man, it was, like a Greek statue. Then over here on the left, at the same time, another arm was drawing a bull's head, with some kind of flowers between the horns. Now the man's body—he was wearing one of those Greek togas or whatever you call them—and the back of the bull curving around up on top—and now the man's arm, and the bull's tail, and now the other arm, and the bull's hind legs—

There it was. A picture of a man throwing flowers at this bull, who was kind of leaping and looking at the man over his shoulder. The arms of the machine stopped moving and then pulled back out of sight. The lights went out and the switch clicked by itself back to "Av."

Fish took the paper and looked it over, excited but a little disappointed. He didn't know anything about *art*, of course, but he knew this was no good—all flat-looking and kind of simple, like a kid would draw. And that bull, who ever saw a bull dancing like that? With flowers between its horns?

Still, if the machine would draw this, maybe it would draw something better; he couldn't quite see the angle—where would you sell drawings, even good ones?—but it was there somewhere. Exhibit the machine, like in a fair of science and industry? No, his mind hurriedly buried the thought—too exposed, too many questions. If Vera found out he was still alive, or if the police in Scranton—

Drawings. A machine that made drawings. Fish looked at it, all eight lumpy black-enameled massive pieces of it scattered around his living room. It seemed like a lot of machinery just to make *drawings*. He admitted it, he was disappointed; he had expected—well, metal stampings or something like that, something real. Crash, bang, the big metal jaw comes down, and tink, the bright shaped piece falls out into the basket. There was machinery for you; but this—

Fish sat back and pondered, twitching the paper disapprovingly between his fingers. Things were always letting him down like this. Really, his best line was marriage—he had been married five times and always made a little profit out of it—he smoothed the vest down over his suety front; between times, he turned to whatever was handy, Marital Counseling some years, or gave Life Readings if he could get enough clients; or Naturopathy, it all depended, but somehow every time it looked as if he had a real gold mine, it slipped out from under his hand.

He reddened with discomfort as he thought of the one winter he had been forced to go to work in a *shoe store*.

Having this house had softened him up, too. He had been getting lazy, just a client or two a week for Life Readings. He ought to be getting busy, working up new contacts before his money ran out.

The thought of poverty, as it always did, made him ravenously hungry. He kneaded his stomach. Time for lunch. He got his jacket hurriedly, and as an afterthought rolled up the drawing—it would not fold—and tucked it under his arm.

He drove to the barbecue place three blocks down the boulevard where he had been eating a lot of his meals lately, to save funds. The counterman was a young fellow named Dave, lean and pale, with a lock of straight dark hair falling over his forehead. Fish had got into friendly conversation with him and knew he was going to art school nights, over in Pasadena. Fish had tried to get him over for a Life Reading, but the youngster had said frankly that he "didn't believe in it," in such an honest and friendly way that Fish bore him no ill will.

"Bowl of chile, Dave," he said cheerfully, hoisting himself up on a stool with the rolled drawing precariously on his lap. His

feet dangled; the paper was squeezed tight between vest and
counter.

"Hello, Doc. Coming up." Fish hunched forward over the bowl,
loosening his collar. The one other customer paid and left.

"Say, Dave," said Fish indistinctly, munching, "like to get your
opinion of something. Unh." He managed to get the rolled paper
free and opened it on the counter. "What do you think—is it any
good?"

"Say," said Dave, coming nearer. "Where'd you get *that?*"

"Mm. Nephew of mine," Fish answered readily. "He wants me
to advise him, you know, if he should go on with it, because—"

"Go on with it! Well, say— Where's he been studying, anyhow?"

"Oh, just by himself, you know—back home." Fish took another
mouthful. "Ver' bright boy, you understand, but—"

"Well—gee, if he learned to draw like that by himself—why, he
must be a world-beater."

Fish forgot to chew. "You really mean it?"

"Why, sure. Listen, are you sure he drew this himself, Doc?"

"Oh, certainly." Fish waved the imputation of dishonesty away.
"Ver' honest boy, I know'm well. No, 'f he tells me he drew it,
why—" he swallowed—"he drew it. But now don't fool me, is it—
do you really think it's as *good*—"

"Well, I tell you the truth, when I first saw it, *I* thought Picasso.
You know, his classical period. Of course I see now it's different,
but, my gosh, it's good. I mean, if you want *my* opinion, why—"

Fish was nodding to indicate that this only confirmed his own
diagnosis. "M-hm. M-hm. Well, I'm glad to hear you say it, son.
You know, being a relative of the boy, I thought— Of course, I'm
very impressed. Very impressed. I thought of Picasso, too, same
as you. Of course, now from the money end of it—" he wagged
his head dolefully—"you know and I know—"

Dave scratched his head under the white cap. "Oh—well—he
ought to be able to get commissions, all right. I mean, if I had a
line like that—" He traced in air the strong outline of the man's
lifted arm.

"Now when you say *commissions*—" Fish said, squirming with
eagerness.

"Oh, well, for portraits, or industrial designs, or you know, whatever he wants to go in for." Dave shook his head in admiration, staring at the drawing. "If this was only in color—"

"How's that, Dave?"

"Why, I was just thinking—see, there's a competition up in San Gabriel for a civic center mural. Ten-thousand-dollar prize. Now I don't know, it might not win, but why don't you have him render this in color and send it in?"

"Color," said Fish blankly.

The machine wouldn't color anything, he was sure. He could get a box of water color paints, but—

"Well, now, the fact is," he said, hastily revolving ideas, "you know, the boy is laid up. Hurt his hand—oh, not serious," he said reassuringly (Dave's mouth had fallen into a circle of sympathy), "but won't be able to draw any more pictures for a while. It's a shame, he could use the money, you know, for doctor bills—" He chewed and swallowed. "Tell you, this is just a wild idea now, but—why couldn't you color it up and send it in, Dave? Course, if it doesn't win, I couldn't pay you, but—"

"Well, gee, I don't know how he'd like that, Doc. I mean, suppose he'd have something else in mind, like, some other color scheme altogether. You know, I wouldn't like to—"

"I'll take full responsibility," said Fish firmly. "Don't you worry about that, and—if we win, why, I'll see that you're paid handsomely, Dave. Now, there, how's that?"

"Well, sure, then, Doc. I mean sure," said Dave, nodding and blushing. "I'll do it tonight and tomorrow, and get it right off in the mail, okay? Then—oh, uh, one thing, what's your nephew's name?"

"George Wilmington," said Fish at random. He pushed the cleaned chile bowl away. "And, uh, Dave, I believe I'll have an order of ribs, with french fries on the side."

Fish went home with a vastly increased respect for the machine. The mural competition, he was positive, was in the bag. Ten thousand dollars! For one drawing! Why, there was millions in it!

He closed and locked the front door carefully behind him, and pulled down the venetian blinds to darken the gloomy little living room still further. He turned on the lights. There the machine still was, all eight gleaming pieces of it, scattered around on the floor, the furniture, everywhere. He moved excitedly from one piece to another, caressing the slick black surfaces with his palm. All that expensive machinery—all his!

Might as well put it through its paces again, just to see. Fish got another sheet of creamy paper from the stack, put it in position, and turned the switch to "Pa." He watched with pleasure as the dials lighted, the hooked arms drifted out and began to move. Lines grew on the paper: first some wavy ones at the top, could be anything. And farther down, a pair of long up-curved lines, kind of handlebar-shaped. It was like a puzzle, trying to figure out what it was going to be.

Under the wavy lines, which Fish now perceived to be hair, the pointer drew eyes and a nose. Meanwhile, the other one was gliding around the outline of what, it became clear in a moment, was a bull's head. Now here came the rest of the girl's face, and her arm and one leg—not bad, but kind of beefy—and now the bull's legs, sticking out all different ways, and then, whoops, it wasn't a bull: there was the whatyoumaycallum—a cow. So, a girl riding on a cow, with flowers between the horns like before.

Fish looked at the drawing in disappointment. People and cows —was that all the thing could *do?*

He scrubbed his beard in vexation. Why, for heaven's sake, suppose somebody wanted a picture of something *besides* cows and people? It was ridiculous—eight big pieces of machinery—

Wait a minute. "Don't go off half-cocked, Gordon," he told himself aloud. That was what Florence, his second, always used to say; except she always called him "Fishy." He winced with discomfort at the memory. Well, anyway, he noticed now that the same buttons he had pressed down before were still down. That must have something to do with it.

Struck by another thought, he trotted over and looked at the machine marked "Bank 1." Now this list here, number 3 was "Folk," and number 4 was "Djur." Those were the numbers he had pressed on the big machine, so—maybe "folk" meant *people,* and "djur," why, that might be some crazy word for *cattle.* Then if he pressed a different set of buttons, why, the machine would have to draw something else.

In fifteen minutes, he verified that this was the case. Pressing down the first two buttons, "Land" and "Planta," gave him drawings of outdoors scenes, just hills and trees. "Folk" was people and "Djur" seemed to be animals; now he got goats or dogs instead of cows. "Byggnader" was buildings. Then it got more complicated.

A button marked "Arbete" gave him pictures of people at work; one labeled "Kärlek" produced scenes of couples kissing—all in the same kind of Greek-looking clothes, and the landscapes and buildings were sort of vague and dreamy. Then there was a whole row of buttons under the heading "Plats," and another headed "Tid," that seemed to control where and when the pictures were about. For instance, when he pressed "Egyptisk" and "Gammal," along with "Folk," "Byggnader," and on a hunch, "Religion," he got a picture of some priests in Egyptian headdresses, bowing in front of a big statue. Now *there* was something!

The next day he nailed up the crates again, leaving the tops loose so that he could remove them whenever he wanted to use the machines. In the process, he came across the little yellow booklet he had thrown away. There were diagrams in it, some of which made sense and some didn't, but the printing was all in the same unfamiliar language. Fish put the booklet away in a bureau drawer, under an untidy heap of clothes, and forgot about it.

Grunting and sweating, he managed to push the smaller crates into corners, and rearranged the furniture so there was room to put the big one against the wall. It still looked terrible, but at least he could get around, and have clients in, and he could see the TV again.

Every day he ate lunch at the barbecue place, or at least stopped in, and every day, when Dave saw him come in, he shook his head. Then all afternoon he would sit with a glass of beer, or maybe a plate of nuts or fudge, watching the machine draw. He used up all the papers in the stack and started turning them over to use the other sides.

But where was the money to come from? After some thought, Fish built a simple magic-writing box and used it with his Egyptian drawings—he had a dozen, all of different gods, but after the first one the machine didn't draw any priests—to show clients what they had been up to in previous incarnations. He began to get a little more business, and once or twice his instinct told him he could raise the fee on account of the drawings, but that was only pocket money. He knew there was *millions* in it, he could almost taste it, but where?

Once it occurred to him that maybe he could take out a patent on the machine and sell it. Trouble with that was he didn't have any idea how the thing worked. It seemed like the little machines must have pictures inside, or pieces of pictures, and the big machine put them together—how?

Fuming with impatience, Fish took the big crate apart again, moved furniture out of the way, and fumbled at the smooth black side of the machine to see if there was any way of opening it up.

After a moment, his fingers found two shallow depressions in the metal; he pushed experimentally, then pressed upward—and the side plate of the machine came off in his hands.

It weighed almost nothing. Fish put it aside, staring doubtfully into the interior of the machine. It was all dark in there, nothing but a few very tiny specks of light, like mica dust hanging motionless. No wires, nothing. Fish got a sheet of paper and put it in position, and turned the machine on. Then he squatted down. The tiny specks of light seemed to be moving, circling slowly around one another in time to the motion of the drawing arms. It was darker in there, and looked farther away somehow, than it had any right to.

Holding the front of the machine, Fish touched another shallow depression, and without really meaning to, he pushed upward. The whole front of the machine fell off, and the other side with it.

He sprawled backward frantically to get out of the way: but the top of the machine didn't fall. It stayed there, rock-steady, although there was nothing holding it up but the back panel.

And underneath, nothing. No framework, just the thick darkness, with the little stars going slowly around as the machine drew.

Fish hastily picked up the front and side panels and put them back. They slid easily and perfectly into place, and fitted so closely that he couldn't see any line between them.

After that, he put the crate back together and never tried to look inside the machines again.

Dave hurried around the end of the counter to him. "Doc! Where have you been?" He was drying his hands on his apron and grinning nervously, with a sort of pole-axed expression around his eyes. A customer around the other side of the counter looked up, then went on chewing with his mouth open.

"Well, I had quite a lot of things to do," Fish began automatically. Then he began to feel excited. "Say! You don't mean—"

Dave fished a long white envelope out of his back pocket. "Came yesterday! Look here!" The envelope crackled in his nervous fingers. He pulled out a folded letter and Fish seized it. Dave looked over his shoulder, breathing heavily, as he read.

Dear Mr. Wilmington:

It is my very great pleasure to inform you that your design has been awarded the First Prize in the San Gabriel Civic Center Mural Competition. In the opinion of the judges, the classic simplicity of your entry, together with its technical mastery, made it far superior to anything else submitted.

Enclosed please find our check for three thousand dollars ($3,000.00) . . .

"Where?" cried Fish, looking up.

"Right here," said Dave, with a grin that looked painful. He held up a salmon-colored strip of paper. The red-printed lettering read: "EXACTLY 3,000.^{00****} DOLLARS*****."

Fish hugged Dave, who hugged him back, and then looked at the letter again.

the remainder to be paid when the design is executed to the satisfaction of the Committee.

"Executed?" said Fish, with a sinking feeling. "What's that mean? Dave, what's it mean here, where it says—"

"When he paints the mural on the wall. Gee, Doc, I just can't tell you—"

"Who?"

"Your nephew. George Wilmington. See, when he paints the mural—"

"Oh," said Fish. "Oh. Well, you see, Dave, the fact *is*—"

Dave's long face grew solemn. "Oh, gosh, I never thought. You mean he's not well enough to draw yet?"

Fish shook his head, mournfully. "No, sir. It's a terrible shame,

Dave, but—" He folded the check absently and slipped it into his pocket.

"I thought you said, I mean, it wasn't serious or anything—"

Fish continued to shake his head. "Turned out there was more to it than they thought. It looks like now they just don't know when he'll ever be able to draw again."

"Oh, Doc," said Dave, stricken.

"That's the way it is. These things—the doctors don't know as much about 'em as they'd like you to think, Dave."

Fish went on staring fiercely at the letter, barely listening to the sound of his own voice. *To be paid when the design is executed* . . .

"Look here," he said, interrupting Dave's murmurs of commiseration. "It don't say *who* has to execute it, now does it? Notice right there? Says 'when the design is executed'—"

"How about a glassa water over here?" called the customer.

"Coming right up, sir. Look, Doc, I think you got an idea." Dave retired sidewise toward the counter, still talking. "You know, anybody could scale that up and do the actual painting—any competent artist, I mean. Gee, I'd do it myself, I mean if George didn't mind. And if it was all right with the committee, why, you know, it would be an opportunity for me." He gave the customer his water, mopped the counter blindly and came back.

Fish leaned over the counter, beard in hand, frowning. "Wilmington" was just a name—Dave could take the part just as well as not, and it would be a lot better in one way, because then Fish himself could stay out of sight—

But, whoops, if they did that, then Dave would *be* Wilmington, and he might want to take off on his own . . .

"Well, Dave," he said, "are you a *good* artist?"

Dave looked embarrassed. "Gee, Doc, you put me on the spot, but—well, anyway, they liked how I rendered the design, didn't they? See, I used a color scheme of deep aqua and a kind of buff, with accents of rose—you know, to make it cheerful? And, gee, if I did it on the paper, I could do it on a wall—"

"Sold!" said Fish heartily, and clapped Dave on the shoulder. "George don't know it yet, but he just got himself an assistant!"

A slim female figure popped up at him suddenly from beside a potted palm. "Mr. Wilmington? If I could just have a moment—"

Fish paused, one hand going to his chin in the old gesture, although he had shaved off the beard over a year ago. He felt exposed without it and his features tended to twitch when he was startled like this. "Why, yes, uh, Miss—"

"My name is Norma Johnson. You don't know me, but I have some drawings here—"

She was carrying a big black portfolio, fastened with tapes. Fish sat down beside her and looked at the drawings. They looked all right to him, but skimpy, like the kind of thing he turned out mostly himself. What he *liked* was pictures with some meat to them, like Norman Rockwell, but the one time he had set the machine to draw something like that, his agent—the first one, Connolly, that crook!—had told him there was no market for "genre stuff."

The girl's fingers were trembling. She was very neat and pale, with black hair and big expressive eyes. She turned over the last drawing. "Are they any good?" she asked.

"Well, now, there's a good deal of spirit there," said Fish comfortably. "And a very fine sense of design."

"Could I ever be successful at it?"

"*Well*—"

"See, the thing is," she said rapidly, "my Aunt Marie wants me to stay here in San Francisco and come out next season. But I don't want to. So she agreed, if you said I had real talent, that she would send me abroad to study. But if you didn't, I'd give up."

Fish looked at her intently. Her fingernails were short but looked cared for. She was wearing a simple white blouse and a little blue jacket and skirt; there was a whiff of woodsy perfume. Fish smelled money.

He said, "Well, my dear, let me put it this way. Now you could go to Europe and spend a lot of money—ten thousand, twenty thousand dollars—" She watched him without blinking. "Fifty thousand—" said Fish delicately. "But what would be the *point* of it? Those fellows over there don't know as much as they'd like you to think."

She fumbled blindly for her purse and gloves. "I see." She started to get up.

Fish put a pudgy hand on her arm. "Now what *I* would suggest," he said, "why don't you come and study with me for a year instead?"

Her pale face lenghtened. "Oh, Mr. Wilmington—*would* you?"

"Well, anybody with as much talent as these drawings—" Fish patted the portfolio on her knee—"why, we have to do something, because—"

She stood up excitedly. "Will you come tell that to Aunt Marie?"

Fish smoothed down the front of his pink shirt. "Why, gladly, my dear, gladly."

"She's right here in the lounge."

He followed her and met Aunt Marie, who was a handsome woman of about fifty, plump but beautifully tailored in brown linen. They agreed that Norma would take a studio near Mr. Wilmington's home in Santa Monica, and that Mr. Wilmington would look in several times a week and give her the full benefit of his great experience, in return for ten thousand dollars per annum. It was, as Fish pointed out to them, less than half the amount he usually got now for major commissions; but never mind, every little bit helped. Murals, institutional advertising, textile designs, private sales to collectors—God, how it was rolling in!

The only thing that really worried him was the machine itself. He kept it now in a locked inner room of the house he was renting—twenty rooms, furnished, terrific view of the Pacific Ocean, lots of room for parties—and up to a point he could work it like a kiddy-car. One time or another, he had figured out and memorized every one of the dozens of labeled buttons on the "Bank" machines, and just by combining the right ones, he could get any kind of a drawing he wanted. For instance, that commission for stained glass for a church—"Religion," "People," "Palestine," "Ancient," and there you were.

The trouble was the machine wouldn't draw the same thing twice in a row. On that church window job, he got one picture of Christ and then couldn't get another, no matter how long he tried, so he had to fill out with saints and martyrs. The church put up a beef, too.

Then sometimes at night, for his own amusement, he used to put the machine through its paces—such as setting it for "Historical figures" and "Romantisk," which seemed to be the machine's name for the present era, and then push the button marked "överdriva," and watch the famous faces come out with big cartoony noses, and teeth like picket fences.

Or he would set it for "Love," and then various interesting times and places—ancient Rome gave him some spicy ones, and Samoa was even better.

But every time he did this, the machine turned out fewer drawings; and finally it wouldn't do any more like that at all.

Was there some kind of censor built into the thing? Did it *disapprove* of him?

He kept thinking of the funny way those men in purple uniforms had delivered the thing. They had the right address, but the wrong—time? Whatever it was, he knew the machine wasn't intended for him. But whom was it meant for? What was a "dvich"?

There were eight pieces—six banks, the master machine, and one which he had discovered would enlarge any detail of a drawing to almost full size. He could handle all that. He could manage the controls that governed the complexity or simplicity of a drawing, gave it more or less depth, changed its style and mood.

The only buttons he wasn't sure of were the three red ones marked "Utplana," "Torka," and "Avsla." None of them seemed to *do* anything. He had tried all three both ways, and they didn't seem to make any difference. In the end, he left them the way they had been, "Torka" down, the other two up, for lack of any better idea. But, big and red like that, they must be important.

He found them mentioned in the booklet, too: *"Utplana en teckning, press knappen 'Utplana.' Avlägsna ett mönster fran en bank efter användning, press knappen 'Torka.' Avsla en teckning innan slutsatsen, press knappen 'Avsla.'"*

Press knappen, press knappen, that must be "push button." But when? And that business about "mönster," that made him a little nervous. He had been pretty lucky so far, figuring out how to work the whole machine without any accidents. Supposing there was still something that could go wrong—suppose the booklet was a *warning?*

He prowled restlessly around the empty house—empty, and untidy, because he wouldn't have any servants in the place. You never knew who was going to spy on you. A woman came in two days a week to clean the place up, all but the locked room, and once in a while he'd bring a couple of girls up for a party, but he always threw them out the next morning. He was busy all right, seeing a lot of people, traveling around, but he'd had to drop all his old friends when he decided to become Wilmington, and he didn't dare make any new ones for fear of giving himself away. Besides, everybody was out for something.

The fact was, dammit, he wasn't *happy*. What good was all the money he was making, all the things he'd bought, if they didn't make him happy? Anyhow, pretty soon now, that oil stock would start paying off—the salesman had assured him that the drillers were down within a few hundred feet of oil right now—and then he'd be a millionaire; he could retire, move to Florida or some-place—

He paused in front of his desk in the library. The booklet was still there, lying open. The thing was, even suppose that *was* some language anybody had ever heard of, whom would he dare show it to? Whom could he trust?

An idea occurred to him and he leaned over, staring at the yellow pages with their incomprehensible text. After all, he could already figure out some of the words; he didn't have to show anybody the whole book, or even a whole sentence. Then there was that information business that came with his deluxe set of the *Encyclopaedia Britannica*—he ought to have it right here somewhere—

Fish hunted in the file drawers and finally came up with a folder and a sheet of gummed yellow stamps.

Grunting, he sat down at the desk, and after much cigar-chewing, scribbling and crossing out, he typed the following:

Dear sirs:
Kindly inform me as to what language the enclosed words are, and also what they mean. Kindly give this matter your best attention, as I am in a hurry.

On a separate sheet, he wrote all the doubtful words from the paragraph about the red buttons, cannily mixing them up so no one could guess what order they came in.

Feeling a little foolish, he carefully drew in all the tiny strange dots.

Then he addressed an envelope, stuck one of the yellow stamps to his letter, and mailed the thing off before he could regret it.

"My rhetorical question is," said Fish craftily to the young physicist, shouting over the hum of cocktail-party conversation, "purely in interests of science, could you make a machine that would draw?" He beamed over his glasses at the horn-rimmed blur of the young man's face. He had had three martinis, and whew! he was floating. But fully in command of senses, of course.

"Well, draw what? If you mean charts and graphs, sure, or something like a pantograph, to enlarge—"

"No, no. Draw *beau'ful* pictures." The last word sprayed a little. Fish rocked forward and back again. "Purely rhetorical question." He put his glass down with precision on a passing tray and took another one which spilled icy liquid down his wrist. He gulped to save it.

"Oh. Well, in that case, no. I would say not. I assume you mean it would originate the drawings, not just put out what was programmed into it. Well, that would mean, in the first place, you'd have to have an incredibly big memory bank. Say if you wanted the machine to draw a horse, it would have to know what a horse looks like from every angle and in every position. Then it would have to select the best one for the purpose out of say ten or twenty billion—and then draw it in proportion with whatever else is in the drawing, and so on. Then, for God's sake, if you wanted *beauty* too, I suppose it would have to consider the relation of every part to every other part, on some kind of esthetic principle. *I* wouldn't know how to go about it."

Fish, thick-fingered, probed for his olive. "Say it's impossible, hey?" he asked.

"Well, with present techniques, anyhow. I guess we'll be staying out of the art business for another century or two." The blur smiled and lifted its highball glass.

"Ah," said Fish, putting a hand on the young man's lapel to support himself and keep the other from moving out of the corner. "Now suppose you had machine like that. Now—suppose that machine kept forgetting things. What would be reason for that?"

"Forgetting things?"

"What I said." With a disastrous sense that he was talking too much, Fish was about to go on, but a sudden hand on his arm forestalled him. It was one of the bright young men, beautiful suit, beautiful teeth, beautiful handkerchief in pocket. "Mr. Wilmington, I just wanted to say what an absolutely marvelous piece of work that new mural is. One enormous foot. I don't know what the significance is, but the draughtsmanship is marvelous. We must get you on *File Seven* some afternoon and have you explain it."

"Never go on television," said Fish, frowning. He had been fending off invitations like this one for almost a year.

"Too bad. Nice to have met you. Oh, by the way, somebody asked me to tell you there's a phone call for you over there." He waved his arm and drifted away.

Fish excused himself and set an adventurous course across the room. The phone was lying on one of the side tables, giving him a black look. He picked it up jauntily. "Hello-o."

"Dr. Fish?"

Fish's heart began to knock. He put the martini glass down. "Who's that?" he demanded blankly.

"This is Dave Finney, Doc."

Fish felt a wave of relief. "Oh, Dave. I thought you were in Boston. Or I suppose you *are,* but the connection—"

"I'm right here in Santa Monica. Look, Doc, something's come up that—"

"What? What're you doing here? Now I hope you haven't quit school, because—"

"This is summer vacation, Doc. Look, the fact is I'm here in Norma Johnson's studio."

Fish stood with the sweaty black phone in his hand and said nothing. Silence hummed in the wires.

"Doc? Mrs. Prentice is here too. We've been kind of talking things over and we think you ought to come over and explain a few things."

Fish swallowed, with difficulty.

"Doc, you hear me? I think you ought to come over. *They're* talking about calling the police, but I wanted to give you a chance first, so—"

"I'll be right over," said Fish hoarsely.

He hung up the phone and stood bemused, with his hand to his flushed forehead. Oh, Lord, three, no four martinis and this had to happen!

He felt dizzy. Everybody seemed to be standing at a slight angle on the kelly-green carpet, all the bright young men in glossy summer jackets and the pastel women in cocktail dresses with bright phony smiles on their faces. What did they care if all he could get out of the machine any more was parts of bodies? His last one a big clenched fist, and now a foot, and don't you think the committee didn't beef, they beefed plenty but they had to take it, because they already announced the commission. Now this morning his agent called up, some church group in Indiana, they wanted *sample* sketches.

So it was all going down the drain while he watched, and now this. Dave, good God, you'd think at least he would stay stuck off in Boston, and how the *hell* had he ever run into Norma?

One of the newspaper reporters turned away from the free lunch and planted himself in Fish's path as he lurched toward the door. "Mr. Wilmington, what would you say was the real significance of that foot?"

"Gow my way," said Fish, staggering around him.

He took a cab home, told the driver to wait, ducked in for a quick shower and a cup of black coffee, and came out again, shaky but not as drunk as before. Those damn cocktails . . . He used to never get like this when he just drank beer. Things were better back on Platt Terrace. How did he ever get mixed up in this crazy art game?

His stomach felt hollow. He hadn't eaten any lunch, he remembered. Well, too late now. He braced himself together and rang the bell.

Dave opened the door. Fish greeted him with cries of pleasure, shaking his limp hand. "Dave, boy! Good to see you! How long has it been, anyway?"

Without waiting for a reply, he bustled on into the room. It was a gray, windowless place that always made him feel trapped. Instead of a roof, there was one big slanting skylight, high overhead; the light filtered down cool and colorless through the translucent panes. There was an easel in one corner, and some drawings pinned up on the otherwise bare walls. Down at the far end, Norma and her aunt were sitting on the red-padded bench.

"Norma, how are you, honey? And Mrs. Prentice—now this is a real pleasure!"

That wasn't hard to say—she really did look good in that new dark-blue suit—he could tell he was projecting the old charm, and he thought he saw her eyes glint with pleasure. But it was only for an instant, and then her expression hardened. "What's this I hear about your not even coming to see Norma?" she demanded.

Fish registered deep surprise.

"Why—why, Norma, didn't you explain to your aunt? Excuse me a minute." He darted over to the drawings on the wall. "Well. Now these are really excellent, Norma. There's a good deal of improvement here. The symmetry, don't you see, and the dynamic *flow*—"

Norma said, "Those are three months old." She was wearing a man's shirt and dungarees, and looked as if she might have been crying recently, but her face was carefully made up.

"Well, honey, I wanted to come back, even after what you said. I did come around, twice, you know, but you didn't answer your bell."

"That's not so."

"Well, I suppose you might have been out," said Fish cheerfully. He turned to Mrs. Prentice. "Norma was upset." His voice dropped. "About a month after we started, she told me to get out and not come back."

Dave had drifted back across the room. He sat down beside Norma, without comment.

"The idea of taking the poor child's money for *nothing*," said Mrs. Prentice vehemently. "Why didn't you give it back?"

Fish pulled up a folding chair and sat down close to her. "Mrs. Prentice," he said quietly, "I didn't want Norma to make a mistake. I told her, now, if you'll live up to your agreement and study with me for a year, I said, and then if you're not satisfied, why, I'll gladly refund every cent."

"You weren't doing me any *good*," said Norma, with a hysterical note in her voice.

Fish gave her a look of sorrowful patience.

"He'd just come in and look at my work and say something like, 'This has a good feeling,' or 'The symmetry is good,' or some *meaningless* thing like that. I was getting so nervous, I couldn't even *draw*. That's when I wrote you, Aunt Marie, but you were in Europe. My golly, I had to do something, didn't I?" Her hands were clenched white in her lap.

"There, dear," Mrs. Prentice murmured, and gave her arm a little squeeze.

"I've been going to day classes at the Art Center," Norma said between her teeth. "It was all I could *afford*."

Mrs. Prentice's eyes sparkled with indignation. "Mr. Wilmington, I don't think we have to discuss this much longer. I want you to return the money I paid you. I think it's disgraceful, a well-known artist like you *stooping—*"

"Mrs. Prentice," said Fish, pitching his voice lower again, "if it wasn't for my faith in Norma's great future as an artist, why, I would hand you over ev-ry cent. But, as it is, she would be making a great mistake, so I suggest again—"

"Doc," said Dave rudely, "you give her back that money now, and pretty damn quick." He leaned forward to speak to the older woman. "You want to know what his real name is? It's *Fish*. Anyhow, it was when I met him. This whole thing is just a joke. Why, he's no artist. The real George Wilmington is his nephew; he's an invalid out in Wisconsin—and Doc here has just been fronting for him, because he's too sick to stand the publicity and all. Now that's the truth. Or as much of it as I know."

Fish said sorrowfully, "Dave, is this the thanks I get for putting you through art school?"

"You got me the scholarship, but it didn't cost you anything. I found that out from the director. I guess you just wanted to put me out of the way, so I wouldn't talk too much. Well, gee, Doc, that was all right. But when I met Norma over at your place yesterday—"

"What? When was that?"

"About ten o'clock." Fish winced; he had been in bed with a bad head and hadn't answered the bell. If he'd only known! "You weren't home, so we got to talking and—well, pretending to be your nephew, that's one thing, but when you promise to teach somebody—when you can't even draw a line yourself!"

Gordon Fish raised a hand. "Now, Dave, there's a thing or two you don't know. You say my real name is Fish. Now did you ever see my birth certificate, or did you know anybody that knew me as a child? How do you know my name is Fish?"

"Well, you *told* me."

"That's right, Dave, I did. And you say the real George Wilmington is an invalid out in Wisconsin. You ever see him, Dave? You ever been in Wisconsin?"

"Well, no, but—"

"Neither have I. No, Dave—" he lowered his voice solemnly— "every single thing I told you about that was just a lie. And I admit it." Now here was the place for a tear. Fish turned his mind to the creditors, the trouble with the machine, the oil stock salesman who had gone south with his money, the lawyers who were robbing him blind trying to get it back, the ungratefulness of everybody. A warm trickle crept out onto his cheek, and lowering his head, he knuckled it away.

"Well, what—" said Dave, bewildered.

Fish said with an effort, "I had reasons. Certain reasons. You know it's—it's hard for me to talk about 'em. Mrs. Prentice—I wonder if I could see you alone."

She was leaning forward a little, looking at him with concern. It never failed—a woman like that couldn't stand to see a man cry.

"Well, it's certainly all right with *me*," said Norma, getting up. She walked away and Dave followed her. After a moment, the door closed behind them.

Fish blew his nose, dabbed unobtrusively at his eyes, straightened up bravely and put his handkerchief away. "Mrs. Prentice, I don't s'pose you know that I'm a widower." Her eyes widened a little. "It's true—I lost my dear wife—I don't usually talk about it, as a matter of fact, but somehow—I don't know if you've been bereaved yourself, Mrs. Prentice—"

She said nervously, "Didn't Norma tell you? I'm a widow, Mr. Wilmington."

"No!" said Fish. "Isn't that strange? I felt something—you know, a *vibration*. Well, Mrs. Prentice—can I call you Marie?—you know, after my loss—" time for another tear now; once started, they came easily—"I just went to pieces. I couldn't touch a pencil for a year. And even to this day, I can't draw a line if there's anybody watching me. Now—there's the reason for this whole mixup. That business about my nephew and all, that was just a story I made up to make things a little easier. That's what I *thought*. I don't know, I'm so clumsy where it takes a little tact, I'm just like a bull in a china closet, Marie. And that's the whole story."

He sat back, blew his nose vigorously again.

Mrs. Prentice's eyes were moist, but her handsome face had a wary expression. "I honestly don't know what to think, Mr. Wilmington. You say you can't draw in public—"

"Call me George. You see, it's what psychologists call a *trauma*—"

"Well, how would this be? I'll step outside for a few minutes and you draw a picture. Now I think that would be—"

Fish was shaking his head sadly. "It's worse than I told you. I can't draw *anywhere* except in one room in my house—I've got it fixed up with her picture, and some mementoes—" He gulped hard, but decided against a third tear. "I'm sorry, I'd do it for you if I could, but—"

She sat quietly in thought for a moment. "Then let's say this. You go home, Mr. Wilmington, and draw something—a sketch of me, my face, from memory. I believe any competent artist could do that?"

Fish hesitated, not liking to say yes or no.

"Now, you see, that will settle it. You couldn't get a snapshot of me and send it off to Wisconsin—there wouldn't be time. I'll give you, oh, half an hour."

"Half an—"

"That should be enough, shouldn't it? So that when I come to call on you, in half an hour from now, if you have a sketch of me—a likeness—why, then, I'll know that you're telling the truth. If not—"

Boxed in, Fish made the best of it. He got to his feet with a confident smile.

"Well, now, that's fair enough. One thing, I know I could never forget *your* face. And I want to tell you how relieved I am that we had this little talk, incidentally, and— Well, I better go and get that drawing started. I'll expect you in half an hour, Marie!"

He paused at the door.

"I'll be there—George," she said.

Grunting and twitching, Fish stormed into the house, banging doors behind him. Place was a mess—sofa cushions and newspapers all over the living room—but never mind, she might marry him to clean up his house. Thing was—he unlocked the private room, feverishly swept the cover off the big machine, and began pushing buttons on one of the banks—thing was, get that sketch made. One chance in—how many? But better than no chance at all.

He switched on the machine, watched in helpless impatience while the arms drifted out and hung motionless.

A face—and a likeness! Only hope he had was to put it together from bits and pieces. Nothing left now that would work in the whole machine but some useless items, mechanical drawings and architecture, and a few scraps of anatomy. Let there be enough for one more face—and let it be something like Marie's face!

The machine clicked suddenly and began to trace a line. Fish stood over it in hand-wringing anxiety, watching how the combined motion of the two revolving pivots translated the straight push of the arm into a subtle line. Pretty thing to watch, even if he never could like what it made. Now here it came curving around —now the arm was lifting, going back—

A nose! It was drawing a nose!

It was a kind of Greek statue nose, shapely but thick, not much like Marie's fine curved nose, but never mind, he could talk her into it—give him the raw material, he could always sell—let there be *any* kind of female face, so long as it wasn't ugly—

Come on now, an eye!

But the arms stopped and hung motionless again. The machine hummed quietly; the dials were lit; nothing happened.

Eaten by impatience, Fish looked at his watch, clapped his palm over it, swore, wandered rapidly out of the room. Sometimes, lately, the machine would just sit like that for minutes at a time, as if it were trying and trying to work, but somehow not succeeding, and then click, away it would go again. He hurried back, looked—still nothing—and went off, pacing the empty rooms, looking for something to do.

There was some mail in the basket under the letter drop, he noticed for the first time. Mostly bills—he threw them behind the sofa—but one was a long, bulky brown envelope with "Encyclopaedia Britannica Library Research Service" in the corner.

It had been so long ago, it took him a moment to remember. A couple of weeks after he sent in his letter, there had been a polite printed postcard acknowledging it, then nothing for months. Somewhere along the line he had decided he wasn't going to get an answer; there wasn't any such language . . .

Well, let's see. He picked the end of the envelope open.

His restless eye was caught by the dining room clock. Look at the *time!* Clutching the envelope forgetfully, he rushed into the private room again. The machine was still sitting motionless, humming, lit. There was nothing on the paper but a nose.

Fish pounded on the side of the big machine, with no result except to his fist, and then on the bank that was in use. Nothing. He turned away, noticed he was still holding the envelope, and irritably plucked out the papers inside.

There was a stiff orange folder, stapled at the top. When he lifted the cover, there was a single sheet of paper inside. At the top, the Britannica letterhead, and "V. A. Sternback, Director." Then, in the middle, "SWEDISH WORDS."

His eyes ran down the list, startled. There were all the words he had copied off, and, opposite each one, a word in English. *Teckning* . . . drawing. *Mönster* . . . pattern. *Utplana* . . . to erase. *Användning* . . . application, use.

Fish looked up. Then that was why nothing had happened when he pressed the "Utplana" button—he'd always tried it before the machine made a drawing, never while there was a finished one on the board. Now why hadn't he thought of that? Yes, and here was *Avsla* . . . to reject. And *slutsatsen* . . . completion. "To reject a drawing before completion, press . . ." He'd never done that, either.

What about the middle button? *Torka* . . . to wipe. To wipe? Let's see, there was another word—*Avlägsna*, that was it—sometimes the phrase "*Avlägsna ett mönster*" would be running through his head when he was half awake, like a whispered warning. Here it was. *Avlägsna . . .* to remove.

His hands were shaking. "To remove a pattern from bank after use, press button 'Wipe.'"

He let the folder fall. All this time, not knowing, he'd been systematically using up the precious patterns in the machine, throwing them away one by one, until now there was nothing left—just eight big hunks of useless machinery, made for somebody somewhere who spoke Swedish . . .

The machine clicked softly and the other arm began to move. It traced a graceful upright line, some distance in front of the nose. It looped over and came back down again, then up . . .

Somewhere distant, the doorbell rang imperiously.

Fish stared mesmerized at the paper. The moving point traced another graceful open loop, then another, like a squeezed-together roller coaster. Then another one, moving inexorably and without hurry: now there were four. Without pausing, it extended the last line downward and then brought it across. The line met the tip of the nose and curved back.

The four open loops were fingers. The fifth one was a thumb.

The machine, humming quietly, withdrew its arms into their recesses. After a moment, the lights went dark and the hum stopped.

Outside, the doorbell rang again, and went on ringing.

Personnel Problem

BY H. L. GOLD

Dowd caught hold of a stanchion and braced himself—it was easier to be forceful when you didn't float off the ground with every word.

He said persuasively: "You can still change your mind, Eggleston. Where are you going to get another job like this? Look, you've been getting ten shares—how about if we make it twelve? The committee will go along. That's eighty thousand dollars a year, man!"

"No," said Eggleston.

"Be reasonable! Ceres isn't as bad as all that. As asteroids go, it's in a class by itself. Maybe we're a little cramped, but we're still getting organized—why, next year we'll have it fixed up so you can get annual leave on Earth and—"

"No!" said Eggleston, even more positively than before.

Dowd blew through his nostrils, once, hard, a snort of anger and exasperation. Being general manager of the miners' co-op that had the Ceres franchise was an unrelieved headache. Here he was promising this nincompoop Eggleston twelve shares—he himself had only three, and an able-bodied vacuum-miner, risk-

ing his life and his health every day, got only one. And all because Eggleston had an engineering degree!

"It isn't the money," Eggleston said. "*You* know what it is."

"No," said Dowd grimly. "I don't know."

Eggleston looked longingly at the open port of the ship. He hesitated and set down his bag—eight hundred and fifty pounds of
personal belongings and equipment. It would weigh that much
on Earth; here it was only a feather-light balloon.

He said tiredly: "I've told you dozens of times. I don't see why
I'm bothering to tell you again. You didn't understand it before
and you won't understand it now."

"Try me!" said Dowd. "Maybe I'll finally get it!"

"All right. There's no work for me here, Dowd. And who wants
to live inside a chunk of rock?"

"Two thousand of us do!"

"Then do it!" snapped Eggleston. "Not me! I'm tired of never
seeing the sun—except through filters, after I put on a spacesuit.
I'm tired of breathing last year's air. I'm tired of living with two
thousand miners and their squalling brats, all cooped up in an
oversized mine shaft. And when it comes right down to it, Dowd,
I'm tired of you! That's why I'm leaving—right now, at fourteen
twenty-two hours on June third, mean solar time, and you can
take your twelve shares and—"

"Okay, okay," Dowd broke in. "So long."

He slipped his shoes back into the magnetic galoshes that held
him to the floor and clumped, teetering, away.

Behind him, he heard the shrill mechanical whine of the lock
motors, sealing off the chamber where the rocket ship lay, and
then the pumps that sucked the air out of the giant lock. When
the lock was empty, the outer panels whined open, the noise
coming shrilly through the rock; there was a sharp, shattering jar
as the rockets started—then silence.

Dowd didn't even look around. It wasn't very interesting any
more. Eggleston wasn't the first engineer to depart in a huff. He
was the seventeenth, and the whole process was becoming un-
pleasantly familiar.

Dowd took the elevator down and reported failure to the rest of the managing committee. They accepted the news without comment; they were getting used to it too.

Manson, the gray-haired supply manager, was the nearest to cheerful of the lot—it wasn't his problem. Except that, of course, production was everybody's problem; if there wasn't enough production, there wasn't enough pay. Still, he was able to say: "Well, that's that. What do we do now?"

Dowd said glumly: "Call a general meeting. We'll have to put it up to the whole membership."

Traffic Manager Pickett scowled. "Put what up? We haven't got an engineer and we're not likely to get one. What's to discuss?"

Dowd shrugged, wishing he had the guts to call the ship back and join Eggleston in leaving this place. "The only thing we can do, as I see it, is try to get along without an engineer for a while. But that's a matter of Policy."

Manson nodded. Policy required a general meeting; everybody knew that. He reached over, picked up the P.A. microphone, flipped it on and spoke into it: "Attention, everyone. Attention, everyone. General meeting in the Common at—" he glanced at his watch—"fifteen hundred hours exactly."

The committee was down at the mouth, but the miners didn't seem perturbed. It was a kind of holiday for them. There wasn't much doing inside the 488-mile diameter of Ceres, and even a general meeting, that invariable precursor of trouble, was better than nothing.

The miners and their families came up out of the rock-built "houses"—really cubicles. *Really*, said the more disgruntled inhabitants, caves. They were laid out in geometrically straight streets in the great, high-ceilinged chamber under the surface of the asteroid. They were not notably pretty or comfortable, but they would do. Enormous sun lamps hung, violet-glowing, on spindly cables from the ceiling; giant street ventilators sucked out the old air and pumped in—well, the same air, but dried, cooled, de-carboned and re-oxidated.

It sounded like the noise of wind in trees—or, anyway, that's what Dowd was in the habit of saying in his wheedling letters to prospective members of the co-op. Actually, what it sounded like was ventilators.

As general manager, Dowd led the committee toward the Common at the center of town. It was the community's showplace—synthetic grass, imitation trees, even a small pool that used to have the unpleasant habit of creeping up over its margins and drenching everything around. This was due to a combination of the high surface-tension of water and the low gravity in the interior of Ceres; and the only thing that could be done about it was to roof the thing over with glass, which more or less spoiled the effect. From a distance, though, it didn't look bad, particularly when you observed the surrounding shops, the theater, the restaurant.

Dowd couldn't see any grass at all this time, not even the glassed-over pool. Every square foot of the Common was covered with people. Dowd climbed to the bandstand—once there really had been a band there, and dancing on the green; but that hadn't worked too well either, because the low gravity made even the best dancers prone to fall all over their partners.

He picked up the loud-hailer and addressed the crowd. In a few brief words, he told the miners what they already knew, and outlined the problem they had already faced: "We don't have an engineer. We aren't likely to get one. We have to try to get along without one; and that's the size of it. Now," Dowd went on, "I'll entertain a motion that we proceed on our own power."

He got his motion and it was passed unanimously—if you could call it that. At least, there weren't any "nay" votes, but there were also only a scattering of "ayes;" and if the expressions on the faces of the two thousand miners and their families had been ballots, the whole Ceres Mining Cooperative would have faced a veto that afternoon.

The committee went back to its work. The miners returned to their homes. The whole community kept its fingers crossed, fearing the worst—

And, two days later, an oversize blast went off and one-nineteenth of the asteroid of Ceres was blown away into space.

First concern was casualties. Dowd raced into a pressure suit and headed a party that grappled and clung its way around the mottled rock surface of the asteroid to where the accident had occurred. They found the miners—sheepish enough, pinioned under what, on Earth, would have been tons of rock, some of them; but unhurt.

The second concern was the airtightness of the living quarters —and that, thank heaven, thought Dowd, was still all right. The blast had occurred seventy miles from the town-cavern.

The third concern was—the Solar System Conservation Society.

Dowd returned to the main operations area and boarded a scout rocket with Manson and Simon Brodsky, the accountant. They jetted a few miles out into space, arrested their relative motion and took a good long look.

Asteroid Ceres looked like a cake with a big chunk hacked out of it.

"Oh, my God," groaned Brodsky. "Now we're in for it."

Dowd said shortly: "I know."

Manson said: "What happened? Did you find out?"

Dowd shrugged. "They had the charge all figured, and then they got worried it wasn't enough, so they added more. They were so busy arguing, they tied in with the stored explosive and the whole business went up. Lucky they weren't all killed—maybe all of the rest of us, too."

"You can say lucky if you want to," Brodsky complained. "I'm not so sure. This is going to cost us our franchise, you know."

Manson said: "You mean the Solar System Conservationists?"

"What else? Our contract said we couldn't do anything that would affect the external appearance or the orbit of Ceres. Believe me, this does both. *Look* at it!"

They looked, in an atmosphere of gloom. "Curse them," Dowd said angrily. "It's a bloody big slice, all right."

It was. The raw cut was as deep and wide as a sea, and the undiffused sunlight cast a space-black shadow that made it seem even deeper and more naked among the jagged asteroidal peaks.

"There's no doubt about it," Dowd added. "Palomar will spot that next time they look this way—if a liner from one of the outer planets doesn't beat them to it."

"Wait a minute," said Brodsky thoughtfully. "There *aren't* any liners this time of year—none of the big planets are in opposition."

"Well?"

"And Palomar isn't going to bother with us till it has to. Listen," Brodsky went on, growing excited, "what if we get that piece and stick it back?"

Dowd stared. "Do *what?*"

"You heard me," Brodsky insisted. "Why not?"

Dowd looked at him in astonishment. He began to laugh—until he realized that Brodsky was serious, and then he got annoyed. "That's crazy. We're miners, Brodsky. We dig out; we don't put back."

Manson interrupted: "No, listen to him. Why shouldn't we?"

Dowd rubbed his square jaw, squinting down at the asteroid. "Well—I don't know, maybe it's an idea. Certainly we couldn't be any worse off—"

"Let's try it," Brodsky urged eagerly. "What can we lose?"

It was a very good question and they all knew the answer. "All by ourselves," Dowd mused. "No engineer to tell us what to do; no experience in this sort of thing . . . Well, you're right, Brodsky. We don't have any choice, do we?"

What had happened to Ceres was this: A wedge of rock had flown off into space, like an axehead hurled off the handle; it was getting farther away every second, and it had picked up a fair amount of spin. Moreover, the remaining eighteen-nineteenths of Ceres had acquired, by natural law, an equal and opposite thrust, seriously disturbing its own orbit.

The ore freighter department head checked in. "Yeah, we've got the ships," he said. "We've got eight that we can use for towing, which is enough. We can kill the spin, sure. Don't worry about that. We'll get the chunk back to Ceres, right over the cavity. Then it's up to the ground crews to take over. Of course," he added, "we'll need an engineer to check our acceleration and bearings and all that, you know. Say, when is the new engineer going to—"

"Thanks," Dowd said bitterly. "Thanks a lot. Just stand by. I'll let you know."

The loading section foreman was less confident, but he grudgingly agreed that the problem of getting the chunk back down in place wasn't impossible. He dragged Dowd to his drafting office and showed him the plans his section had made. They all gathered around his desk, arguing over a diagram.

"See," the foremen said, "I guess we could winch it down, like. From the bottom and sides, you understand? It might mean losing a few winches underneath, but I guess it's cheaper than losing the franchise."

"Hold on," Dowd said sharply. "You *guess* you can winch it down? It *might* mean losing a couple of winches?"

"Well, what do you expect me to say?" the foremen demanded righteously. "I'm no engineer."

"Damn it," exploded Dowd, "you've been doing this kind of work for twenty years! All Eggleston would have done is check over your own diagram. Why can't you do that?"

The foreman said stubbornly: "Stress factors, things like that— what do I know about them, Dowd? It *looks* all right, but how can I say for sure?"

Dowd pulled his lips over his teeth and sought out the head blaster.

The blaster pointed out: "I ain't an engineer, but the way it looks to me, we can fuse the wedge in place once the loading section gets it down. See, like we did when we put in the cargo lock for the rockets, remember?"

Dowd asked: "And do you think fusing it would hold it in place permanently, allowing for orbital spin and gravitational—"

The blaster spread his hands. "How do I know? Now if I were an engineer—"

"That's what I thought," said Dowd. "I'll let you know."

Dowd called the Managing Committee meeting to order in the board room. He locked the door and started the tape recorder; for several minutes, it recorded only his profane remarks about lack of guts and self-confidence.

"Hold it, Dowd," Manson said at last. "We've most of us dug all our lives—all but Brodsky. That's why he doesn't know the problems in a job like this. There are all kinds of tricky things involved."

"Like what?" Dowd savagely wanted to know.

Manson snapped: "If I could tell you that, I'd be an engineer."

Dowd drummed his fist on the desk. "Ah, what's the use?

Sometimes I wish this wasn't a co-op. If I was a real boss, I'd just give the orders—and they'd damn well do what they were told, engineer or no engineer."

Pickett glanced up at him thoughtfully, and then returned to what he was doing—paring his cuticles with a little knife. He said: "You can't, Dowd. I'd quit. I don't blame the men; I wouldn't work on anything as ticklish as that hunk of rock without an engineer. That's the way it is. On routine operations, maybe we could get along—but this isn't routine."

"Oh, the hell with it," Dowd said in disgust. "Here, let me tell you something. You know why we can't keep an engineer? *Because we don't need one.* Our boys have done everything that *can* be done with our equipment so often that they can do it in their sleep—yes, even like dragging a hunk of Ceres back to where it belongs! It's only the same things they've been doing, on a slightly larger scale. They only want an engineer to yes them because they don't have confidence. That's why we've lost seventeen engineers, one after another—they want *work*, not just a soft berth."

"So?"

"So—I don't know." Dowd spread his hands, baffled. "I don't blame the engineers. When a man gets a degree, he wants to use it. Not just look at radar soundings—which are read for him—and approve charge formulas—which are all worked out for him—and read loading schedules and shoring diagrams and—hell, the entire job! That's why we can't keep them. And that's why we don't need them, even now."

Pickett didn't look up. "No engineer, no job," he said softly, and the rest of the room murmured agreement.

Dowd sat down heavily and stared at the ceiling. It was an impasse.

Brodsky cleared his throat. "You know," he said, "my sister Molly has a boy, David. He wanted to be a violinist, but she made him go to mining college."

Manson lifted his head questioningly. "He's probably got some nice job in a nice place," he grumbled. "You don't think he'd quit some other place just to—"

"Oh, he doesn't have a job yet," said Brodsky. He counted on his fingers, nodding. "Yes, he's just getting out of school now. I remember because my niece Leah got married when he was in his sophomore year and—"

"All right! All right! What are you getting at, Brodsky? You think you can get the kid before somebody else signs him up?"

Brodsky looked surprised. "Yes."

Manson looked interested. "What do you think, Dowd?"

Dowd banged the table. "Brodsky," he roared, "why didn't you say something about this before? Get to it, man! If he's a relative, maybe there's a chance he'll stick—anyway, even if he only stays long enough to get the damned asteroid stuck together again, that's something! Look—" he figured rapidly—"we'll get one of the oreboats to haul you to where you can pick up a liner. Pickett, you get on the radio and find out who's in port. Manson, you get the freight section ready to take Brodsky in. Move!"

"Right!" Manson smiled. "Then we've got a chance. With a mining engineer, we can do the job."

"Yeah." Suddenly Dowd sat back again. "But only the job," he said wearily. "Then we're on our own. Relative or not, he'll never stay."

"Oh, he'll stay," Brodsky promised. "I guarantee he'll stay."

As usual in unusual situations, the membership of the Ceres Mining Cooperative was in the community square when Brodsky brought his nephew, David Bookbinder, down from the landing area.

David was a tall boy, not entirely filled out yet, with light hair that had four great waves in it—a feature that the miners' wives and daughters approved—and a long, sensitive face. He wore strong contact lenses—a feature that the minors approved; it was evidence of studiousness.

Brodsky proudly introduced him first to the managing committee and then to the foremen of the various crews, who took him around to meet the members and their families. David held a violin case in his left hand and shook with his right, smiling gently and looking a little overwhelmed. He had to show his handsome diploma over and over to the awed and respectful miners.

Dowd, Brodsky, Pickett and Manson stood near the bandstand

and watched the lad answer questions, moving shyly from one group to another.

"They like him," said Dowd.

Brodsky nodded, pleased. "He was worried about that. I told him once in a while, say a couple of times a month, he could give a violin concert here. That would keep him happy. And who knows, people might enjoy it."

"They'll enjoy *anything* he does," Dowd said enthusiastically. "Speaking of keeping him happy, we ought to work that out in detail."

Brodsky waved his hand. "Later, later. First we put Ceres back together. Then we worry about that."

"Oh, that's no problem now," Dowd assured him. "We're all set. The wedge is being towed back—the crews began that the minute we got your spacegram, saying you and David were on the way. Now he's got the data from the other sections to go over —but that won't take long."

"No, that's true," Brodsky agreed. "He'll be glad to look it over."

"And then what?" asked Manson. "Do we lose him like the others? I'll tell you what. I'm for voting him fifteen shares, Dowd. Why not? We could build him a big rock house down in some nice section of town—put in a bar, a ballroom, whatever he wants. And we can get him a little electrocar—maybe even a chauffeur, if he wants—"

"Sure!" added Pickett. "Listen, why not get a little private rocket? It could be his—let him go to Mars once in a while. You know? Maybe the rest of us could use it when he didn't mind— but it would be his all the same. And we can put through that leave plan right away—what the devil, why not give the guy a couple months a year on Earth or Mars? With pay, naturally. And the town looks a little drab—we could spray-paint it. And a mist machine up at the ceiling to give us a blue sky and white drifting clouds—"

"You're crazy!" cried Dowd, outraged. "He's just an engineer, you idiots! No engineer is worth it!"

Manson scowled blackly. "You say that?" he demanded. "After we've messed ourselves up trying to get along without one?"

Brodsky was polishing his glasses. "Gentlemen," he begged,

looking distressed. "Please, we don't have to go to all that trouble. He's just a boy. The place is fine—maybe we could dress it up a little, like you say. But for us, not for David. David will stay, I assure you, and he'll be happy with the usual ten shares and our old engineer's quarters."

Wonderingly, Pickett said: "You've got more influence with your relatives than me with mine."

"Sure," said Brodsky. "Say, Dowd, can I talk to you for a minute?"

Dowd shrugged. The others nodded and walked off toward the group around the colony's new engineer.

Dowd said suspiciously: "Well?"

Brodsky cleared his throat. "The fact is," he said, "David wanted to be a violinist, as I told you. But he went to mining college to please his mother—"

"As you told me. I know. What about it?"

"Well," Brodsky said hesitantly, "there was just a little trouble about his grades." He took a petty cash voucher out of his pocket. "I have here—"

"Wait a minute! What are you trying to tell me, Brodsky? He's an engineer, isn't he? I saw his diploma with my own eyes!"

"Oh, yes," Brodsky assured him. "Of course you did. Everybody did—a beautiful diploma, right? Nice sheepskin. Nice lettering. That's what this bill I have here is—five dollars for parchment, forty dollars hand lettering. I also," he added, "invested quite a lot for rosin and violin strings and things like that, but I want to pay for those myself. Call it a present for my nephew."

"A graduation present?" Dowd asked, more than a bit baffled.

"Well—" Brodsky was a little embarrassed—"not exactly. You see, there was the thing with his grades. So I promised him that here things would be all right—he could practice his fiddle as much as he wanted; all we'd want from him is that once in a while he had to look over whatever the foremen brought him and say yes. Easy? He thought so. But it's worth it to us."

Dowd swallowed hard. "You mean—" he started, and had to pause to swallow again. "You mean he isn't really—"

Brodsky shrugged. "A technicality. He's been to school? He's got a degree? What more does he need?"

"But—but suppose the data's wrong! Suppose the foremen make a mistake and—"

Brodsky was shaking his head. "Never!" he said positively. "Besides, David isn't entirely ignorant. He may not be an engineer to other engineers, but to a miner, believe me, he's an engineer."

The Number of the Beast

BY FRITZ LEIBER

"I wish," said the Young Captain, police chief of High Chicago, the turbulent satellite that hangs over the meridian of the midwestern groundside city, "I wish that sometimes the telepathic races of the Galaxy weren't such consistent truth-tellers and silence-keepers."

"Your four suspects are all telepaths?" the Old Lieutenant asked.

"Yes. I also wish I had more than half an hour to decide which one to accuse. But Earthside has muscled into the case and the pressure is on. If I can't reason it out, I must make a guess. A bare half-hour they give me."

"Then perhaps you shouldn't waste it with a pensioned-off old louey."

The Young Captain shook his head decisively. "No. You think. You have time to now."

The Old Lieutenant smiled. "Sometimes I wish I hadn't. And I doubt if I can give you any special angles on telepaths, Jim. It's true I've lately been whiling away the time on informal study of alien thought systems with Khla-Khla the Martian, but—"

"I didn't come to you looking for a specialist on telepathy," the Young Captain asserted sharply.

"Very well then, Jim. You know what you're doing. Let's hear your case. And give me background. I don't keep up with the news."

The Young Captain looked skeptical. "Everyone in High Chicago has heard about the murder—not two furlongs from here—of the representative of the Arcturian peace party."

"I haven't," the Old Lieutenant said. "Who are the Arcturians? I tell you, for an oldster like me, the Now is just one more historical period. Better consult someone else, Jim."

"No. The Arcturians are the first non-related humanoid race to turn up in the Galaxy. Non-related to Earth humans, that is. True, they have three eyes, and six fingers on each hand, but they are hairless mammalian bipeds just the same. One of their females is the current burlesque sensation of the Star and Garter."

"The police found that a good spot to keep their eyes on in my day too," the Old Lieutenant recalled, nodding. "Are the Arcturians telepaths?"

"No. I'll come to the telepathy angle later. The Arcturians are split into two parties: those who want to enter the Commerce Union and open their planets to alien starships, including Earth's —the peace party, in short—and those who favor a policy of strict non-intercourse which, as far as we know, always ultimately leads to war. The war party is rather the stronger of the two. Any event may tip the balance."

"Such as a representative of the peace party coming quietly to Earth and getting himself bumped before he even gets down from High Chicago?"

"Exactly. It looks bad, Sean. It looks as if *we* wanted war. The other member peoples of the Commerce Union are skeptical enough already about the ultimate peacefulness of Earth's intentions toward the whole Galaxy. They look on the Arcturian situation as a test. They say that we accepted the Polarians and Antareans and all the rest as equals simply because they *are* so different from us in form and culture—it's easy to admit theoretical equality with a bumblebee, say, and then perhaps do him dirt afterward.

"But, our galactic critics ask, will Earthmen be so ready or willing to admit equality with a humanoid race? It's sometimes harder, you know, to agree that your own brother is a human being than to grant the title to an anonymous peasant on the other side of the globe. They say—I continue to speak for our galactic critics—that Earthmen will openly work for peace with Arcturus while secretly sabotaging it."

"Including murder."

"Right, Sean. So unless we can pin this crime on aliens—best of all on extremists in the Arcturian war party (something I believe but can in no way prove)—the rumor will go through the Union that Earth wants war, while the Arcturian Earth-haters will have everything their own way."

"Leave off the background, Jim. How was the murder done?"

Permitting himself a bitter smile, the Young Captain said wistfully, "With the whole Galaxy for a poison cabinet and a weapon shop, with almost every means available of subtle disguise, of sudden approach and instantaneous getaway—everything but time machine, and some crook will come along with that any day now—the murder had to be done with a blunt instrument and by one of four aliens domiciled in the same caravansary as the Arcturian peace-party man.

"There's something very ugly, don't you think, in the vision of a blackjack gripped by the tentacle of an octopoid or in the pinchers of a black Martian? To be frank, Sean, I'd rather the killer had been fancier in his *modus operandi*. It would have let me dump the heavy end of the case in the laps of the science boys."

"I was always grateful myself when I could invoke the physicists," the Old Lieutenant agreed. "It's marvelous what colored lights and the crackle of Geiger counters do to take the pressure off a plain policeman. These four aliens you mention are the telepaths?"

"Right, Sean. Shady characters, too, all four of them, criminals for hire, which makes it harder. And each of them takes the typical telepath point of view—Almighty, how it exasperates me! —that we ought to *know* which one of them is guilty without asking questions! They know well enough that Earthmen aren't telepathic, but still they hide behind the lofty pretense that every intelligent inhabitant of the Cosmos *must be* telepathic.

"If you come right out and tell them that your mind is absolutely deaf-dumb-and-blind to the thoughts of others, they act as if you'd made a dreadful social blunder and they cover up for you by pretending not to have heard you. Talk about patronizing—! Why, they're like a woman who is forever expecting you to know what it is she's angry about without ever giving you a hint what it is. They're like—"

"Now, now, I've dealt with a few telepaths in my time, Jim. I take it that the other prong of your dilemma is that if you officially accuse one of them, *and you hit it right*, then he will up and confess like a good little animal, using the ritual of speech to tell you who commissioned the murder and all the rest of it, and everything will be rosy.

"But *if you hit it wrong*, it will be a mortal insult to his whole race—to all telepaths, for that matter—and there will be whole solar systems moving to resign from the Union and all manner of other devils to pay. Because, continuing the telepath's fiction that you are a telepath yourself, you must have known he was innocent and yet you accused him."

"Most right, Sean," the Young Captain admitted ruefully. "As I said at the beginning, truth-tellers and silence-keepers—intellectual prigs, all of them! Refusing to betray each other's thoughts to a non-telepath, I can understand that—though just one telepathic stoolpigeon would make police work ten mountains easier. But all these other lofty idealistic fictions do get my goat! If I were running the Union—"

"Jim, your time is running short. I take it you want help in deciding which one to accuse. That is, if you *do* decide to chance it rather than shut your mouth, lose face and play for time."

"I've got to chance it, Sean—Earthside demands it. But as things stand, I'll be backing no better than a three-to-one shot. For you see, Sean, every single suspect of the four is just as suspect as the others. In my book, they're four equally bad boys."

"Sketch me your suspects then, quickly." The Old Lieutenant closed his eyes.

"There's Tlik-Tcha the Martian," the Young Captain began,

ticking them off on his fingers. "A nasty black beetle, that one. Held his breath for twenty minutes and then belched it in my face. Kept printing 'No Comment' white-on-black on his chest to whatever I asked him. In Garamond type!"

"Cheer up, Jim. It might have been Rustic Capitals. Next."

"Hlilav the Antarean multibrach. Kept gently waving his tentacles all through the interrogation—I thought he was trying to hypnotize me! Then it occurred to me he might be talking in code, but the interpreter said no. At the end, he gives a long insulting whistle, like some shameless swish. Whistle didn't signify anything either, the interpreter said, beyond a polite wish for my serenity.

"Third customer was Fa the Rigelian composite. Took off a limb—real, of course, not artificial—and kept fiddling with it while I shot questions at him. I could hardly keep my mind on what I was saying—expected him to take his head off next! He did that too, just as he started back to his cell."

"Telepaths can surely be exasperating," the Old Lieutenant agreed. "I always had great trouble in keeping in mind what a boring business a vocal interview must be to them—very much as if a man, quite capable of speech, should insist on using pencil and paper to conduct a conversation with you, with perhaps the further proviso that you print your remarks stylishly. Your fourth suspect, Jim?"

"Hrohrakak the Polarian centipedal. He reared up in a great question-mark bend when I addressed him—looked very much like a giant cobra covered with thick black fur. Kept chattering to himself too, very low—interpreter said he was saying over and over again, 'Oh, All-father, when will this burden be lifted from me?' Halfway through, he reaches out a little black limb to Donovan to give him what looks like a pretty pink billiard ball."

"Oh, naughty, naughty," the Old Lieutenant observed, shaking his head while he smiled. "So these are your four suspects, Jim? The four rather gaudy racehorses of whom you must back one?"

"They are. Each of them had opportunity. Each of them has a criminal reputation and might well have been hired to do the murder—either by extremists in the Arcturian war party or by some other alien organization hostile to Earth—such as the League of the Beasts with its pseudo-religious mumbo-jumbo."

"I don't agree with you about the League, but don't forget our own bloody-minded extremists," the Old Lieutenant reminded him. "There are devils among us too, Jim."

"True, Sean. But whoever paid for this crime, any one of the four might have been his agent. For to complete the problem and tie it up in a Gordian knot a yard thick, each one of my suspects has recently and untraceably received a large sum of money—enough so that, in each case, it might well have paid for murder."

Leaning forward, the Old Lieutenant said, "So? Tell me about that, Jim."

"Well, you know the saying that the price of a being's life anywhere in the Galaxy is one thousand of whatever happens to be the going unit of big money. And, as you know, it's not too bad a rule of thumb. In this case, the unit is gold martians, which are neither gold nor backed by Mars's bitter little bureaucracy, but—"

"I know! You've only minutes left, Jim. What were the exact amounts?"

"Hlilav the Antarean multibrach had received 1024 gold martians, Hrohrakak the Polarian centipedal 1000 gold martians, Fa the Rigelian composite 1728 gold martians, Tlik-Tcha the Martian coleopteroid 666 gold martians."

"Ah—" the Old Lieutenant said very softly. "The number of the beast."

"Come again, Sean?"

" 'Here is wisdom,' " quoted the Old Lieutenant, still speaking very softly. " 'Let him that hath understanding count the number of the beast: for it is the number of a man'; *Revelation* chapter thirteen, verse eighteen. *Revelation*, Jim, the last book in the Bible."

"I know that," the Young Captain burst out excitedly. "I also know the next words, if only because they're a favorite with numerology crackpots—of whom I see quite a few at the station. The next words are: 'and his number is Six hundred threescore and six.' Almighty, that's Tlik-Tcha's—that's the number of his gold martians! And we've always known that the League of the Beasts got some of its mumbo-jumbo from Earth, so why not from its Bible? Sean, you clever old devil, I'm going to play your hunch." The Young Captain sprang up. "I'm going back to the station and have the four of them in and accuse Tlik-Tcha to his face."

The Old Lieutenant lifted a hand. "One moment, Jim," he said sharply. "You're to go back to the station, to be sure, and have the four of them in, yes—but you're to accuse Fa the Rigelian."

The Young Captain almost sat down again, involuntarily. "But that doesn't make sense, Sean," he protested. "Fa's number is 1728. That doesn't fit your clue. It's not the number of the beast."

"Beasts have all sorts of numbers, Jim," the Old Lieutenant said. "The one you want is 1728."

"But your reason, Sean? Give me your reason."

"No. There's no time and you mightn't believe me if I did. You asked for my advice and I've given it to you. Accuse Fa the Rigelian."

"But—"

"That's all, Jim."

Minutes later, the Young Captain was still feeling the slow burn of his exasperation, though he was back at the station and the moment of decision weighed sickeningly upon him. What a fool he'd been, he told himself savagely, to waste his time on such an old dodderer! The nerve of the man, giving out with advice— orders, practically!—that he refused to justify, behaving with the whimsicality, the stubbornness—yes, the insolence!—that only the retired man can afford.

He scanned the four alien faces confronting him across the station desk—Tlik-Tcha's like a section of ebon bowling ball down to the three deeply recessed perceptors, Hrohrakak's a large black floormop faintly quivering, Fa's pale and humanoid, but oversize, like an emperor's death mask, Hlilav's a cluster of serially blinking eyes and greenish jowls. He wished he could toss them all in a bag and reach in—wearing an armor-plated glove—and pick one.

The room stank of disinfectants and unwashed alienity—the familiar reek of the oldtime police station greatly diversified. The Young Captain felt the sweat trickling down his flushed forehead.

He opened wide the louvre behind him and the hum of the satellite's central concourse poured in. It didn't help the atmosphere, but for a moment he felt less constricted.

Then he scanned the four faces once more and the deadline desperation was back upon him. *Pick a number*, he thought, *any number from one to two thousand. Grab a face. Trust to luck. Sean's a stubborn old fool, but the boys always said he had the damnedest luck . . .*

His finger stabbed out. "In the nexus of these assembled minds," he said loudly, "I publish the truth I share with yours, Fa—"

That was all he had time to get out. At his first movement, the Rigelian sprang up, whipped off his head and hurled it straight toward the center of the open louvre.

But if the Young Captain had been unready for thought, he was more than keyed up for action. He snagged the head as it shot past, though he fell off his chair in doing it. The teeth snapped once, futilely. Then a tiny voice from the head spoke the words he'd been praying for: "Let the truth that our minds share be published forth. But first, please, take me back to my breath source . . ."

Next day, the Old Lieutenant and the Young Captain talked it all over.

"So you didn't nab Fa's accomplices in the concourse?" the Old Lieutenant asked.

"No, Sean, they got clean away—as they very likely would have, with Fa's head, if they'd managed to lay their hands on it. Fa wouldn't rat on them."

"But otherwise our fancy-boy killer confessed in full? Told the whole story, named his employers, and provided the necessary evidence to nail them and himself once and for all?"

"He did indeed. When one of those telepath characters does talk, it's a positive pleasure to hear him. He makes it artistic, like an oration from Shakespeare. But now, sir, I want to ask the question you said you didn't have time to answer yesterday—though I'll admit I'm asking it with a little different meaning than when I asked it first. You gave me a big shock then and I'll admit that I'd never have gone along and followed your advice blind the way I did, except that I had nothing else to go on, and I *was* impressed with that Bible quotation you had so pat—until you told me it didn't mean what it seemed to!

"But I *did* follow your advice, and it got me out of one of the worst jams I've ever been in—with a pat on the back from Earthside to boot! So now let me ask you, Sean, in the name of all that's holy, how did you know so surely which one of the four it was?"

"I didn't know, Jim. It's more accurate to say I guessed."

"You old four-flusher! Do you mean to say you just played a lucky hunch?"

"Not quite, Jim. It was a guess, all right, but an educated guess. It all lay in the numbers, of course, the numbers of gold martians, the numbers of our four beasts. Tlik-Tcha's 666 did strongly indicate that he was in the employ of the League of the Beasts, for I understand they are great ones on symbolic actions and like to ring in the number 666 whenever they can. But that gets us just nowhere—the League, though highly critical of most Earthmen, has never shown itself desirous of fomenting interstellar war.

"Hrohrakak's 1000 would indicate that he was receiving money from some organization of Earthmen, or from some alien source that happens also to use the decimal system. *Anyone* operating around Sol would be apt to use the decimal system. Hrohrakak's 1000 points in no one direction.

"Now as to Hlilav's 1024—that number is the tenth power of two. As far as I know, no natural species of being uses the binary system. However, it is the rule with robots. The indications are that Hlilav is working for the Interstellar Brotherhood of Free Business Machines or some like organization, and, as we both know, the robots are not ones to pound the war drums or touch off the war fuses, for they are always the chief sufferers.

"That leaves Fa's 1728. Jim, the first thing you told me about the Arcturians was that they were hexadactylic bipeds. Six fingers on one hand means 12 on two—and almost a mortal certainty that the beings so equipped by nature will be using the duodecimal system, in many ways the most convenient of all. In the duodecimal system, 'one thousand' is not 10 times 10 times 10, but 12 times 12 times 12—which comes out as 1728 exactly in our decimal system.

"As you said, 'one thousand' of the going unit is the price of a being's life. Someone paid 'one thousand' gold martians by an Arcturian would have 1728 in his pocket according to our count.

"The size of Fa's purse seemed to me an odds-on indication that he was in the pay of the Arcturian war party. Incidentally, he must have felt very smart getting that extra 728—a more principled beast-criminal would have scorned to profit from a mere difference in numerical systems."

The Young Captain took some time before he answered. He smiled incredulously more than once, and once he shook his head.

Finally he said, "And you asked me to go ahead, Sean, and make my accusation, with no more indication than that?"

"It worked for you, didn't it?" the Old Lieutenant countered briskly. "And as soon as Fa started to confess, you must have known I was right beyond any possibility of doubt. Telepaths are always truth-tellers."

The Young Captain shot him a very strange look.

"It couldn't be, Sean—?" he said softly. "It couldn't be that you're a telepath yourself? That that's the alien thought system you've been studying with your Martian witch doctor?"

"If it were," the Old Lieutenant replied, "I'd tell—" He stopped. He twinkled. "Or would I?"

the IFTH of OOFTH

BY WALTER S. TEVIS, JR.

Farnsworth had invented a new drink that night. He called it a mulled sloe gin toddy. Exactly as fantastic as it sounds—ramming a red-hot poker into a mugful of warm red gin, cinnamon, cloves and sugar, and then *drinking* the fool thing—but like many of Farnsworth's ideas, it managed somehow to work out. In fact, its flavor had become completely acceptable to me after the third one.

When he finally set the end of his steaming poker back on the coals for rest and regeneration, I leaned back warmly in my big leather chair—the one he had rigged up so that it would gently rock you to sleep if you pressed the right button—and said, "Oliver, your ingenuity is matched only by your hospitality."

Farnsworth blushed and smiled. He is a small, chubby man and blushes easily. "Thank you," he said. "I have another new one. I call it a jelled vodka fizz—you eat it with a spoon. You may want to try it later. It's—well—exceptional."

I suppressed a shudder at the thought of eating jelled vodka and said, "Interesting, very interesting," and since he didn't reply, we both stared at the fire for a while, letting the gin continue its pleasant work. Farnsworth's bachelor's home was very comfortable and relaxing, and I always enjoyed my Wednesday night visits there thoroughly. I suppose most men have a deep-seated love for open fires and liquor—however fantastically prepared—and deep, comfortable leather armchairs.

Then, after several minutes, Farnsworth abruptly bounced to his feet and said, "There's a thing I wanted to show you. Made it last week. Didn't pull it off too well, though."

"Really?" I said. I'd thought the drinks had been his usual weekly brainchild. They seemed quite enough.

"Yes," he said, trotting over to the door of the study. "It's downstairs in the shop. I'll get it." And he bounced out of the room, the paneled door closing as it had opened, automatically, behind him.

I turned back to the fire again, pleased that he had made something in the machine shop—the carpentry shop was in a shed in the backyard; the chemistry and optical labs in the attic—for he was his most proficient with his lathe and milling machines. His self-setting, variable-twist thumb bolt had been a beautiful piece of work and its patent had netted him, as had several other machined devices, a remarkable sum.

He returned in a minute, carrying a very odd-looking thing with him, and set it on the table beside my chair. I examined it silently for a minute while Farnsworth stood over me, half-smiling, his little green eyes wide, sparkling in the reflected, flickering light from the fire. I knew he was suppressing his eagerness for my comment, but I was uncertain what to say.

The thing, upon examination, appeared simple: a more or less cross-shaped construction of several dozen one-inch cubes, half of them of thin, transparent plastic, the other half made of thin little sheets of aluminum. Each cube seemed to be hinged to two others very cunningly and the arrangement of them all was somewhat confusing.

Finally, I said, "How many cubes?" I had tried to count them, but kept getting lost.

"Sixty-four," he said. "I think."

"You *think?*"

"Well—" He seemed embarrassed. "At least I *made* sixty-four cubes, thirty-two of each kind; but somehow I haven't been able to count them since. They seem to . . . get lost, or shift around, or something."

"Oh?" I was becoming interested. "May I pick it up?"

"Certainly," he said, and I took the affair, which was surprisingly lightweight, in my hands and began folding the cubes around on their hinges. I noticed then that some were open on one side and that certain others would fit into these if their hinging arrangements would allow them to.

I began folding them absently and said, "You could count them by marking them one at a time. With a crayon, for instance."

"As a matter of fact," he admitted, blushing again, "I tried that. Didn't seem to work out. When I finished, I found I had marked six cubes with the number one and on none of them could I find a two or three, although there were two fours, one of them written in reverse and in green." He hesitated. "I had used a red marking pencil." I saw him shudder slightly as he said it, although his voice had been casual-sounding enough. "I rubbed the numbers off with a damp cloth and didn't . . . try it again."

"Well," I said. And then, "What do you call it?"

"A pentaract."

He sat back down again in his armchair. "Of course, that name really isn't accurate. I suppose a pentaract should really be a four-dimensional pentagon, and this is meant to be a picture of a five-dimensional cube."

"A *picture?*" It didn't look like a picture to me.

"Well, it couldn't *really* have five-dimensionality—length, width, breadth, ifth and oofth—or I don't think it could." His voice faltered a little at that. "But it's supposed to illustrate what you might call the layout of an object that did have those."

"What kind of object would that be?" I looked back at the thing in my lap and was mildly surprised to see that I had folded a good many of the cubes together.

"Suppose," he said, "you put a lot of points in a row, touching; you have a line—a one-dimensional figure. Put four lines together at right angles and on a plane; a square—two-dimensional. Six squares at right angles and extended into real space give you a cube—three dimensions. And eight cubes extended into four physical dimensions give you a tesseract, as it's called—"

"And eight tesseracts make a pentaract," I said. "Five dimensions."

"Exactly. But naturally this is just a picture of a pentaract, in that sense. There probably isn't any ifth and oofth at all."

"I still don't know what you mean by a *picture*," I said, pushing the cubes around interestedly.

"You don't?" he asked, pursing his lips. "It's rather awkward to explain, but . . . well, on the surface of a piece of paper, you can make a very realistic picture of a cube—you know, with perspective and shading and all that kind of thing—and what you'd actually be doing would be illustrating a three-dimensional object, the cube, by using only two dimensions to do it with."

"And of course," I said, "you could *fold* the paper into a cube. Then you'd have a real cube."

He nodded. "But you'd have to *use* the third dimension—by folding the flat paper *up*—to do it. So, unless I could fold my cubes up through ifth or oofth, my pentaract will have to be just a poor picture. Or, really, eight pictures. Eight tesseracts, pictures of four-dimensional objects, stuck together to make a picture of five dimensions."

"Well!" I said, a bit lost. "And what do you plan to use it for?"

"Just curiosity." And then, abruptly, looking at me now, his eyes grew wide and he bumped up out of his chair. He said breathlessly, "What have you done to it?"

I looked down at my hands. I was holding a little structure of eight cubes, joined together in a small cross. "Why, nothing," I said, feeling a little foolish. "I only folded most of them together."

"That's impossible! There were only twelve open ones to begin with! All of the others were six-sided!"

Farnsworth made a grab for it, apparently beside himself, and the gesture was so sudden that I drew back. It made Farnsworth miss his grab and the little object flew from my hands and hit the floor, solidly, on one of its corners. There was a slight bump as it hit, and a faint clicking noise, and the thing seemed to crumple in a very peculiar way. And sitting in front of us on the floor was one little one-inch cube, and nothing else.

For at least a full minute, we stared at it. Then I stood up and looked in my chair seat, looked around the floor of the room, even got down on my knees and peered under the chair. Farnsworth was watching me, and when I finished and sat down again, he asked, "No others?"

"No other cubes," I said, "anywhere."

"I was afraid of that." He pointed an unsteady finger at the one cube in front of us. "I suppose they're all in there." Some of his agitation had begun to wear off—you can, I suppose, get used to anything—and after a moment he said thoughtfully, "What was that you said about folding the paper to make a cube?"

I looked at him and managed an apologetic smile. I had been thinking the same thing. "What was that *you* said about having to go into another dimension to do it?"

He didn't smile back, but he got up and said, "Well, I doubt if it can bite," and bent over and picked the cube up, hefting its weight carefully in his hand. "It seems to weigh the same as the —sixty-four did," he said, quite calmly now. Then he looked at it closely and suddenly became agitated again. "Good heavens! Look at this!" He held it up.

On one side, exactly in the center, was a neat little hole, about a half-inch across.

I moved my head closer to the cube and saw that the hole was not really circular. It was like the iris diaphragm of a camera, a polygon made of many overlapping, straight pieces of metal, allowing an opening for light to enter. Nothing was visible through the hole; I could see only an undefined blackness.

"I don't understand how . . ." I began, and stopped.

"Nor I," he said. "Let's see if there's anything in here."

He put the cube up to his eye and squinted and peered for a minute. Then he carefully set it on the table, walked to his chair, sat down and folded his hands over his fat little lap.

"George," he said, "there *is* something in there." His voice now was very steady and yet strange.

"What?" I asked. What else do you say?

"A little ball," he said. "A little round ball. Quite misted over, but nonetheless a ball."

"Well!" I said.

"George, I'll get the gin."

He was back from the sideboard in what seemed an incredibly

short time. He had the sloe gin in highball glasses, with ice and water. It tasted horrible.

When I finished mine, I said, "Delicious. Let's have another," and we did. After I drank that one, I felt a good deal more rational.

I set my glass down. "Farnsworth, it just occurred to me. Isn't the fourth dimension supposed to be *time*, according to Einstein?"

He had finished his second sloe gin highball, unmulled, by then. "Supposed to be, yes, according to Einstein. I call it ifth—or oofth—take your pick." He held up the cube again, much more confidently now, I noticed. "And what about the *fifth* dimension?"

"Beats me," I said, looking at the cube, which was beginning to seem vaguely sinister to me. "Beats the hell out of me."

"Beats me, too, George," he said almost gaily—an astonishing mood for old Farnsworth. He turned the cube around with his small, fat fingers. "This is probably all wrapped up in time in some strange way. Not to mention the very peculiar kind of space it appears to be involved with. Extraordinary, don't you think?"

"Extraordinary," I nodded.

"George, I think I'll take another look." And he put the cube back to his eye again. "Well," he said, after a moment of squinting, "same little ball."

"What's it doing?" I wanted to know.

"Nothing. Or perhaps spinning a bit. I'm not sure. It's quite fuzzy, you see, and misty. Dark in there, too."

"Let me see," I said, realizing that, after all, if Farnsworth could see the thing in there, so could I.

"In a minute. I wonder what sort of time I'm looking into—past or future, or what?"

"And what sort of space . . ." I was saying when, suddenly, little Farnsworth let out a fantastic shriek, dropped the cube as if it had suddenly turned into a snake, and threw his hands over his eyes.

He sank back into his chair and cried, "My God! My God!"

I was apprehensive when the cube hit the floor, but nothing happened to it. It did not fold up into no cube at all, nor proliferate back into sixty-four of itself.

"What happened?" I asked, rushing over to Farnsworth, who was squirming about in his armchair, his face still hidden by his hands.

"My eye!" he moaned, almost sobbing. "It stabbed my eye! Quick, George, call me an ambulance!"

I hurried to the telephone and fumbled with the book, looking for the right number, until Farnsworth said, "Quick, George!" again and, in desperation, I dialed the operator and told her to send us an ambulance.

When I got back to Farnsworth, he had taken his hand from the unhurt eye and I could see that a trickle of blood was beginning to run down the other wrist. He had almost stopped squirming, but from his face it was obvious that the pain was still quite intense.

He stood up. "I need another drink," he said, and began heading unsteadily for the sideboard, when he stepped on the cube, which was still lying in front of his chair, and was barely able to keep himself from falling headlong, tripping on it. The cube skidded a few feet, stopping, hole-side up, near the fire.

He said to the cube, enraged, "Drat you, I'll show you . . . !" and he reached down and swooped up the poker from the hearth. It had been lying there for mulling drinks, its end resting on the coals, and by now it was a brilliant cherry red. He took the handle with both hands and plunged the red-hot tip into the hole of the cube, pushing it down against the floor.

"I'll show you!" he yelled again, and I watched understandingly as he shoved with all his weight, pushing and twisting, forcing the poker down with angry energy. There was a faint hissing sound and little wisps of dark smoke came from the hole, around the edges of the poker.

Then there was a strange, sucking noise and the poker began to sink into the cube. It must have gone in at least eight or ten inches—completely impossible, of course, since it was a one-inch cube—and even Farnsworth became so alarmed at this that he abruptly yanked the poker out of the hole.

As he did, black smoke arose in a little column for a moment and then there was a popping sound and the cube fell apart, scattering itself into hundreds of little squares of plastic and aluminum.

Oddly enough, there were no burn marks on the aluminum and none of the plastic seemed to have melted. There was no sign of a little, misty ball.

Farnsworth returned his right hand to his now puffy and quite bloody eye. He stood staring at the profusion of little squares with his good eye. His free hand was trembling.

Then there was the sound of a siren, becoming louder. He turned and looked at me balefully. "That must be the ambulance. I suppose I'd better get my toothbrush."

Farnsworth lost the eye. Within a week, though, he was pretty much his old chipper self again, looking quite dapper with a black leather patch. One interesting thing—the doctor remarked that there were powder burns of some sort on the eyelid, and that the eye itself appeared to have been destroyed by a small explosion. He assumed that it had been a case of a gun misfiring, the cartridge exploding in an open breech somehow. Farnsworth let him think that; it was as good an explanation as any.

I suggested to Farnsworth that he ought to get a green patch, to match his other eye. He laughed at the idea and said he thought it might be a bit showy. He was already starting work on another pentaract; he was going to find out just what . . .

But he never finished. Nine days after the accident, there was a sudden flurry of news reports from the other side of the world, fantastic stories that made the Sunday supplements go completely mad with delight, and we began to guess what had happened. There wouldn't be any need to build the sixty-four-cube cross and try to find a way of folding it up. We knew now.

It *had* been a five-dimensional cube, all right. And one extension of it had been in time—into the future; nine days into the future—and the other extension had been into a most peculiar kind of space, one that distorted sizes quite strangely.

All of this became obvious when, three days later, it happened on our side of the world and the Sunday supplements were scooped by the phenomenon itself, which, by its nature, required no newspaper reporting.

Across the entire sky of the Western hemisphere there appeared—so vast that it eclipsed the direct light of the Sun from Fairbanks, Alaska, to Cape Horn—a tremendous human eye, with a vast, glistening, green pupil. Part of the lid was there, too, and all of it was as if framed in a gigantic circle. Or not exactly a circle, but a polygon of many sides, like the iris diaphragm of a camera shutter.

Toward nightfall, the eye blinked once and probably five hundred million people screamed simultaneously. It remained there all of the night, glowing balefully in the reflected sunlight, obliterating the stars.

A thousand new religious cults were formed that night, and a thousand old ones proclaimed the day as The One Predicted for Centuries.

Probably more than half the people on Earth thought it was God. Only two knew that it was Oliver Farnsworth, peering at a misty little spinning ball in a five-dimensional box, nine days before, totally unaware that the little ball was the Earth itself, contained in a little one-inch cube that was an enclave of swollen time and shrunken space.

When I had dropped the pentaract and had somehow caused it to fold itself into two new dimensions, it had reached out through fifth-dimensional space and folded the world into itself, and had begun accelerating the time within it, in rough proportion to size, so that as each minute passed in Farnsworth's study, about one day was passing on the world within the cube.

We knew this because about a minute had passed while Farnsworth had held his eye against the cube the second time—the first time had, of course, been the appearance over Asia—and nine days later, when we saw the same event from our position on the Earth in the cube, it was twenty-six hours before the eye was "stabbed" and withdrew.

It happened early in the morning, just after the Sun had left the horizon and was passing into eclipse behind the great circle that contained the eye. Someone stationed along a defense-perimeter station panicked—someone highly placed. Fifty guided missiles were launched, straight up, the most powerful on Earth. Each carried a hydrogen warhead. Even before the great shock wave from their explosion came crashing down to Earth, the eye had disappeared.

Somewhere, I knew, an unimaginably vast Oliver Farnsworth

was squirming and yelping, carrying out the identical chain of events that I had seen happening in the past and that yet must be happening now, along the immutable space-time continuum that Farnsworth's little cube had somehow by-passed.

The doctor had talked of powder burns. I wondered what he would think if he knew that Farnsworth had been hit in the eye with fifty infinitesimal hydrogen bombs.

For a week, there was nothing else to talk about in the world. Two billion people probably discussed, thought about and dreamed of nothing else. There had been no more dramatic happening since the creation of the Earth and Sun than the appearance of Farnsworth's eye.

But two people, out of those two billion, thought of something else. They thought of the unchangeable, pre-set space-time continuum, moving at the rate of one minute for every day that passed here on our side of the pentaract, while that vast Oliver Farnsworth and I, in the other-space, other-time, were staring at the cube that contained our world, lying on their floor.

On Wednesday, we could say, *Now he's gone to the telephone.* On Thursday, *Now he's looking through the book.* On Saturday, *By now he must be dialing the operator . . .*

And on Tuesday morning, when the Sun came up, we were together and saw it rise, for we spent our nights together by then, because we had lost the knack of sleeping and did not want to be alone; and when the day had begun, we didn't say it, because we couldn't. But we thought it.

We thought of a colossal, cosmic Farnsworth saying, "I'll show you!" and shoving, pushing and twisting, forcing with all of his might, into the little round hole, a brilliantly glowing, hissing, smoking, red-hot poker.

The Genius Heap

BY JAMES BLISH

The fight began, really, with a simple comment that Mordecai
Drover offered to nobody in particular while watching Dr. Helena
Curtis, the Bartók Colony's resident novelist, trying to finish her
research before nightfall. He couldn't fathom why the remark
had set off such an explosion.

After all, all *he* had said was, "I can never quite get used to it."

"What?" Henry Chatterton asked abstractedly.

"Seeing a woman using an index. It's as outlandish a sight as a
chimpanzee roller-skating."

At this precise moment, Callisto slid into Jupiter's shadow and
the nighttime clamor of the Bartók Colony began to rise rapidly
toward its sustained crescendo. Typewriters began to rattle one
after the other, pianos to compete discordantly, a phonograph to
grunt out part of *Le Sacre du Printemps* for Novgorod's chore-
ography pawns, and collapsible tubes to pop air-bubbles as paint
was squeezed onto palettes. The computer, too, began humming
deep in its throat, for Dr. Winterhalter of the Special Studies section was trying to make it compose a sonata derived entirely
from information theory.

The clamor would last four hours and 53.9 minutes before beginning to taper off.

Helena, however, made no move toward her typewriter. She closed her reference book with a savage snap, as though trying to trap a passing moth, and stood up. Mordecai, who had already plunged deep into Canto XVII of *The Drum Major and the Mask*, failed to notice her glare until he became aware of an unprecedented silence in the Commons Room. He looked up.

Helena was advancing on him, step by step, each pace made more menacing by the peculiar glide Callisto's slight gravity enforced. She was graceful under any circumstances; now she looked positively serpentine, and her usually full lips were white. Alarmed, Mordecai put down his pen.

"Just what did you mean by that?" she asked.

By what? Mordecai searched his memory frantically. At first, all he could come up with was the last strophe he had written, only a few seconds ago, and as yet he had no idea what he meant by that; the thing was badly flawed and needed revision before even its author could know what it meant.

Then he remembered the remark about women and indexes —indices?—already hours away in the fleet subjective time of Callistan night.

"Why, it wasn't anything," he said wonderingly. "I mean you know how it is with chimpanzees—"

"Oh, I do, do I?"

"Well, maybe I didn't—what I mean is, they get to be very skillful at unusual tasks—it's just that you don't expect them to be —Helena, it was only a joke! What good is a joke after it's explained? Don't be obstinate."

"Meaning don't be ostinately stupid?" she said through her teeth. "I've had enough of your nasty innuendoes. If there's anything I loathe, it's a would-be genius with no manners."

Henry Chatterton's smock was already spattered with egg tempera from top to bottom and the painting on his canvas was nearly a quarter finished. Slashing away at one corner of it with a loaded brush, he said out of the corner of his mouth:

"We've had to put up with that viper's tongue of yours long enough, Helena. Why don't you go hitch your flat frontispiece over your decolleté novel and let the rest of us work?"

"Now wait a minute," John Rapaport said, flushing heavily and looking up from the dural plate on which he had been sketching. "By what right does an egg-coddler go out of his way to insult a craftsman, Chatterton? If you have to dip that brush of yours in blatherskite, save it for your daubs—never mind smearing it over Helena."

Chatterton swung around in astonishment and then began to smirk.

"So *that's* how it's going to be! Well, Johnny boy, congratulations. But I predict that you'll find five hours makes a very, very long night. Don't say an expert didn't warn you."

Rapaport swung. His engravers' point flew accurately at Chatterton's left eye. The painter ducked just in time; the tool stuck, quivering, in his canvas. He took one look at it and rushed on Rapaport, howling. Mordecai would have been out of the way with no difficulty, if Helena's open hand had not caught him a stinging blow across the chops at the crucial moment. Then he and Chatterton went over.

The noise quickly attracted the rest of the happy family. Only fifteen minutes after Mordecai's innocent remark, the Commons Room was untidily heaped with geniuses.

It looked like a long night.

Because Mordecai, a month before, had fumbled so long and so helplessly with his spacesuit until an impatient crewman had decided to help him dog it down, he had almost been dumped out of the airlock, and the ship's captain barely gave him time to get clear before taking off again. Within a few seconds, it seemed, he had been more alone than he had ever been in his life.

He had stood still inside the suit, because he could do nothing else, and fumed. Actually, he knew, he was more afraid than angry, though he was thoroughly furious with himself, and with Martin Hope Eglington, his mentor. It certainly hadn't been Mordecai's idea to come to Jupiter IV. He had never even been in space before, not even so far as the Moon, and had had no desire to go.

Nevertheless, here he was, under a sky of so deep a blue that it was almost black and full of sharp cold stars, even though it was midday. The Sun was a miniature caricature of itself, shedding little light and no apparent heat. There was nothing else to be seen but a wilderness of tumbled rocks, their sharp edges and spires protruding gauntly through deep layers of powdery snow, all the way to the near horizon. The fact that Mordecai could hear a faint sighing whistle outside his suit, as of the saddest and weakest of all winds, did not cheer him.

It had begun, as such things usually did with Mordecai, with what had seemed an innocent question, this time one asked by someone else. Eglington had been helping him with the prosody of *The Drum Major and the Mask*, Mordecai's major poem thus far, cast as a sirvente to Wallace Stevens. They had swinked at it all day in Eglington's beautiful and remote Vermont home. Mordecai had now been Eglington's only protégé; there was a time when the Pulitzer Prize winner had maintained a sort of salon of them, but now he was too old for such rigors.

"That's enough for now," Eglington had said, shortly after dinner. "It's really shaping up very well, Mordecai, if you could just get yourself past trying to compress everything you know into one phrase. In a poem of this length, at least a little openness of texture is desirable—if only to let the reader into it."

"I see that now. Whew! When I first got started, nobody told me poetry could be such hard work."

"All real poetry is hard work; that's one of its telltales. Tell me something, Mordecai—when do you do most of your work? I don't mean your best work, necessarily; at what hours of the day do you find that you work most easily, can concentrate best, put the most out?"

That had been easy to answer. Mordecai's work habits had been fixed for fifteen years. "Between about eight at night and two in the morning."

"I thought so. That's true of most creative people, including scientists. The exact hours vary, but the fact is that most of the world's creative work—and creative play; it's the same thing—is done at night."

"Interesting," Mordecai had said. "Why is that, do you suppose?"

"Oh, I don't have to suppose. The answer is known. It's because, during those hours, the whole mass of the Earth is between you and the Sun. That protects you from an extremely penetrating kind of solar radiation, made up of particles called neutrinos. The protection is negligible statistically, because all matter is almost perfectly transparent to neutrinos, but it seems that the creative processes are tremendously sensitive to even the slightest shielding effect."

"Too bad they can't be blocked off completely, then. I'd like to be able to work days. I just can't."

"You can, if you want to undergo some privations in the process," Eglington had said, almost idly. "Ever hear of the Bartók Colony?"

"Yes, it's a retreat of some sort. Never went in for that kind of thing much myself. I work better alone."

"I see you don't know where it is. It's on Callisto."

The notion had startled and somewhat repelled Mordecai, for whom the neutrinos had already been almost too much. He would expect Eglington to know about such things—he was not called "the poet of physics" for nothing—but Mordecai had no interest in them. "On Callisto? Why, for heaven's sake?"

"Well, for two reasons," Eglington had said. "First of all, because at that distance from the Sun, the raw neutrino flux is only about three point seven per cent of what it is here on Earth. The other reason is that for nearly five hours of every two weeks—that is, every Callistan day—you have the small bulk of the satellite plus the whole mass of Jupiter between you and the Sun. For that period, you're in a position to work your creative engine with almost no neutrino static. I'm told that the results, in terms of productivity, are truly fantastic."

"Oh," Mordecai had said. "It seems like an extreme measure, somehow."

Eglington had leaned forward, intensely serious. "Only extreme measures produce great work, Mordecai. Tell me—what was the big change in Man that differentiated him permanently, qualitatively, from all other species?"

"The opposable thumb," Mordecai had said promptly.

"Wrong. The opposable thumb helps Man to handle things, it stimulates curiosity, it gets the world's work done. It is, if you like, a device of daylight. But the ability to think in abstractions is the big skill that Man has and that is an ability that works mostly at night. Second question: why was fire Man's most important discovery?"

"Well, it helped him to get more nourishment out of his food," Mordecai said, but more cautiously now.

"That's minor. What else?"

Mordecai had known he was well out of his depth by that time. He simply shook his head.

"Independence of the Sun, Mordecai. That one gain has permanently arrested Man's evolution. Without it, he was developing a number of specialized types for different environments: the bushman, the pigmy, the Eskimo, and so on. Fire not only halted the process, but reversed it; the devolution set in. Now we don't have to adapt to our environments; we can carry our own wherever we go. In that way, we protect ourselves from adapting away from abstract thinking and toward some purely physical change that will make it unnecessary for us to think."

Eglington had paused and sniffed reflectively at his brandy. Then, with apparent irrelevance, he had added: "Do you tell your relatives what your work hours are?"

"Not by a long shot. They're all alarm-clock types. They think I'm lazy as it is; if I told them I didn't get up until noon, they'd be sure of it."

"Exactly. Daylight encourages monkey-thinking, practicality, conformity, routine operation. It's at night that Man-thinking gets done. During the day, there are the twinges about the regular paycheck, keeping the family fed, making your relatives proud of you, taking no chances, and all the rest of that rot. 'Early to bed and early to rise' is nothing but an invitation to put your head into a horse-collar. The man who stays in bed all day isn't a lazy slob; he's a man who's very sensibly protecting his valuable human brains from the monkey-drive."

"You make a good case," Mordecai had said admiringly.

"I really think you ought to go, Mordecai. I'll give you a letter to the chairman; he's at the Earth headquarters at MIT. I'm quite sure I can swing it."

Mordecai had felt a belated surge of alarm. "But, Martin, wait a minute—"

"Don't worry; you'll be admitted. Anyhow, you've gone as far as you can go with me. Now you need to strike out on your own —and this is the way to do it."

And so Mordecai Drover, on Jupiter IV, frightenedly had been waiting for somebody from the Bartók Colony to pick him up. He did not feel a particle more creative than he had felt at his worst moments back home. Rather less, as a matter of fact.

A stirring in the middle distance drew his attention belatedly. Something like a bug was coming toward him. As it came closer, he saw that it was a sort of snowmobile, with huge fat tires and a completely sealed cabin. He let out a gasp of relief.

"Hello," his suit radio said, in a voluptuous feminine voice. "Stand fast, Mr. Drover; we have you on the radar. Welcome to Bartók Colony."

The voice virtually transformed Callisto for Mordecai; if there was one historical period in which he would most liked to have lived, it was that of Marlene Dietrich. When, half an hour later, he found that Dr. Helena Curtis strongly resembled that—alas!— long-dead Helen of the age before space flight, he had been suddenly, as Eglington probably had expected, ready to stay on Callisto forever.

"Now there are only two rules here," Dr. Hamish Crenshaw, the Colony's director, had begun murmuring in Mordecai's ear while his suit was being stripped off him. "First of all, we have no facilities for children; you'll understand, I'm sure, and forgive us when I tell you that we—uh—Take Steps. Dietary steps; you'll never notice them, but we like to be honest. And the other rule is Get Along. We're all one family here and we try not to quarrel."

"Oh, of course not," Mordecai had said, but he hadn't really been listening.

After the fight, the Colony's surgeon—a staff member, not a guest —gave Mordecai a hyaluronidase injection for his black eye and dismissed him without ceremony. Evidently the brawl in the Commons Room had produced several more serious wounds. Mordecai prowled the corridors morosely for a while, but kept meeting people he had only recently been fighting with—or, at least, trying to fight out from under. He finally went back to his own cubicle and tried to resume *The Drum Major and the Mask*.

It was hopeless. The cacophony of noise in the station had

hardly bothered him after the first strange night, but now he couldn't think through it. He wondered how the others had stood it for so long. Neutrinos or no neutrinos, his own brain was generating nothing but blots.

Besides, he felt amost intolerably guilty. After all, his remark had been unfeeling, especially after what had happened two nights ago (or a month ago, as he kept thinking of it). That had been one of the unexpected effects of night on Jupiter IV: the same shielding that liberated the creative impulse seemed to liberate the libido as well. In four hours and 53.9 minutes, two people could fall in love, become passionately and exclusively attached to each other, and fall explosively out of love before the night was over—a process that would have taken months or years on Earth.

No wonder the Colony, as Dr. Crenshaw had put it, Took Steps against the possibility of children.

But was it Mordecai's fault that Helena was the most beautiful woman in the Colony and hence the most frequent figure in these amours and explosions? Besides, he had suffered, too. He could hardly find it comfortable to be out of love with Dietrich, after having had adored her image hopelessly since he was old enough to distinguish pants from trousers. He doubted that he would ever write another love poem again.

The corridors of the Colony began to resound with a series of hoots and shrieks, as loud as though they were being heard by an insect trapped in a steam calliope. Dr. Winterhalter had once again begun to hope, and had wired the computer's output directly to the Hammond organ; the computer's current notion of what a sonata ought to sound like was rattling the doors in their sockets. The computer had not yet quite solved the music of the spheres. The Cadre to Suppress Dr. Winterhalter, made up of all the musicians in the Colony, would be stampeding past Mordecai's door at any moment.

Yet after all, he told himself, the remark hadn't been any more virulent than many of the things that got said daily in the Colony, and Helena had always been one of the worst offenders; Chatterton had been right about that. Even at home, Mordecai recalled with nostalgia, nighttime was the time you said things that you regretted the next day. He had always attributed that looseness of tongue to the dulling of inhibitions by fatigue (or, of course, alcohol), but since it was so much worse here, maybe the double-damned neutrinos had been responsible for that too. Or maybe they hadn't. If you coop thirty highly individualistic people in one sealed can on a cheerless iceball like Callisto, you should expect tempers to get somewhat frayed.

Whatever the answer, Mordecai wanted out. There was no doubt in his mind that being in the Colony had increased his productivity markedly, but it wasn't worth the constant emotional upheavals.

He peered up and down the corridor to make sure he would not be run over by the Cadre, and then set off determinedly for the office of Dr. Hamish Crenshaw. There was no sense in postponing matters.

As he passed Helena Curtis' closed door, however, he paused. Maybe one postponement could do no harm. There was another question nagging at him, which he suddenly decided was more important. He knocked tentatively.

Helena opened the door and stared at him, her eyes coldly furious. "Beat it," she said.

"I don't mean to interrupt," Mordecai said humbly. "I apologize for my remark. It was nasty and inexcusable. Also, I've got something I'd like to discuss with you."

"Oh?" For a moment, she simply continued to glare at him. Then, gradually, some of the unfriendliness seemed to die away. "Well, it's decent of you to apologize. And that beastly squabble did sour me on Rapaport just in time; maybe I owe you an apology, too. What's on your mind?"

"I want to know what you know about old Walker Goodacre —the man who founded the Colony. I'm beginning to think there's a joker buried somewhere and he may be it."

"Hm. All right, come on in. But no monkeyshines, Mordecai."

"Certainly not," he said innocently. "That's part of the problem, Helena. This setup is supposed to encourage what they call 'Manthinking' and it does seem to have that effect—but it also seems to bring out all the monkey-emotions. I'm starting to wonder why."

"Well," Helena said, sitting down thoughtfully, "they say the neutrinos—"

"Hang the neutrinos! I mean let's just forget about them for the time being and think about what the Colony's supposed to accomplish. We should begin with the history; there's where you can help, right at the beginning. How is the Colony actually run?"

"By a board of directors, administering the Goodacre estate," she said. "The place was originally founded by Goodacre himself; he put ten million dollars into a special trust to build the place and then bequeathed another ten to keep it going. The Colony is run off the interest from the bequest."

"All right. What kind of man was Goodacre?" Mordecai asked. "I mean aside from the fact that he was a rich man. Wasn't he also a scholar of stature? I seem to remember that he was."

"Oh, yes," Helena said. "He was a sociologist, considered one of the most eminent of his time. Mordecai, if you're suggesting that this whole thing is an experiment and we're just experimental animals, you're wasting your breath. The newspapers milked all the melodrama out of that when the Colony was first founded. Of course, it's an experiment; what of it?"

"Of course. But what kind of experiment? Look here, Helena, you know more history than I do. A lot more. Think back on the history of bequests to artists. Do they usually come from men who are artists or scholars themselves? It's my impression that they don't. More usually, they come from men who are not creative themselves and feel guilty or frustrated about it—men whose money was often made by dubious means in the first place, so some of it is given away to the most 'disinterested' people the rich man can imagine, in expiation. Like the Nobel Prizes—money made from dynamite. Only a cultural cipher could dream of an artist as 'disinterested' in that sense."

"I can think of a few exceptions," Helena said, "but only partial ones. In that respect, old Goodacre was an unusual case. I'll grant you that."

"Right. Now it's my judgment that this experiment *as it was outlined to us* is working very badly. Yet Goodacre was a top sociologist, you tell me; why should the biggest experiment he ever designed, being run strictly in accordance with his wishes, be so miserable a failure?"

"Well, sociology's not an exact science—"

"I had the notion that it'd become much more exact since Rashevsky, at least. And I think it might be more sensible to assume that old Goodacre did know what he was doing and that this mess is exactly the outcome he wanted. *Why did he want it?*"

"Mordecai," Helena said slowly, "I apologize again and this time I mean it. Let's see how close we can get to the bottom of this before the night's over."

"Why stop then?" Mordecai urged. "It's only a question of fact —no creativity involved."

In this, of course, he was a little underestimating himself. Deduction is creative; Mordecai had simply had too little experience with it to realize the fact.

During the succeeding days, Dr. Hamish Crenshaw appeared to be indulging in a series of improvised attempts to prevent further brawls by dividing the sheep from the goats, without having quite made up his mind how to tell one animal from the other. His first move was to forbid working in the Commons Room, which did nothing but stop work in the Commons Room; it utterly failed to prevent brawling there, and it was impossible for the director to close the Commons Room entirely.

Then he tried to reshuffle the room assignments so that all the guests whose records carried the fewest marks for quarrels would wind up on one side of the Colony and the most quarrelsome guests on the other. The net gain here was fewer bruises sustained by accident by the least quarrelsome. The most quarrelsome continued to quarrel, more frequently now because they were deprived of the calming effects sometimes exerted by the cooler heads.

After this had become sufficiently obvious to all, Dr. Crenshaw decided to reshuffle the rooms according to talent. This was abortive. Everybody at Bartók Colony, except the staff, was supposed to be a leader in his field, so Crenshaw apparently concluded that the only way to measure talent was by age: young poets, for example, were sheep, old poets goats. Since there was only one poet in the Colony at the moment—Mordecai—the plan foundered on Mordecai's obvious inability to baa and bleat at the same time from opposite sides of the dome.

But nothing seemed to discourage Dr. Crenshaw. He tried to segregate the sexes. This produced the biggest riot in the Colony's history. The next move in the game of musical chairs was to lump all the practitioners of the noisy arts—music, ballet, sculpture—into one group and those who quietly wrote or painted into the other. The concentration of noise made it worse than it had been when diffused and in no way decreased the squabbling.

The most recent solution was a curfew. The rules were that everyone had to be in his room by nightfall and had to stay there until the night was over. All gatherings were forbidden, but exceptions were made for teams ("such as composer-and-librettist," Dr. Crenshaw had added with what he seemed to think was great tact). This move really made a difference; it actually cut the quarreling in half.

It also cut productivity right back down to the daytime level, even in the naturally solitary arts.

"Which I think is what you've been aiming for all along," Mordecai told Crenshaw grimly, in Crenshaw's office. "All the other silly rules were designed to convey an illusion of bumbling desperation, to disguise the curfew as just one more example of the same."

Crenshaw laughed disarmingly but a look at Mordecai and Helena evidently convinced him that neither had been disarmed.

He put his hands together on his desktop and leaned forward confidingly.

"Now that's a peculiar theory," he said, still smiling. "Suppose you tell me why you think so."

"It's in keeping with the whole philosophy," Mordecai said. "Dr. Curtis and I have been doing considerable research lately and we've come up with some conclusions we don't like. Among other things, we talked to Dr. Ford."

Crenshaw frowned. Dr. Ford was the colony's staff physicist. The statement that he had been talking to guests obviously did not please the director.

"We found out a few things about the neutrino notion that we hadn't known before," Mordecai went on. "Dr. Ford says that neutrinos go through ordinary matter as if it weren't there. Back home on Earth, the neutrino flux is so great that there are a hundred neutrinos passing through a space the size of a matchbox at any given instant—yet even detecting their existence was one of the hardest problems physicists ever tackled. He says the difference between the night and the day flux on Earth has never been measured."

"Never by instruments," Crenshaw said smoothly. "But the human brain measures it; it's a very delicate detector."

"That's pure hypothesis," Helena retorted. "Dr. Ford says that to capture the average neutrino would take a lead barrier *fifty light-years thick*. Under those conditions, exceptional captures within a human brain must take place on the order of once every million years or more."

"We considered all this in setting up the Colony," Crenshaw said. "We do have people like Dr. Ford on our staff, after all. Obviously the neutrino-capture theory was not proven. It was a conjecture. But we've been in operation for quite a few years now and the empirical evidence has been adding up all during that time. Your own personal experience should confirm it. There *is* a definite increase in creativity out here and particularly when we are in the Jovian shadow."

He leveled a finger at them or, rather, between them. "This is one reason why I don't like to have physicists like Ford shooting off their mouths to our guests. Physicists don't understand the artistic temperament and artists generally don't know enough about physicists to be aware of their limitations. You didn't know, for instance, the real meaning behind what Ford was telling you. I do know: he was complaining that the neutrino theory is based upon the concept that the brain acts as an organic detector, and the ground rules of his science don't allow organic detectors. Since you had no way of knowing this and, like most lay people, you regard physicists as minor gods, you're shaken up. You've allowed him to discredit not only your belief in the Colony, but even the evidence of your own experience!"

"Very plausible," Mordecai said. "But experience isn't evidence until it's put in order and there's always more than one possible order. Dr. Curtis and I don't know much about physicists, it's true, but we do know something about artists. We know that they're highly suggestible. They have to be or they'd be in some other trade. Convince them that they're going to be more creative in the dark of the moon, or after a course of mescal, or in the Jovian neutrino shadow, and most of them *will* be more creative, whether there's any merit in the actual notion you've sold them or not."

He grinned reminiscently. "I once knew a writer whose work was largely unsalable, so he had to have a regular job to stay alive. He developed the notion that he had to be fired at least once a year in order to maintain his productivity. Sooner or later, toward the end of each job year, he *was* fired—and it *did* increase his writing output for a while. What has that to do with neutrinos?"

"Nothing," Crenshaw said. "A single example never has anything to do with anything except itself. But let's suppose for the sake of argument that the neutrino theory is not only shaky, but entirely wrong. Have you anything better to offer? Until we discover just what creativity actually is—what goes on in the brain to produce it—we'll never really *know* whether it's possible for a neutrino to interfere with that process. In the meantime, the empirical evidence we collect here in the Colony adds up."

"Adds up to what?" Mordecai demanded.

Crenshaw only shrugged.

"Dr. Crenshaw," Helena said, "maybe there is something in the neutrino theory all the same. I'm prepared to admit the possibility—*but I don't think it makes any difference*. We know that artists always produce best under stress, either personal or societal—it doesn't matter what kind. If production increases in this Colony, it's because conditions here for a resident artist are *worse* than those he had to work under back home—not better. No wonder production dropped when you cut down our internecine warfare. You've always had it in your power to reduce those quarrels, but you didn't choose to exercise it until now."

"Why now?" Crenshaw inquired gently.

"To cut down on the amount of our work that gets home, of course," Mordecai said, amazed that the man could continue such an obvious rear-guard defense after his major defenses had been breached. "Dr. Crenshaw, we know that old Goodacre knew what he was doing. He was interested in the role of the artist in society. He was asking himself: Does society really need these creative people? Does it really want them around? Are the things they produce worth having, weighed against the damage that they do just by being alive and impinging upon normal people? So he contrived this experiment."

Crenshaw said, "I don't see the point." But he was sweating.

"We do. Above all, old Goodacre wanted to know this: What would happen to society if, generation after generation, the cream of its artists is skimmed off, the artists sent into exile—and their work returned to Earth only at a measurable, controllable rate? Take architecture, for instance: you skim Gropius off one generation, Wright off another, and so on, and what's left? Draftsmen, renderers, workhorses, without anybody to stir them into a ferment. Sooner or later, Earth has no creativity left in its gene pool but the kind that makes men into engineers and scientists— and mightn't that be just as well, in the long run? *That's* the question this Colony is set up to answer, and brilliantly, too."

Crenshaw sighed.

After a while, Helena said: "Well?"

"Well, what?" Crenshaw asked tiredly. "*I'm* not going to tell you you're right or wrong or way off base. No matter what conclusions you come to, I still have to stay here and administer this madhouse. I'm not Goodacre; I just work here."

"That's what the guards at Dachau said," Mordecai said.

"The question is, what do you plan to do?"

"Go home," Mordecai stated immediately.

"And how do you plan to do that? You signed a contract when you came here. In addition to your legal ties, you can't leave here until I personally say you can. I can simply deny you passage, deny you knowledge of the ship schedules—there are half a hundred other knots I can tie you in. Why not just sit and take it? It won't last forever."

"Of course it won't," Helena said grimly. "But we're not sheep, nor Judas-goats. Suppose the experiment ends by proving that society *can* get along without us? Then we'd never get home at all, no matter what the contract says."

Crenshaw looked down at his hands, and then up again. His expression was now one of frank boredom. "That may well be true. However, I deny it for the record. And now I have work to do. Thank you for coming to see me."

Mordecai grinned. Crenshaw had obviously never thought of him as a conspirator and Mordecai was savoring the surprise.

"There are other people waiting to see you," he said. He got up and opened the door.

There were others, all right. There was Novgorod and his highly muscular group of dancers; Henry Chatterton, his beard bristling and his smock-pockets loaded with eggs far too far gone to make decent egg tempera; John Rapaport with his bottles of acid and his beltful of nastily pointed little engravers' tools; Dr. Winterhalter with a sheaf of papers full of calculations on orbits and schedules to Earth; and quite a few additonal "harmless artists." They looked anything but harmless now.

"We're going home," Mordecai said. "Maybe society would like to get along without us, but we aren't going to let it. It won't catch us again by offering us a nice workroom, where it's always as quiet as three o'clock in the morning. We don't need that kind of phony solitude—we carry the real thing with us wherever we go, even when we're fighting among ourselves. Do you understand that?"

"No," Crenshaw said hoarsely. "I don't think I do understand."

Mordecai took Helena's hand as she rose. "Then you didn't study your experimental animals thoroughly enough. If you had, you would have found that one of them, F. Scott Fitzgerald, knew the flaw in your experiments a whole century ago and wrote it down."

"What—was it?"

"'In a real dark night of the soul,'" quoted Mordecai, "'it is *always* three o'clock in the morning.'"